I'll Be
Seeing U

I'll Be
Seeing U

Dianne Castell

BRAVA

KENSINGTON PUBLISHING CORP.
http://www.kensingtonbooks.com

BRAVA BOOKS are published by

Kensington Publishing Corp.
850 Third Avenue
New York, NY 10022

ISBN 0-7582-1007-8

First Kensington Trade Paperback Printing: November 2006
10 9 8 7 6 5 4 3 2 1

Printed in Mexico

To Gina.
You make me so proud.
What a terrific daughter!

Chapter 1

Driving to O'Fallon's Landing in a fourteen-year-old robin's-egg blue Buick station wagon complete with *God Is Coming and She's Pissed* bumper sticker was not the way Cynthia Landon intended to return home. Where was the stretch limo to ballyhoo her great New York success as a designer? The warm summer day when she could drive proudly through town, waving through the rolled-down windows?

Gone! Along with all of her other great plans and hard work of the last ten years. "Good-by Fifth Avenue, hello backwater Tennessee," she murmured into the darkness as rain splattered the two-lane. She glanced at her eight-year-old son sleeping in the passenger side, head bobbing, seat belt holding him upright. She smiled in spite of the situation. Lawrence made all her messes seem not quite so . . . messy, and he was the only true thing Aaron had ever given her besides bankruptcy and a rotten marriage. If they fished his sorry lying cheating ass out of the East River someday soon that would be just fine with her.

Lightning split the sky, the Mississippi rolled wild and rough to her left, and something darted in front of her. "What the . . ."

She hit the brakes, skidded and swerved. "Damnation!"

"Mom?"

"Hold on, Lawrence!" The car slowed but did a one-eighty and slid into the ditch as the airbag exploded, flattening her to the back of the seat before fizzling across her lap. She looked at Lawrence through the darkness, no white blob on his lap. Oh hell!

Fumbling for the interior lights with one hand she held his chin in her other hand. "No bruises, no bumps, no thanks to the jerk who sold me this car. That—"*no-good, rotten, son of a bitch* she added to herself—"salesman promised me there were airbags on both sides of this car. *Both.* That's why I bought it, certainly not for its aesthetic appeal." Damn him!

Men—from Aaron to her attorney to her accountant and now the used car salesman—had all double-crossed her when they got the chance. "We should get you to a doctor. I can't believe I forgot about Grant."

"Mom, you weren't going fast, the seat belt held me in place. I didn't budge. I'm okay and who's Grant?"

"Meddling Yankee general who's still pissing everyone off around here."

"Mom, the Civil War was a over a hundred and fifty years ago."

"That's what you think." A knock at the window made her jump. Mass-murderer? Kidnapper? But she was only three miles from the Landing, not exactly crime central.

The car door opened to the lower half of a rain-splattered leather jacket and the top half of snug jeans hanging low across lean hips. Male . . . nicely put together male. And she was so done with anything male. Not that all men were pigs, she just attracted the ones who were.

"Anyone hurt?"

She knew that voice. Quaid O'Fallon, local bad boy number one—at least for the younger set. She was forty so that made him about thirty-three. He peered into the car, rain skating off the brim of his cap and across his face. "Cynthia Landon?"

She needed to say something, and not that thirty-three never looked so good.

"Her maiden name is Landon," came Lawrence's voice from next to her. "I think she's in shock from running off the road but we're fine. We're on our way to Ivy Acres. Were you really in the Coast Guard or did you just buy that hat?"

Rain blew in waves, the wind howled, but Quaid didn't seem to notice. He grinned. Why the heck would he do that? This night sucked.

"Used to be Coast Guard. I'm Quaid O'Fallon and on my way home, right down the road from where you're headed." He eyed Cynthia. "My car's across the road. I can drive you."

Terrific green eyes, even in the dim light she could tell, or did she just remember? Where'd a man get eyes like that? Square jaw, stubbled chin she wanted to touch. Really good firm lips, not the squishy kind like Aaron's. Oh, crap, she was doing it again. If there was ever a wrong kind of guy, the adopted son of Rory O'Fallon topped the list.

"No," Cynthia blurted. "I thank you for the offer but Lawrence and I can manage fine on our own." And she could, dammit. Landons depended on no one.

Quaid cut his gaze from one end of the car to the other. "You're stuck knee-deep in Tennessee soup here. This car isn't budging. The sooner you come with me the sooner we all get to someplace dry."

She stepped on the accelerator, the wheels doing the spin thing and Quaid not bothering to move or even close the door in case the car did budge . . . which it didn't. He shook his head in that know-it-all way men do. "It's not going to work, girl."

"I am a woman, not a girl, I can take care of everything." She killed the engine and lights, and reached under the front seat and retrieved her umbrella, holding it up in triumph. "My son and I will walk."

"Mom, Mr. O'Fallon said he'd give us a—"

"We're walking, Lawrence," she growled in her I-am-the-mother voice. "You and me together to your grand-mother's house."

"It's raining, a lot."

"It's August, we won't melt." She stepped into the downpour, forcing Quaid to step back. She popped the umbrella and ignored Lawrence's sighs that suggested she'd clearly lost her mind, as he scooted across the seat. "You're behaving irrationally."

"You're eight. You don't know what irrational is."

"Lacking the power to reason. Contrary to reason. Senseless. Unreasonable. Absurd. In math it means—"

"Never mind. I should have known better than to say that. If it's in a book it's in your brain." She took his hand in hers. The wind rendered the umbrella useless as they splashed across the road more suited for rafts than cars, passing a Jeep, obviously Quaid's. But she was not giving in no matter how nice and dry and new the Jeep looked with its charcoal-gray metallic paint and dual airbags. "We have to stand on our own, Lawrence. Be self-sufficient. That's what Landons do."

"Can't we be self-sufficient when the sun's out?"

She held his hand a bit tighter to make him feel more secure. "We need to start now. A new beginning, just the two of us and your grandmother. That's why we're here." 'Course when she got home she wouldn't mind a little of her mother's pampering to get over the divorce, bankruptcy and the demise of Creations by Cynthia. She so missed her father. He'd know what to do, offer sage advice. The one true man in her life, a man who knew the meaning of family and caring for them, except he was gone three years now. The man had been a rock, a saint among men.

Lawrence said, "It's dark, we'll get hit by a car."

And then it suddenly wasn't dark where they walked. The Jeep followed, yellow caution lights flashing, lighting the way. Lawrence was drenched and he'd been through enough with leaving friends, private school, midtown brownstone, his favorite chocolate cannoli.

She flagged down the Jeep to stop, then slogged her way to the passenger side and pulled open the door. "Get in, Lawrence." She closed the door behind him and he powered down the window. "Now what are you doing, Mom?"

She straightened her shoulders, a rivulet of rain slipping between her shoulder blades, chilling her to the bone. "Walking to Ivy Acres."

Quaid looked from Lawrence to Cynthia Landon, splashing down the road in front of the Jeep, umbrella blowing inside out, rain ruining her skimpy shoes. Even with all that, she moved with the same damn stuck-up prissiness as when he'd seen her that first time nineteen years ago, parading her stuck-up prissy poodle with a rhinestone collar all over town. Quaid had given an appreciative wolf whistle, she'd given him a kiss-my-ass look, and since he was fifteen and horny and she twenty-two and a fox, he would have been happy to oblige.

She wore a yellow sundress then, her hair gold in the sunlight. Tonight her hair clumped together and her dress hung wet and ruined, but she had the same curvy hips, long legs, and she really did have a terrific ass.

Lawrence said, "I think she's delusional."

Quaid thought *she's a damn snob and still hot as hell.* He said, "Tough day?"

"Rotten year." Lawrence slouched into the upholstery, looking small and alone as he stared out the rain-streaked window. "She divorced my dad and her business flopped. We're broke and my dad's a loser. We're screwed."

Quaid ruffled the boy's hair. He knew all about tough times and being alone . . . till Rory O'Fallon came along and made him his son. "Sometimes other people know what's best for you even when you don't." He killed the engine. *Damn, stubborn female.* "Stay put, I'll get your mom."

"She's not going to like you interfering."

"She'll get over it, she's young."

"She's not that young."

Quaid chuckled even though he was tired to the bone from the long drive. He stepped out into the storm. Something was eating Cynthia Landon, something that made her walk home in a Tennessee monsoon. Well, he'd been rescuing people for five years and wasn't about to stop with a change in the geography. Do the job and then go home, that was the drill.

"Hey," he said as he jogged up to Cynthia, headlights silhouetting her against the darkness.

"What?" she yelled over the wind. She shivered but acted as if it didn't happen.

"You're wet, cold and tired, we're all tired. Get the hell in the car and let's get out of here."

She gave him an incredulous look. "No."

"Fuck." He snagged the umbrella and tossed it into the ditch, her eyes rounding. He remembered the color, blue. Ocean blue.

"For your information that was Fendi."

"For your information it's broken and useless and you are a pain in the ass."

"Look, did I ask you to stop? No. Men, they think they know everything." She snorted and spun around and stomped off, splashing water with each step. He moved in front of her, eyes beady, jaw set as she said, "Get out of my way. I'm walking here."

"Not on my watch." He leaned down and flipped her over his shoulder, rescue style, like he'd done a hundred times before on the job . . . except . . . except . . . Holy shit, Sherlock! None of them had been Cynthia Landon over his shoulder. He went hot and hard from head to foot, nearly losing his balance. Some rescue guy he was.

"Put me down!" She wiggled and pushed against his back, making him hold her all the harder. "Are you out of your mind?"

Her stomach rested on his shoulder, hip against his neck, breasts pressed to his back, his arm over her shapely calves. Did she have to wiggle? Every fiber of his body wanted her—pigheaded snob and all—right now in the pouring rain in the middle of the road. Horniness rode him harder now than nineteen years ago and that was going some. He headed to the Jeep and deposited Cynthia neatly into the back seat as she glared, eyes blazing, lips full and lush and tempting as hell. If her son weren't in the front seat he'd take the kiss and put an end to this.

"I can walk! I want to walk! I know—"

He slammed the door shut, climbed into the driver side and headed for Ivy Acres, the only sound the rain hammering the car and Cynthia Landon James grinding her teeth.

The driveway wound to the house with four columns that always impressed the hell out of him. "Here you go, m'lady."

"And I would have gotten here just fine on my own, without your infernal interference."

He turned and faced her mostly because he wanted another look into those eyes. "Why is it so important that you walk? What's the big—" he swallowed *fucking* because of the kid "—deal?"

"I needed the exercise. There, now you know. Happy?"

She stepped from the car, then opened the passenger side and took Lawrence's elbow.

"Thanks for the ride, Mr. O'Fallon."

"Name's Quaid." He took off his hat and slid it on Lawrence's head, the brim sliding down to the top of his glasses and putting a huge grin on his face. Mother and son darted for the front porch, Lawrence waving frantically, Cynthia doing her I-am-princess strut. A brass light suspended from a chain swayed in the wind, making the place look snootier than ever, then the door finally opened letting the two inside.

"Good riddance." Quaid drove back to Cynthia's crammed-full station wagon and locked it up. Why'd she leave New York?—and from the looks of it Cynthia and son really were moving back home.

Home. The word stuck in Quaid's brain as he again passed Ivy Acres, then Hastings House perched on the next rise. He Y'd right then into the drive of the rambling white frame O'Fallon house set on the bluff. Gravel crunched, oaks lined the yard, and he knew the Mississippi rolled just beyond—full of fire and hell on a night like this.

He killed the engine, doused the lights and sat in the dark, losing track of time, feeling himself settle back into the rhythm of life on the river. Four guys, one house and a lot of good times.

Then the not so good time—the before Rory O'Fallon time—clawed its way into his brain. He shivered. Hadn't he buried memories of his asshole grandfather so deep they'd never find their way out? Meeting Lawrence must have triggered it. Eight. Eight was when Pete took him in, when his mother said *to hell with parenthood.* He shoved the memories away, locking them out for good.

The rain slackened, leaving the scent of warm wet earth, humid night air and the river . . . always the river. Max pranced across the yard, tail wagging, yellow ball clamped in his teeth. Quaid got out and scratched Max behind the ears as water dripped from the trees and a tow growled out in the channel. A linehauler, some big mother of a tow, pushing a string of barges upstream against the current in a storm. His blood stirred. He was really home.

"Who gave you the bandana, boy? Says you're a Super Dog? I bet there's no living with you these days."

Max danced in circles then dropped the ball at Quaid's feet. "We'll do catch tomorrow. You go running in the mud and mess up the house and we'll both be in hot water. And I don't know about you but I got my mind set on some of Dad's fried chicken."

He snatched his duffle and ambled across the brick path, dog following. They passed the boxwoods that led to the planter filled with pink flowers by the side door. He'd let himself in, raid the fridge, sleep on the couch, no need waking everyone in the middle of the night . . . least that was the plan till he turned the knob, an alarm split the quiet and the house lit up like a Christmas tree.

Max barked and Quaid stepped back and took in the show. If fireworks blasted from the chimney he wouldn't have been surprised. "I'll be damned. What the hell's going on around here?"

The door flew open on Rory in a pair of blue boxer shorts, no shirt, his granddaddy's Civil War sword firmly in hand and raised for battle. Quaid would have paid a month's salary for a camera.

"Christ in a sidecar, boy, what the hell are you doing here?" He lowered the blade. "You're supposed to be in Alaska, fishing folks out of the drink."

"And you're supposed to be sleeping."

"What the hell do you think I was doing dressed like this, going to church? Kids!" He punched numbers on a keypad by the door that had never been there before. That killed the alarm, except there was another noise, piercing, like an air raid siren.

"Two alarms? What do you have in here, Fort Knox?"

"Piss and vinegar!" Rory groused as he raked his hand through his graying hair, which stuck out in all directions. "I got better than gold, but the sound that can strip varnish from wood is your mighty unhappy little sister cutting up a ruckus, all thanks to you. Now she's awake and no one's getting any more sleep tonight. Damnation!"

"That sound is . . . Bonnie?" Quaid followed Rory inside. "Thought babies cooed and giggled. That's what the ones on TV do."

"Well, this baby never read the damn script." Rory took off for the hall in a jog. "You better come on. 'Bout time you met her, get to lose sleep like the rest of us."

Quaid kicked off his wet shoes and hung his wet jacket over the newel post. He climbed the stairs behind Rory, who yelled to be heard over the din, "Keefe's shooting his last episodes on that soap opera so he's gone back to New York and Callie, his gal, is packing up her stuff in Atlanta to move here. Ryan and Effie are finishing up their business in San Diego and should show up any day now. Thelma and Conrad are working their butts off to make a go of the drydock and turn Hastings House into a bed and breakfast."

Quaid yelled back, "So it's just you and the baby in this big house?"

"And now you. We'll put those survival skills you learned at search and rescue to work, because I sure could use some help. Bonnie's got a real willful streak."

"Can't imagine where she gets that," Quaid said on a laugh as he slapped Rory on the back. They entered the room, Rory switching on a bunny lamp, and Quaid added, "Think you got enough pink stuff in here?"

"After suffering through three boys I got a right." Rory nodded at the squalling Bonnie in a pink pj thing, eyes squinted shut, arms and legs fighting the air. "Go on, pick her up. You woke her, you walk her."

"Huh?"

"House rules. Might as well get used to it if you're staying around for a while."

"You just made that up too." Quaid flexed his fingers, trying to figure out what was the best way to hold a squirming baby.

"She won't break, you know, and you better be doing something quick-like, or the neighbors are going to gripe even if they are down the road a ways. Max is already howling to beat the band."

If he scooped people out of the ocean he could scoop a baby. He held her little bottom in one hand, her head in the other. Warm, soft, wiggly as hell. He thought of Cynthia all wiggly and warm over his shoulder. Nice, very nice . . . and still the princess. "I think I got it."

"Now you change her, another house rule. Whoever holds her does diaper duty. Stuff you need's on that table." He nodded to the corner.

Quaid held tight but not too tight. What was too tight? He thought of his arm across Cynthia's legs, holding her there, tight . . . damn! "I just walked in the door. How can you sucker your own son into changing a baby?"

"Proves I love you, boy. Think of this as a bonding experience." Rory sat in the rocking chair. "So, what are you doing here in the middle of summer? The Coast Guard kick you out?"

Quaid put Bonnie on the table and studied the paraphernalia. "Heard there was this guy with a baby who couldn't keep track of his woman." Quaid glanced at Rory. "Any news on Mimi?"

Rory rocked and Quaid tore off Bonnie's diaper, uncovering the grossest pile of . . . "Dear God in heaven, Rory. What the hell are you feeding this kid?"

"Started vegetables today. Carrots."

"Oh, damn. I'm never eating carrots again."

"As for Mimi we can't find hide or hair of the three guys who headed up that company she worked for. They were fiddling with the books and billing the state for work on levees and docks that never happened. Mimi has disks that prove what was going on."

Quaid located some wipe things. "Why didn't she just go to the DA in the first place?"

"She did, and the next day someone tried to push her in front of a bus and her apartment got busted into. She didn't know who to trust and took the disks and ran. She ended up here at the Landing one rainy night when her car slid in that ditch by Hastings House."

"Grant?"

"Who else. She didn't tell anyone anything that was going on, even me. Dammit all, I could have helped but I think she was too scared. Then one day she just took off again without so much as good-by, probably saw someone she knew who was after her. I didn't know she was carrying my baby and she probably didn't know either."

"How'd you find all this out?"

"A Nashville cop working with the DA's office came looking for Mimi. They tracked her this far. I'd found Bonnie on the back doorstep along with a gold necklace I'd given Mimi and figured she was in some kind of big trouble or she'd never have left Sweet Pea here."

Quaid dropped the diaper and wipes in a plastic bag, the baby quieting a few decibels. "Hard to think sweet when you're doing what I'm doing."

Rory laughed, a low easy sound that filled the room,

making the house a home. "Comes with the territory, you'll get used to it."

"Care to make a little wager on that?" Quaid fastened the tabs on the new diaper, and gazed into the bluest little eyes he'd ever seen. They seemed to be staring right back at him, asking *Who the hell are you?* Then her soft pink lips made a perfect bow and she winked. Quaid felt his breath catch and his heart swell then squeeze tight. Dang! "She looks like you."

"See, Bonnie's got you wrapped around her little finger already. I knew it." Rory let out a sigh. "Now all we got to do is find those three bigshots and get them behind bars before they find my Mimi."

"Any ideas?"

"Like a lump of lead between their eyes?"

"Like where she is." Quaid wiped his hands on the wet things then handed Bonnie to Rory. He rocked, his eyes smiling, the baby cooing . . . finally. "Hard to believe you haven't heard anything from Mimi in three months. Not like a mother to just leave her baby all this time and not make some kind of contact to see how she's doing."

"When are you heading back to Alaska?"

Quaid leaned against the changing table, taking in Rory and his baby daughter. He'd raised one family and was starting on the next. It suited him. He was good at the family thing, damn good, better than Quaid deserved. "I don't know."

The rocking stopped and Rory's gaze met Quaid's across the dim light. "What happened, and I'm betting I'm not going to like the answer."

"Decided my life needed some shaking up."

"Your life's nothing but shook up all to hell and back with the kind of job you have, jumping in the freezing water, saving people's asses. And now you quit doing it to run home and take care of me. I was afraid you'd do a dang-fool thing like that, that's why I didn't tell you right off what was going on around here."

"Ryan called. Said these people who are after Mimi tried to take Bonnie to get to her. Came right into this house and walked out with the baby."

He looked at father and child and his jaw clenched. "Someone stealing your child is not going to happen again. The Guard kept dragging their feet about getting me an extended leave so I helped them make a decision."

"Christ in a sidecar, Quaid. Go get your damn job back right now."

"No." The two men stared at each other for a few beats. Probably the only time in Quaid's life he ever said *no* to Rory O'Fallon. "I'm going to bed, all this baby stuff tires a guy out."

"The Coast Guard's your life, boy."

Quaid grinned and ruffled Rory's hair as he walked by. "Not even half. Good night, Dad." He stopped at the door. "Cynthia Landon's back home."

Rory gave him a sly smile. "A real looker, that one. Proud as all get-out and stuck up, but what do you expect when her parents spoiled her rotten. Bet she fit in just fine with that snooty New York crowd. Heard she had some money problems. Where'd you see her?"

"She ran her car off the road and I drove her and her son home."

"Don't do it, boy."

"Don't do what? Give her a ride?"

Rory chuckled and rocked Bonnie. "You just watch your step with that one, you hear. She's used to pissing in the high cotton."

"Her son's a neat little kid, kind of lost at the moment. But there's no step for me to watch with Cynthia Landon.

I just ran into her on the road and helped her out. She's still a pain."

Rory leaned back and rocked, staring down at Bonnie. "Sometimes running into 'em is all it takes." He put the baby to his shoulder and winked. "I know. I've been there and things can get real complicated real fast."

Chapter 2

Morning sun streamed into the kitchen as Cynthia dried the last dish and put it in the cabinet, wiped off the counter and poured a third cup of coffee. She gazed out the window in the breakfast nook to the weed-infested rose garden. Mother always kept a perfect garden, and if she was too busy with the country club social calendar or heading up another charity event she needed to have the staff help her out. In fact, they needed to do a lot around here, beginning with dusting and vacuuming and washing the windows.

And why were the air conditioner and dishwasher on the fritz? The place was falling apart, and since great-great-granddaddy Landon built it a hundred and sixty years ago, falling apart was not an option.

Even at seven in the morning the shorts and blouse she'd borrowed from Mother already stuck like a spa mudpack and her hair had frizzed into a poodle-do. She wiggled her toes in the electric-green flip-flops she'd had since high school. Except for visits back here every few years she hadn't worn them since she'd packed her things and moved to New York fifteen years ago. A lot had happened in that time; she'd married, had a son, started her own line of women's wear, made money, lost everything . . . except Lawrence, thank God . . . and Quaid O'Fallon was all grown up.

She stopped the coffee cup halfway to her mouth. Where'd that grown-up crack come from? She hadn't thought about the guy in years. But then she'd never been tossed over his shoulder before either.

"You didn't have to do the dishes," her mother said as she shuffled into the kitchen, hand to her forehead, shading her eyes. Her hair had a finger-in-the-light-socket look and her white cotton blouse wasn't pressed. Not Ida Landon's usual neat southern belle appearance. She sat at the oak table, not facing the window. "I could have done them."

Cynthia remembered the brandy decanter on the sideboard in the living room as half empty last night and completely empty when she got up this morning. Mother celebrating her and Lawrence's homecoming? "I don't mind washing dishes but where's Dolly and Bobo and Cook? And why aren't they serving breakfast in the dining room like usual?" Eggs Benedict, hotcakes, maple syrup, fresh orange juice—sounded really good right now. "Did they persuade you into letting them all take vacation together? You know you shouldn't have let them do that. You're too soft a touch."

Cynthia poured coffee into a Haviland china cup, placed it on a saucer and served it to her mother. Ida bit her bottom lip and sighed.

"Are you feeling okay?"

"I will be in a moment, dear. I need a little fortification. Everyone needs fortification now and then." She went to the pantry, pulled a brandy bottle from behind a box of oatmeal, sat down and topped off her coffee. She placed the bottle in front of her. "Oh poop, what the hell." She pulled the cork and drank the brandy straight from the bottle.

"Mother!"

She burped and patted her lips. "Yes, that's better." She looked at Cynthia, her eyes cloudy. "There's a little . . . glitch, dear." Ida took another swig like a person who'd swigged many times before. "I'm afraid things have become rather difficult. You see, I'm financially embarrassed."

"Embarrassed as in can't find your checkbook? Lost your credit card?"

"I'm broke as an out-of-work beggar and haven't a clue what to do about it."

Cynthia's legs went to rubber and she sat across from her mother. "But . . . but Daddy left you money. He was the president of three banks in the area. He's only been gone three years. And there was insurance. Where did it all go?"

"Seems your Father made some rather dreadful financial decisions that I never knew about. Sugar and spice mostly, I believe."

"Commodities? He invested in commodities? That's not like Daddy, they're so risky. Why would he do such a thing?"

"Sugar and Spice are two strippers at the Lord and Lady, a private men's club in Rockton. Seems he had a fetish for leather and threesomes. Even bought a condo and left it to the girls. I paid to keep it out of the papers. You know how gossip spreads in small towns and we do have our pride." Her mother hiccupped and Cynthia grabbed the bottle and downed the brandy. "I had to let Dolly and the rest go and I've taken a mortgage on the house."

She gave a lopsided grin that indicated the booze was having an effect, and Cynthia hoped she'd feel the same way soon. "But I've come up with a truly wonderful idea. Well two, actually. I've decided to turn Ivy Acres into a bed and breakfast and write my memoirs as a southern lady, one of those steel magnolia books."

Cynthia massaged her forehead. "I'm getting a migraine."

Her mother nudged the bottle and continued, "I've already had customers here till I went and burned the breakfast for that nice couple from New Jersey. Then there was that mouse infestation and then that man who pinched my behind and I was forced to deck him with the Royal Doulton vase that used to be in the dining room. For some reason the man seemed to think he had a right. Can you imagine?"

She snatched the bottle from Cynthia. "And I was downright partial to that vase." She took a mouthful. "Belonged to Grandmother Hilary. Seems the word has gotten out that Ivy Acres is less than a pristine place to stay, and then Thelma and Conrad opened Hastings House as a bed and breakfast and they're getting all the business."

"Thelma McAllister? She's an incredible cook. Scones to die for."

"You're not making me feel better, dear. I'm afraid I have made a mess of things."

"Not you Mother, Daddy is the culprit here. How could he . . . Why would he . . ."

"No one's perfect, dear, and I must confess that leather was never my preference. A little spanky once in a while and those Velcro handcuffs now and then, but—"

A car sounded in the drive. Oh, thank God! A discussion on her parents' sex life—that she never would have expected in a million years—was not how she wanted to start the day. The fact that Mother had no money and that her wonderful, saintly father was not so saintly at all was the crowning blow.

Mother said, "Perhaps it's a customer. I put an ad in the *Memphis Times*. See, since you arrived things are getting enormously better already." Ida brightened, and with the booze under her belt that was a lot of bright for seven A.M.

"You stay here," Cynthia said. The whole world didn't

need to know her mother had brandy with her oatmeal. She wondered if they knew about the strippers and the leather. There weren't many secrets in a small town no matter how much hush money her mother paid out. This was so not the setting she expected to come home to. Where was the mint julep on the back porch, homemade ice cream with chocolate shavings, the lazy days of summer, the housekeeper and cook? She really missed Cook.

Cynthia flip-flopped across the hardwood floor that needed refinishing, past the staircase and peered out the leaded-glass sidelights. Her Buick circled the drive and stopped in front of the house. Since it didn't get here by itself that meant Quaid O'Fallon was back.

She was in no mood to deal with a man, any man, especially a smart-ass used to getting his own way. Didn't they all? Why couldn't Quaid O'Fallon just . . . be a girl, then she wouldn't mind him showing up here! She yanked open the front door, ready with *thanks for the car now go away,* when Lawrence joined her, staying close, Coast Guard hat on his head. "Hi, Quaid."

Quaid peered out the rolled-down window. Eyes bright and clear, square jaw, a hint of danger about him. He was so *not* a girl!

He ignored her but said to Lawrence, "Came by to drop off your stuff and see if you want a job."

Cynthia did an eye roll, mostly to keep from staring at Quaid. "He's eight. Doesn't even make his own bed."

"What kind of job?" Lawrence said with more enthusiasm in his voice than she'd heard in a while.

"We have a dog, Max, who needs walking and someone to play with him. My dad and I are too busy and he's getting fat—the dog, not my dad." Quaid grinned and she knew Lawrence was grinning too. For a second she wasn't sure which tickled her more till she remembered that it didn't matter what Quaid did or how he smiled. This was the beginning of the *no men* portion of her life. Besides, at thirty-three all that men wanted was sex . . . though, if she wanted to be honest, that sounded pretty darn good right now.

No! Remember Aaron and his band of merry men who screwed over her big time. That was the only kind of screwing she should think about.

"So, what do you say, Lawrence?" Quaid unfolded himself from the car. He seemed taller than last night, black hair longer than she expected for a military man, and a five-o'clock shadow that seemed a permanent condition no matter when or how often the man shaved.

His olive T-shirt molded to fine abs and terrific shoulders. She knew about those shoulders first hand since she'd been there, head down, derriere in the air, Quaid's arm across her legs. How embarrassing, how humiliating, how . . . unforgettable? Embarrassing and humiliating she could deal with, she'd been through so much of that in New York she was numb. But the unforgettable part, his hands on her . . . *oh boy*. This was all a direct result of being without a guy for a while—a long, long, long while.

She added up the months, or was it a year now . . . or two? Two! Dear God. Quaid said something to Lawrence that made him laugh then added, "Pays two bucks an hour. A guy needs to have some folding money in his pocket."

Lawrence pushed his glasses up the bridge of his nose like he always did when nervous. He shuffled down the four front steps, hands stuffed in the pockets of his khaki pants. "You're really going to pay me to walk your dog?"

"And play with him. He has a favorite yellow ball."

"Neat."

At least Lawrence found something neat; she couldn't remember the last time she felt that way. Maybe when she'd opened her own design loft in New York, Aaron was her prince, her father was a god, and Quaid O'Fallon was not on her doorstep making her hotter than the August sun.

"Why are you doing this?" she blurted. She and Quaid weren't exactly friends, not even in school together. She'd been in second grade when he was born. Good Lord, was she old or what!

"Something wrong?" Quaid asked. "You've been looking at me like I have two heads."

And he did and she was obsessing over both!

"Can I have the job, Mom? Please. I'll get folding money of my own. I can save up for a microscope."

"You've never been around dogs. You could be allergic."

"I promise not to sneeze and I'm a fast learner."

She'd taken so much away from Lawrence these past few months, she couldn't say *no* now when he was finally excited about something in O'Fallon's Landing, Tennessee, which must seem like the end of the earth compared to New York City. "Okay, you can take the job."

"Yes!" Lawrence did a little jump—and he never jumped, actually he didn't even walk fast, as if always putting his energy into thinking.

Ida came out onto the porch, hand to her forehead, shading her eyes. "Is that you, Quaid O'Fallon? What brings you here at this hour of the morning?"

"Making a delivery."

Wobbling, she shooed him away. "I don't rightly remember ordering anything but I do remember that you stole that blueberry pie right off Cook's windowsill, and did you ever graduate from high school and aren't you supposed to be in . . ." She hiccupped. "The Arctic?"

Quaid's brow arched at the hiccup and a grin played at

his mouth, his very nice mouth that Cynthis wished she'd stop thinking about. He said, "Got a diploma and everything, it just took a while."

Ida harrumphed and Cynthia said, "Mother, that pie incident was twenty years ago." Now why did she stick up for Quaid O'Fallon? He didn't look the sort of man who needed her help on anything. Maybe because she knew what it was like to make mistakes and then get reminded of them. She said to Ida, "Why don't you go back inside and pour us coffee, Mother? Lawrence, help your grandmother cook breakfast. I'll be in in a minute to lend a hand."

"Grandmother can cook? You can cook? Really?" Lawrence stared, till she gave him *the* look and added, "Go."

Quaid held out his hand to Lawrence. "Is it a deal?"

Lawrence shook, his small hand dwarfed by Quaid's much larger one, the very one he'd used to hold her legs as she'd dangled down his back. She prayed for amnesia and Lawrence said, "I'll come over right after breakfast. Where do you live?"

"Your mom knows. There's a good path through the woods that's safer than the two-lane. But you have to watch out for Grant."

"Grant? Ulysses S.? Mom said something about him last night."

Quaid winked. "Quartered his troops right where we're standing. Probably ran you off the road last night. He does things like that, especially in the rain and with Southerners coming down the road."

"We have our own ghost? Oh, this is really good. There's no scientific proof that ghosts exist . . . but there's none to prove they don't, either." Lawrence beamed, skipped up the stairs and followed Ida into the house. Cynthia said in a low voice, "What the heck do you think you're doing?"

"Returning your car?"

"Good Lord, why'd you tell him about Grant?"

"Sounds like you already did that. And I figure the Landing's got to have something over New York, and kids love ghosts."

And she'd thought that very same thing. Quaid looked as if he intended to leave but then didn't. He folded his arms across his broad chest, the sunlight playing in his black hair as he leaned against the car, grinning. Damn, did he have to grin?

"What's with Ida?"

"Hasn't had her coffee yet and just out of curiosity, how'd you start my car? Bet they don't teach that in the Coast Guard."

"Something from my checkered past, like stealing pies."

"And you're offering my son and not some other kid in town this job because . . . ? We're not charity, you know."

"Lawrence is the new kid. Taking care of Max will give him something to do and he's got an instant friend." Quaid's eyes darkened a shade, not that anyone else would notice but being a designer, colors were her business. "I had a dog when I was his age, a mangy cur that roamed the docks—like me, except he was better looking."

She bit back a laugh. Quaid O'Fallon was too smooth, much too easy to get along with . . . like Aaron at the beginning, and her attorney, and all the rest of the guys in her life, including her own father. They gained her trust then let her down. She and Ida shared a genetic flaw, poor male selection. Well, she wasn't selecting now and she did still have her pride. "I intend to repay you."

"Lawrence is working for me. I don't know how you all do things in New York City but down here that means I get to pay him."

"You pulled us off the riverbank last night and gave my son a job that makes him happy, and moving to nowhere USA was not on his list of things to do this summer." Avoiding temptation by not looking at Quaid, she came down the steps and opened the car door. "I should warn you that Lawrence is rather cerebral and has the eye-hand coordination of a bat."

She rummaged in the back seat till she found her sewing basket, the one her mother gave her when she went off to Parsons for fashion design, the one she snuck out of the loft along with an old sewing machine and a few bolts of material, before the bank auctioned the loft contents to pay off Aaron's debts. She fished a tape measure from the top tray. To get his size she needed to look at him, touch him. Think . . . mannequin. She took in Quaid, toe to neck. Oh, crap! "Stand up straight and hold out your arms like a T."

"Excuse me?"

I am a professional; I can do this; I will not salivate over the customer nor tackle him to the grass and fornicate on the front lawn. "I'll make you a sport coat."

"You can do that?"

"They don't fall off the sports coat tree, O'Fallon." She put the tape to his wrist—warm, sturdy, lightly sprinkled with black curls of hair that continued up his arm. Maybe she should just make him a cake. Could she sew a cake, because she sure couldn't bake one.

The scent of musky soap and something fresh and male filled her head. She stretched the tape from wrist to broad shoulder, the one she knew intimately, the one covered in soft cotton now, the one she wanted to touch. Swallowing a carnivorous whine she said, "Thirty-seven."

"You don't have to sew me a coat."

"It makes us even. You can go your way and I go mine. You've heard of wireless, well I'm going manless. I don't want them in my life and that includes you." She could feel the heat from his skin under her fingertips. Every inch of Quaid firm, tight, totally hunky.

"Is this what you did in New York?"

"Huh?" She nearly dropped the tape measure. "Do what?"

"Make men's clothes? Is that why you don't like them? Got tired of dressing them?"

"Got tired of them messing up my life. It doesn't start out that way but that's what happens so I'm through with men." She took the tape across his back, his very broad back that tapered to his waist and lean hips. *Think of something else.* "I had a loft, Creations by Cynthia. I designed business chic for the larger woman. So much of what's out there in the bigger sizes has a masculine tone that makes women look like Donald Trump with better hair and earrings."

"So what happened?"

What happened was that she darn near melted into a blob being so close to Quaid. "Aaron, my dear husband, borrowed money against my business for his favorite pastime, Texas Hold'em, and I'm not from Texas and he sure wasn't holding me. The bank foreclosed on my loft and I foreclosed on Aaron."

She walked around to Quaid's front, keeping her eyes from his, looking at her flip-flops. If he realized how turned on he made her it would be embarrassing. He was young and she wasn't and that made her even more uncomfortable. What would he think? "I'm starting over at the ripe old age of forty."

She held the white cloth tape against his chest; his muscles flexed. Sweat prickled at her neck, her hands now at his belt, his breath in her hair, her forehead grazing his shirt. "Mother and I are opening Ivy Acres as a bed and breakfast and—"

"Cynthia?"

"And we should have customers and—"

"Cynthia!"

"What!" She snapped her head up, looking straight into

his eyes, now the color of antique Chinese jade. He took her chin on his forefinger, his touch gentle and caring, making her go all . . . soft. Soft and this man was not the way to start the day. She stood, her face to his.

This time he swallowed. "I have to get going. Now . . . right now." His voice was strained and low. "Rory's expecting me at the docks to help out. There's no need for you to make me anything. You don't owe me."

He backed up but she grabbed the front of his shirt, holding him still, then kissed him full on his warm, very receptive and incredibly yummy lips. God, he had great lips.

She stepped back, her eyes wide and mouth open. She snapped it shut. "Oh, crap! I don't want anything to do with you, Quaid O'Fallon. Nothing at all, I swear it. Stay away from me. Stay out of my business. Try and be . . . a little ugly." She turned and raced up the steps like an embarrassed teenager and slammed the door shut behind her, leaning against it as if to keep what was on the outside from coming in—except it was the nutty woman inside causing all the trouble.

She peeked though the sidelight, catching a glimpse of Quaid walking down the drive. He rounded the bend by the sugar maple that had been there as long as she could remember. Then he was gone.

Like heck he was gone. Quaid O'Fallon's presence was like the scent of a dead skunk. Not that he smelled like a carcass . . . she wished . . . but he was around even when she couldn't see him and wasn't likely to go away no matter how darn much she wanted him to. And she really, really wanted him gone.

Quaid could feel Cynthia watching him as he ambled down the Landon's driveway. He hadn't ambled in a long time, maybe his whole damn life, and the only reason he did the slow walk now was thanks to his dick being hard as a chunk of three-day-old bread.

He'd been around a lot of women, kissed most of them and never had this damn embarrassing problem. Then again, being stationed on Kodiak Island for the last three months had kept female contact to nonexistent and a kiss like the one just planted on him was enough to give a saint a hard-on. Quaid O'Fallon was nowhere near sainthood.

Like Rory said, Cynthia was not a woman for him. She was one uptown gal, and he was one down-home boy. The good part was she didn't want men in her life, so that ended anything brewing between them and he could turn all his attention to finding Mimi . . . except his attention kept focusing on that kiss. Why would a prissy woman who didn't want men in her life, especially the local badass, kiss him like that anyway? And man could she kiss!

Quaid headed up the road, past the O'Fallon house, a light breeze off the river swaying the treetops. He turned for town. How many sodas and candy bars had he snitched from the market? A ton. He hoped that sending Betty Lindel flowers and a check on her birthday for the last ten years sort of made up for it.

A thin curl of smoke drifted from the back porch of Slim's. A hint of the best barbecue on earth hung in the air. The porch floorboards still sagged and the door stood open, letting the odor of beer out and fresh air and sunlight in. In an hour the Landing would go to sizzle, the door close and the AC back on full tilt. But now it was a summer morning in the South and not to be missed.

Sally Donaldson sat on a stool, head bent, poring over papers strewn across the bar. John Lee Hooker's "One Bourbon, One Scotch, One Beer" purred in the background from the green and yellow jukebox in the corner, that some antique dealer in the city would shed blood to own. Same worn oak chairs, same paint-chipped tables dotted the room. An upright by the wall with a guitar propped against it waited for someone to get an urge and bring them to life.

Quaid pulled up behind Sally and yanked her chestnut hair. She yelped, bolted straight up, spun around, fire in her big brown eyes and a hint of pink across her perfect mahogany cheeks. She grinned. "Well, I'll be damned. Lock up your daughters and get out the shotguns, Quaid O'Fallon's back in town."

He nodded at the papers. "'Bout time you put that high-faluting Harvard education of yours to use."

"Hush, boy. Snobby places like that give this fine establishment a bad name." She slid from the stool, flung her arms around his neck and kissed him full on the mouth. A friendly kiss, not like the one he'd gotten from Cynthia. Sally's eyes danced and he felt as if he were exactly where he was supposed to be.

"What brings you here in the middle of the summer?"

"A pretty girl and a kiss like that would bring any man crawling home."

"You are so full of baloney. You're here for Dad's barbecue and you know it."

"There is that. I've eaten so much damn fish I think I have gills. I need some serious cholesterol-inducing meat on a hot grill."

She laughed as she stepped to the back of the bar and pulled a frosted glass pitcher of tea from the fridge, condensation dripping down the sides, lemon slices floating on top. Quaid smacked his lips. "Well there you go, sweet tea. Only in the South can you get the good stuff."

"And that's me you're talking about, big boy?" She twitched her hips and laughed then filled two glasses. "Besides being a rabid carnivore, I'm guessing the reason you're home is a certain baby sister and her missing mama."

"Do you have any idea what's going on? I asked Rory about Mimi and he just changed the subject."

Sally hitched herself back onto the stool and Quaid claimed the one beside her as she said, "Maybe it's just too painful to have Bonnie and not her mother around."

Sally leaned back against the bar, legs crossed at the knee, showing off long brown legs. Every guy on the Landing had a crush on Sally Donaldson at one time or another . . . including him and his brothers, thank God at different times. O'Fallon men always did have great taste in women and right now he couldn't get his mind off Cynthia. Dang!

"No one knows where Mimi is and everyone in town's watching out for Bonnie and the Martians just abducted her in their spaceship and are heading for Pluto."

"Huh?"

She set her tea on the bar. "What are you thinking about, Quaid O'Fallon, because with that faraway look in your eyes it sure isn't me or what I'm saying. It's a woman. You got that *woman* look about you. And I'm betting Cynthia Landon is in the mix somewhere."

"I just got into town."

"And Cynthia just got into town at the same time, least that's what the chit-chat is this morning. Sounds like destiny's working overtime down on the two-lane."

"Only if destiny comes in the form of a Yankee ghost prowling in a rainstorm just like he's been doing for over a hundred years now. More coincidence than karma."

"Maybe, but I doubt that Grant has anything to do with Cynthia planting a lip-lock on you that singed your eyebrows?"

Quaid did a double take. "How'd you know?"

She flashed a sassy grin. "I didn't . . . till now. You best watch your step with that one."

"She just got here. I just got here."

"I know. That's what worries me. What the heck's going to happen next?"

A big guy in an apron came in through the back door. His dark eyes went from Sally to Quaid as he put his hand on his hip and shook his head. "I'm out back sweating my butt off over an open fire, girl, and here you are two-timing me with the locals."

Sally got up and kissed the guy full on the lips, adding some tongue and sexy attitude—kind of like the kiss Cynthia slipped him. Did he have to keep thinking about her? Why did she kiss him like there was no tomorrow? And why in the hell did he let Sally trip him up?

Because Cynthia Landon had turned his brain to fish bait.

Sally pulled the man over. "Demar Thacker, cop with the attorney general's office, meet Quaid O'Fallon, search and rescue, U.S. Coast Guard."

Quaid shook Demar's hand. "Formerly Coast Guard. Now mostly unemployed river rat."

"I'm on vacation and cooking barbecue. That makes us about even."

"I understand what got you here in the first place was Mimi. Any leads?"

Demar let out a deep breath. "I know time's running out. The three guys who headed up River Environs, the company Mimi worked for, are hunting for her and her disks. The guys escaped when the DA went after them. Their assets are frozen, but without Mimi's testimony the DA really has no evidence that will stick and they'll have to drop the case. We need to find the bad guys before they get to Mimi, and we have to lock them up or she'll stay hidden forever. She fears for her life, that's why she ran."

"Do we know what these guys look like?"

"Two of them. They were in the papers a lot. But the third was the accounting honcho, very low-key, kept out of the limelight, no family, from Pennsylvania. No pictures of him anywhere except driver's license—it's so nondescript it doesn't help at all. Brown eyes, brown hair, average height, average weight, has a thing for good food and saddle shoes. He's probably using a disguise. But make no mistake, these guys are ruthless. If they pull this off they'll get away with millions."

"Hello," came a voice from the doorway, as a short middle-aged man in shorts and a blue Hawaiian shirt strolled in. He held out his card. "Hope I'm not interrupting anything. Preston Wright here, private investigator from Memphis. Well, I'm really from Milwaukee and moved to Memphis for the weather . . . and the folks. More friendly in the South. I think it's because of the good food. I got a thing for good eating. Anyway, Rory O'Fallon hired me to find the mother of his little girl and I thought the local watering hole was a good place to start."

Sally took the card, and Preston ran his hand through his thinning curly hair. "You all wouldn't know anything about that, would you? I don't have a picture of the lady but she used to work for Mr. O'Fallon. About thirty-eight, auburn hair, brown eyes."

Demar craned his neck forward as if examining a bug. "Rory hired *you*?"

Preston beamed. "You bet your boots. This is my second case, my first was in Rockton, but I can't tell you what it was about because that's privileged information for us private investigators. I used to be a high school history teacher and now I'm retired. Been watching detective shows all my life. Magnum's my favorite."

Preston jabbed himself in the chest. "Now I know what you're thinking . . ." His grin grew. "That's what Magnum always says on TV . . . Now I know what you're thinking . . . where'd I get this great shirt." He held up the collar for inspection. "Bought it on eBay, the real thing, had it shipped all the way from Hawaii. Got myself a red Beetle, couldn't afford a Ferrari on a retired teacher's salary. Even grew a mustache." He twitched the fuzz under his nose.

Quaid resisted the urge to shake his head to figure out what the hell was going on. Why would Rory hire Preston Wright to find Mimi? The guy was nice enough but . . . a wannabe TV character?

"Can you all give me directions to a place to stay for a few days? Nothing too pricey. I'll be hanging around for a while." His gaze swept the room. "Great bar. Barbecue smells as if it's got a hint of cinnamon, touch of cloves and maybe some chocolate. Chocolate in barbecue is the secret."

Demar nodded and laughed. "You got a good nose for good food, my man. And if I don't get back to my grill I'm going to be serving up burnt hockey pucks for lunch."

Demar left and Quaid said, "There's Ivy Acres, it's a bed and breakfast run by Ida Landon. You can stay there."

"Landon? No kidding. Heard that name mentioned over in Rockton. It's got a certain reputation. Is this a . . . house?"

"The family's well known in the area and they have a really great house. You'll like Ivy Acres. A little run-down but it makes up for that in hospitality. You'll feel right at home. The women who run it will take good care of you, very friendly."

"Really?"

"You bet. Whatever you heard in Rockton is absolutely true. Just follow the road to the river, take a hard left to the white house a few miles down. Four columns in front, you can't miss it." Least he could give Cynthia some business out of this . . . whatever *this* was. Raising a child was not cheap and she was out of a job. "And as long as you're staying there you get free dinners here."

Sally gave him an evil look and Preston arched his brows Tom Selleck style. "Well now, I think I'll check out this Ivy Acres. Never visited a place like that before, though I've been tempted. Never knew Southern hospitality could be so . . . hospitable."

Preston strolled out the door, his beat-up loafers slapping the floor. Sally glanced at the card in her hand, shook her head and drank her tea down in one gulp. She said in a low voice, "Rory's cracked under the pressure. This Mimi thing has scrambled and fried his brain like an omelet. Why else would he hire . . . Magnum? And what's with this free dinner stuff?"

"I need to find Rory." Quaid stared out the doorway, the old red convertible coughing and sputtering its way down the main street of town. "Bill me for the dinners. I just wanted to throw some business Cynthia's way."

"Well, if Thelma finds out you sent a paying customer to Ivy Acres instead of Hastings House you'll never get another piece of her pecan pie as long as you live." Sally's eyes twinkled. "And if there's nothing between you and Cynthia why'd you give her business?"

"She has a son, they need money. There are a lot of strangers in town, now that the place is getting spruced up. Thelma will get her share. Ida wouldn't be doing the bed and breakfast thing if she didn't need money. The place looked worn when I was there. Not the way I remember. Preston might need encouragement to stay, so I threw in the dinner."

Sally said, "Everyone in town thought Ida was doing the bed and breakfast because she was lonely in that big house all by herself. When her Edward died there was talk of something going on in Rockton but no one knows what happened exactly. No scandal for the Landons. I'm guessing it was a cute young cupcake on the side but everything got real hush, hush."

Sally looked Quaid straight in the eyes. "Kind of like you and Cynthia. A big old fat mystery."

Quaid flashed a grin as he headed for the door. "And that's exactly the way it's going to stay."

Chapter 3

The next morning Sally stood in the middle of the bar and studied the architect plans Ryan O'Fallon drew up on expanding Slim's, except she wasn't really thinking about the building project so much as Quaid and Cynthia. What was going on between those two? And something sure was. Quaid's poker face didn't give much away but there was a spark there when he talked about Cynthia— and she was so not the one for Quaid.

Demar came up behind her, she could tell before he even spoke. She could feel his presence. 'Course she could also smell the odor of hickory smoke and barbecue sauce that seemed to follow him everywhere.

He nuzzled her neck, sending both chills and roaring heat clear through her. She turned and he pressed her close to his broad chest, her favorite place to be. His arousal nestled against her, and her hands rested against his derriere. Demar Thacker was the most handsome, well-built man God ever set on the earth in or out of a barbecue-smeared apron. "Cynthia is not the gal for Quaid but I am so the girl for you."

"Are you still thinking about that?"

"That I'm the girl for you? Heck yes!" She laughed and gave him a quick kiss.

"Why does it bother you so much that Quaid and this Cynthia person are an item—if they even are? Who is she and what's wrong with her?"

"She's the local snob, even had Conrad Hastings beat in that department till he fell for Thelma and entered the real world."

Demar ran his lips lightly across hers and she kissed him because she had to. "Quaid's my friend, Cynthia isn't. The two together gives me a bad feeling."

"And I'll just have to change that feeling." His tongue licked her lips, her mouth parting. He tasted warm and male and of pure sex. His tongue mated with hers as he slid his big arms around her, making her feel as if all was right with the world, at least her corner of it. She'd found the man for her, her Prince Charming, her soul mate, her—

"My, my, as I live and breathe, if it isn't Demar Thacker doing what he does best." A woman swayed her way up to them, black hair braided back, khaki slacks hugging slim hips and thighs, white blouse open to the third button. "I've been looking my eyeballs out for you, big boy."

The stranger flashed a smile, perfect white teeth against perfect ginger complexion and a really great makeup job Christian Dior would be proud of. "If the gang at the station could see you now all decked out in an apron they'd laugh their behinds off."

Demar's eyes widened and his arm slipped away from Sally. He stepped back. "Jett? What the hell are you doing here? And nobody from that station would be laughing, they'd be wanting me to cook for them."

Laughing, Jett ran to Demar, jumped into his arms, wrapping her arms around his neck. "What in the world are you doing in this place?"

This place? Sally felt steam curl from her ears.

"That's my line."

"Had to see for myself that you really were spending your vacation standing over a grill."

She slid down his front as if this was not the first time she'd taken that particular path. Demar said, "I make the best barbecue east of the Mississippi . . . except for Slim." Then as if he suddenly remembered, he nodded at Sally. "Uh, this is . . . Slim's daughter."

Slim's daughter? She'd been relegated to someone's *daughter* with no name of her own, in the space of five seconds, a front-body slide and a sexy come-on?

"This is Jett Compton, another cop from Nashville."

Good old Jett had a name. Demar didn't hesitate a beat in who she was.

He said to Jett, "And I know you didn't come here to watch me cook."

She rolled her shoulders, her well-toned body moving in all the right places. Sally sucked in her stomach, stuck out her boobs, what there was, and swore off sausage and chocolate chip cookies. She stood tall—though being five-three didn't give her much to work with, especially compared to a lanky five-ten with good caps and augmentation . . . those puppies had to be augmented.

Ms. Cleavage said, "Thought if this town is where you took your vacation I should too."

"You're staying?" Demar said, too much happy in his voice.

"Why not," she purred as Cynthia Landon came in and took a seat at the bar.

What the heck was Cynthia Landon doing here? Sally wondered. Slim's was not the usual haunt of the rich and snobby, or cops from Nashville.

Cleavage continued, "I've never seen the Mississippi

River or Graceland, and Memphis isn't far away. You know how I love Delta blues and I have some R and R time coming."

"Well, then I'll just have to show you around," Demar volunteered, looking like a kid at Christmas.

"I have to tend the bar," Sally offered.

Jett waved her hand in dismissal, not even glancing Sally's way. "We'll catch up with you later, dear."

Dear?

A spark lit Demar's eyes, a look he'd reserved only for her, Sally thought. Except he wasn't looking at her. He gazed at Jett and said to her, "We need to take a walk down by the river. Nothing like the river in the summer. I'll pack lunch and we'll catch up." He checked his watch. "Meet me at the landing in two hours."

He gave Sally a quick kiss that was more autopilot than meaningful then headed for the back door, calling over his shoulder, "The road takes you down to the water, Jett. I'll snag us a boat and show you the Mississippi up close and personal like."

"I showed him the river when he got here," Sally muttered to herself while watching Demar's retreating back. She faced Cleavage. What to say? Welcome. Nice boobs? What the hell are you really doing here with my man?

Jett smiled sweetly, too sweetly, and she didn't budge. "I guess you're wondering why I'm here?"

"Ordering breakfast? We don't do breakfast. You'll have to find another place." Like back in Nashville.

"Demar and I used to be lovers."

Sally willed herself not to react because that's what Jett wanted, she knew that with every jealous fiber of her body. Jett added, "Actually, we were engaged two years ago."

"Congratulations?" This conversation was not improving.

"And I suppose you should know that I intend to get Demar back. I made a mistake breaking up with him. He's drop-dead handsome and thoughtful and a girl could do a whole lot worse than getting it on with Demar. So why don't you be a good little country frau and let him go and save us both a lot of time and trouble."

A homicide in the bar would not be good for business but it was damn tempting. "I think that's up to Demar."

Jett let out with one of those *that's what you think* kind of laughs. "It's up to the woman to catch the man she wants and I want that man. Always have, always will."

"Except you broke up with him."

"I'm just doing you a favor and telling you up front what's happening." She patted Sally's cheek and Sally considered slapping her silly. "You're no match for me, dear. You should know that."

Sally folded her arms. "I may be a hillbilly from Tennessee but I'm also a Harvard hillbilly, and floor broker on the stock exchange. If I can handle that I can handle anything, *dear*."

"But you didn't handle it, did you," sneered Jett. "Or you wouldn't be back here in nowhere Tennessee serving drinks to the locals."

Ouch! The truth hurt. Three years on the exchange, two prescriptions for ulcers and landing flat on her back in the ER and she knew it was time to pack it in. She wasn't cut out for the Wall Street scene.

Sally Donaldson *couldn't hack it just like Jett said.* Self-esteem took a dive and she couldn't think of a comeback to save her life.

"See you around, girl. Think about what I said, save yourself some grief."

"Wait a minute," Cynthia said, suddenly standing in front of Jett, anger in her eyes, surprising the hell out of

Sally. "What makes you think you have the right to come in here, insult the owner and threaten to take her man? No one died and left you boss, girl."

Jett's eyes narrowed. "What's it to you?"

Cynthia's eyes drew together, her lips thinned and Sally took a step back. Whoa. Cynthia Landon, pissed off woman. Who would have thought? "I've had my fill of people taking what belongs to others and I didn't come home to get more of the same."

"I'll remember that. But you remember that Demar Thacker is mine and I'm going to do whatever it takes to have him."

Jett stepped around Cynthia and strutted her stuff all the way to her little white sports car. It headed down the street in a spray of gravel and Cynthia said, "I have an ex who'd be a perfect match for that witch. We should get them together, pray they don't breed."

"Why . . . why did you do that?"

Cynthia's brows arched as if she didn't quite know herself. "I think I snapped." She raked her hair from her face. "It's no fun to have someone come into your place and run off with the things you cherish most, man or loft."

"Loft?"

"Long story. I didn't mean to butt into your business but that woman's a snake. You better watch your back."

This was probably the most Cynthia Landon had ever said to Sally in her life. "Well, thanks for saying what you did. She kind of caught me off guard." She didn't think she'd ever be thanking Cynthia Landon for anything. "Did you need something?"

Cynthia drew in a deep breath and smiled, though it seemed forced. "My mother may stop in here for a drink and I'd like for you to call me if she does. She's taking medication and it doesn't mix well with alcohol and she tends to get a little wobbly but . . ."

"What kind of medication? Is Ida ill?"

Cynthia gave a deer-in-the-headlights look. "Ill?"

"Medication? Your mother? Are you okay?"

Cynthia sighed and her shoulders slumped. "Okay, There is no medication, I lied and I'm really bad at it. I need to give it up. The truth is my dad made some unwise investments and Ida's numbing it all by tipping the sauce. There it is, I said it, it's the truth."

"Ida's a . . . drunk?"

"More like a drink followed by another and another. I got rid of all the alcohol in the house so she may come here because I hid her car keys and she can't drive into Memphis. I don't want her dependent on liquor and I'm working on breaking her habit. If she starts distilling gin in the bathtub I'm in trouble. I can pay you." She opened her purse and took out a checkbook.

"Ida doesn't exactly frequent this place."

"Well thank heavens for that," Cynthia said as she fished in her purse. She stopped and looked up. "That came out all wrong. I mean I'm thankful that Ida's not coming here to imbibe and . . . Oh, what's the use?" She dropped her checkbook in her purse and turned for the door. "You have no reason on earth to help me. I'm not exactly the Landing's answer to Ms. Congeniality. I spent most of my childhood with my nose in the air wondering who I was. I'll handle this myself."

Now who was being the snob? thought Sally. Besides, Cynthia had stood up for her. She caught up with Cynthia and touched her arm. "If Ida comes in I'll call you, or feed her barbecue till you get here. I really appreciate your help with Jett."

"Sorry you're having man troubles. I can relate. I think I wrote the book on troubles with the opposite sex."

Sally shrugged, pushing aside the tension from Jett. She grinned. "Not from what I hear. Word has it you and the opposite sex in the form of one Quaid O'Fallon are getting along real well." And that didn't bother her now as much as it did ten minutes ago. In fact, maybe Cynthia Landon was someone who could actually handle Quaid, or at least stand up to him. Surprise, surprise! "You two are an item?"

Cynthia laughed, suddenly looking not so stressed. And she blushed. Sally bet it took a lot for a forty-something from New York to blush but Quaid did the trick. Cynthia said, "Gossip rules in small towns. Even when you think no one's looking someone always is. How could I forget?" She pushed back her hair from her face. "But just for the record, there is nothing going on between Quaid and me. I've had my fill of men, any and all of them. I simply quit."

"Yeah, yeah, that's what we all say and it never happens. Kind of like a diet, you swear off chocolate and then you see a delicious six-foot chunk that you can't live without."

"Men have so screwed up my life, but if you want your chocolate you'll have to fight for him. Jett is not the kind who gives up easily . . . and . . ." She pursed her lips and looked thoughtful. "And there's something else going on with that woman. Jett's beautiful, more model than cop. Why all the way out here to get Demar?"

"Girl, Demar is gorgeous."

"But there are hunks of gorgeous especially in Nashville . . . with it being country-western music central. Demar's got something she wants and not just what's below his belt."

Sally raised her brow. "You've never seen what's below that man's belt."

Cynthia chuckled and patted Sally's hand in big sister fashion that wasn't patronizing so much as a shared experience. "If you want Demar below and above the waist, leave what happened to you in New York in New York.

You need to forget about it, shake it off and remember you're better than that. You are a talented woman and don't let Jett belittle you with her poison. She's counting on that, just like my ex did with me, they make you feel bad so they can get away with murder."

Cynthia left and Sally sat down at the bar where she'd been serving barbecue and drinks forever. What a morning. Jett, Cynthia, Demar salivating like Pavlov's dog. Cynthia was right about another thing: if Jett wanted a fight, Sally Donaldson would give it to her and win. Oh, she could go to Demar and whine that Jett was here to get him back but that made Sally look pathetic and gave Jett a leg up as strong and capable. Nope, she had to win Demar fair and square. 'Course that meant she'd win him for keeps.

The question was, did she love Demar enough to go after him? Did she really want him that much? For keeps was a really long time.

Demar hustled down the gravel road to the O'Fallon docks as late morning sun inched overhead, gearing up for another August inferno. Nothing moved, not a leaf on the maples or blades of the cattails at the shoreline. A box turtle hid in the mud under a chunk of driftwood and even the Mississippi seemed to move slower.

He had a few hours to spend with Jett before getting back for the dinner crowd. He liked the bar, Slim was the best and Sally was pretty and fun, sassy and sexy as hell and . . . and suddenly Demar caught sight of Jett on the dock talking on the payphone, and every thought in his brain vanished. Desire he thought dead and gone wasn't gone at all. Hell, one look at Jett and he was horny as a three-puckered billy goat.

Dang, he'd been here six weeks and spoke Tennessee like a pro but what really bothered him was the horny part. He had Sally now and she was terrific and he really cared for her. Jett had ditched him big time, broke his heart and if he had an ounce of sense he should have nothing to do with her ever again, and run like hell in the other direction.

But he couldn't do that, his legs wouldn't move. And that was okay because . . . because he and Jett were simply old friends. Yeah, that was it. But she didn't look old. She looked damn sweet in pink shorts, a sleeveless shirt tied at the ends, showing off her belly button, and a small rose tattoo that hadn't been there before. He tripped, she laughed and waved and walked to him. She touched his hand, throwing him completely off balance, nearly plunging him into the river.

"Took you long enough to get down here," Jett said as the deckhands loading supplies onto a tow gave her the once over. Demar bet his badge they'd been giving her the eye since she showed up and he wasn't the only one who'd nearly tripped off the dock today.

Jett flashed a perfect grin and pulled up in front of him, the heat from her chest searing his. He resisted the urge to run his fingers through her hair. She had great hair with a touch of gold highlights. "You trying to drive every man on this dock insane."

"Only one man here I care about." Her hand in his felt nice. "Think you can find us a boat like you promised and maybe we can get lost for a while?"

He nodded to the Mississippi, wide and brown, making its way to New Orleans. "Going to be hot as hell out there in an hour."

"Then we'll find us a nice cool place to relax and catch up on what's happening in our lives. I really want to catch up with you, Demar." She pulled him to the back of the dock out of earshot from the workers, under the shade of a birch tree hugging the shore. She nibbled her bottom lip, not like her confident self at all. She gazed up at him, her big brown eyes not bright but sad. "I know I didn't treat you well and I want to set it straight between us. That's why I came here. I needed to find you."

His gut tightened as he remembered losing Jett. "You ran off to Bermuda with my best friend. That was pretty straightforward."

"And that wasn't cool and I'm sorry. I want us to be friends again. You're important to me, Demar."

"Is this part of your twelve-step program to being a better person?"

"I want to make it up to you for being a creep." She looked sullen, in a seductive sort of way. "I want us to spend time together and get things back the way they were. Breaking up with you was the biggest mistake of my life. I'm sorry. Can . . . can you forgive me for that?"

He studied her for a moment, his heart beating fast, hormones doing the same. "This is a big turnaround from the mincemeat you made of me a year and a half ago."

"I didn't want to hurt you . . . I was scared of the way I felt about you so I ran away."

"Honey, you sure took your old sweet time getting back to me."

"That's because I didn't know what I wanted and now I do." She touched his cheek and he couldn't breathe. "I want you, Demar. I want us to be together again. We're good together."

He tried to think clearly but when it came to Jett he couldn't string two intelligent thoughts together. That's how she affected him from the first time he saw her, when they worked together on that case and nearly got trapped in a burning building. "I have someone special in my life. Sally and I are an item, Jett."

"And I'll have to live with that but I wanted you to know how I feel about us."

Us! A year ago he'd have skinned a dead cat to hear her say it. This time he touched her, her skin soft against his fingertips as his dick swelled. Think Sally! Sally, Sally, Sally. He dropped his hand away and took a step back. "You and I work in the same office, Jett. We can be friends. We'll always be friends."

She gave him a sweet innocent smile. "That's all I ask. I wanted to be truthful."

He nodded. "Right. Truthful. How long are you going to be here?"

"As long as it takes for us to be friends again. Am I convincing you?"

She was doing something to him and it wasn't good. He couldn't just stand here and gawk at her like a lovesick fool. "I'll ask Rory if we can use his chase boat for a few hours."

"Rory O'Fallon?" Her eyes rounded.

"You know him?"

She shrugged. "Uh . . . his name's on the sign coming down here. I didn't realize you knew the man himself, sugar." She'd always called him sugar and he'd loved it. His heart skipped a few beats.

"Everybody around here knows everybody else. Part of being in a small town." This was good. They were talking about other stuff besides the two of them and he needed to keep it that way. He led the way across the dock, Jett at his side, her breast against his arm. It had to be over a hundred in the shade today. He looked down at Jett, smiling and radiant. More like two hundred in the shade.

She nodded to the *Liberty Lee* gleaming in the sunlight at the end of the dock. "Well, this pretty boat sure isn't one of your towboats. It looks like something right out of the old South."

"The *Lee's* a showboat. In a few weeks they're going to put on *Arsenic and Old Lace*."

She flashed her smile and his brain melted. "That's my favorite play. I'll stay around. We'll have to go."

"Sally's probably working the bar that night, I should be doing dinner—"

Jett framed his face between her palms and her lips went pouty. He was a sucker for those lips. "Come on, sugar. Take me to the play, for old times' sake."

Oh, damn. His dick felt hard as a fence post.

"Don't you miss the real shows, the Nashville scene? The action, the music? Just being a real cop in a real city? You're not a cook."

What he was, was a bastard for being this way with Jett when Sally was his woman. "I'm just hanging out on vacation, Jett."

"And that means you're coming back to Nashville soon?"

Right now he barely knew his name but he sure knew Jett's.

"What are you doing here anyway, Demar?"

Losing his flipping mind, that's what.

"This place is so not you and I know you pretty darn well, I'd say better than anyone. I know you're ticklish as all get out and that you like to be kissed on the back and I know that just putting my hand on your leg—"

"I'm helping some people I've gotten friendly with." *Concentrate . . . but not on the lips.* And after this afternoon he would steer clear of Jett. He had to. "Being a cop was making things complicated so I decided to not be a cop for a while." He nodded at the building on the dock. "I'll introduce you to some great folks I've met."

"Why, sure, like Rory O'Fallon? If they're your friends I want them to be my friends too."

He didn't expect that. Jett wasn't exactly the folksy type. Then again maybe she really had changed. Hell, she'd come all the way to Tennessee after him. And she really was after him big time. He never would have expected that. Before he could stop himself he said, "Damn, girl! It *is* great seeing you again, Jett."

She took his hand to her lips and kissed his palm, her mouth against his skin setting his blood on fire, making up for the rotten way she'd ditched him. Her eyes darkened and her voice was like a sensual song kicking his heart into high gear. "It's good being here, Demar. With you is exactly where I want to be, forever."

Sally paced behind the bar, the late afternoon sun sneaking in each time the door opened as Thelma and Conrad, Nick and Nellie, and everyone else came for dinner, except Demar. Where the heck was he? And what the heck was he doing?

Nothing good, she'd bet on that. The Tennessee tart had him in her clutches. Sally waved to Joe and Betty as they took a table to grab a bite before play practice down at the *Lee*. Demar should be here, and not just to help at the bar, anyone could do that, but because . . . because he was her main squeeze, darn it. She wanted him to be that forever, and she was in no mood to share.

And to celebrate this momentous decision of declaring her undying love she had something for Demar under this black T-shirt, like a lacy push-up bra. She'd been saving it for a special occasion. This was definitely special except the darn thing was gradually inching it's way up to her chin because she didn't have enough endowment to hold it down. Jett didn't have hold down trouble. Jett had enough endowment to anchor the *QE II*.

"Sally?" Quaid asked.

"What?" she snapped, then instantly regretted it. "You

are the third person I've done that to in the last half hour. I need a tomato."

His eyes laughed but he managed to keep a straight face. "Since when is a tomato your stress food of choice? What happened to chocolate chip cookies? You were always a cookie kind of girl."

"I buried them in the back yard, couldn't just toss them in the trash with no respect. I joined Fat Fighters today." She patted her not-as-flat-as-it-used-to-be stomach. "Too much barbecue, corn on the cob, and of course the cookies."

"Sounds like Demar problems."

"Nope, his gut is still firm and flat. Men are like that. They give up their afternoon doughnut and lose ten pounds in twenty-four hours. Life is so not fair." She pulled a cherry tomato from behind the counter, chomped and made a face. "And this is so not a cookie. But, since you brought up the Demar issue, have you seen him or that good-for-nothing skinny bimbo with the large melons he left with?"

"Wow."

"Cookie deprivation."

"What's Demar doing with this less-than-desirable woman if he has you around?"

Sally discreetly tugged at her undergarments.

"Bugs biting?"

Guess not discreetly enough. "Garter belt's riding up to my rib cage."

Quaid's eyes rounded as she continued, "I guess I can tell you. I have enticement for Demar, if he ever gets himself back here."

"Enticement?" Quaid leaned his elbows on the bar, rubbed his chin and chuckled.

Sally held out a longneck. "And since you find this all so

amusing you can take this to the table in the corner." She leaned close and whispered under the din of "Chattanooga Blues" humming from the jukebox, "I'm wearing stilettos. If I walk that far I'll kill myself or get people talking. I don't know which is worse."

"Doesn't sound like attire from your New York days on the Exchange."

"Wore them for a gig I did in Memphis along with Keefe's fiancée. It's a long story."

"What happened to the Harvard snob?"

"She's eating tomatoes."

He sat back. "Well I'll be damned, this sounds serious. The great Sally Donaldson, queen of investments and all things barbecue has fallen off the singles wagon and Demar's the luckiest man on the planet."

"His old ex-girlfriend showed up this morning and right now I don't think he remembers I'm *on* the planet." Sally took a gulp of Quaid's beer because everyone knew snitched food had no calories.

"You show him that garter belt and he'll remember real quick."

"But I don't want him to want me just because we have great chemistry in the bedroom. I want to be on his mind all the time." She shrugged. "At the moment I think the man has amnesia."

"No way. He'll remember—"

"Who's going to remember what?" Demar said as he came up behind Quaid.

Sally's heart jumped and her bra slid higher. She reached across the bar and took Demar's arm. "I want to show you something."

"I've got to relieve Slim."

She yanked him toward the back room, tossing Quaid her bar towel. "Hold the place down for a minute? Don't eat all my tomatoes." She dragged Demar back toward the kitchen, stopping at the storage cupboard. Shoving him inside she turned on the overhead bulb, slid the bolt home, locking them in, and flattened herself against the door.

Demar gave her a *what the hell's going on* look. "Since when is there a lock in here?"

"Since this afternoon. I'm very handy."

"Because . . ."

She yanked her T-shirt over her head, twirled it around on her index finger and sent it sailing off onto a case of paper napkins. She did a suggestive pose and twitched her hips. "Do you like?"

"Holy hell, what brought this on? I'm supposed to be working."

She pressed her hands to his fly. "I'd say you're working just fine."

She slid her thumbs into the waistband of her skirt and skimmed the red peasant skirt over her hips, tossed it over a keg of beer, then hiked one leg onto a box of potato chips . . . she'd kill for a potato chip. Instead, she took Demar's hand and pressed it to her soft patch of curls. "I'm not wearing panties."

"I noticed." He swallowed; beads of perspiration suddenly dotted his upper lip. Now that's the reaction she was looking for. The discomfort of wearing fishnet hose in ninety-plus weather was worth it. She grabbed a handful of his shirt and brought his face to hers, nose-to-nose, eye-to-eye. She kissed him, adding lots of tongue, her legs parting as his fingers pressed into her wetness.

"Oh, Demar," she panted, feeling dizzy, thankful she still held onto his shirt for balance. Perched on one skinny heel did not offer much support. She gasped as his fingers slid into her a bit more and his tongue claimed her mouth. Demar growled deep in his throat and he stepped closer between her legs. "Slim's going to wonder where I am. I should . . ."

She kissed him again and said against his lips, "Take me. Hurry."

His eyes went black as she unbuttoned his belt, her hands finding his arousal, hard and throbbing in her palms. "I want you so bad."

He eased his fingers from her, yanked off his shirt and dropped it on top of a box. He grinned, his left brow raising a fraction. " A case of Hot sauce." His low wicked chuckle gave her goose bumps. "And that's exactly what you are, girl. You are so hot, so lovely . . . and a little naughty."

His muscles glistened in the dim light. "You make me nuts, babe."

She cradled his tight testicles in her palm. "And you have such a fine set." She eased his briefs over his hips, freeing his erection and filling her with pure lust. "You are so fine, Demar."

"And flattery will get you everywhere." He lifted her and sat her on his shirt, then fitted himself between her legs. She ran her fingers over his broad chest, appreciating his smooth dark skin and firm broad shoulders.

"I hate rushing this, but . . ." His breathing quickened. "But what you do to me . . ."

The scent of sex saturated the small cluttered space as she pulled a condom from inside her bra and held it up. "I thought of everything." She tore the package and rolled the latex over his penis. "What's a nice guy like you doing with a big thing like this?"

"I'll be glad to show you." He kissed her and suddenly she couldn't think of anything besides Demar's hands on her buttocks, holding tight while sliding himself into her, filling her with one long even stroke. Her hair felt as if it were on fire. Her lungs threatened to burst as he pumped into her again, going deeper. So hard, so incredibly male. She spread her legs wider, arching against him as he pushed into her one more time. She gasped and he kissed her, as she gripped his shoulders with each thrust until her world exploded, leaving only Demar, the man she truly loved.

Chapter 4

*D*amn, Cynthia thought as she yanked off work gloves and looked at the garden she'd slaved over for the last two days. Not that it looked bad—actually, it looked pretty good—but all this work didn't do what it was supposed to. Weed pulling, hedge cutting, even rock dragging and mole chasing hadn't made her forget that she threw herself at Quaid O'Fallon and kissed him. How in the heck could she do such a thing?

She sat on the front steps as evening fell and Ida turned on the lights inside the house. A peaceful time . . . least it should be. Cynthia was not peaceful. Why couldn't Quaid rejoin the Coast Guard and leave? How could she have the hots so badly for this guy? She was forty, for God's sake. Over the *hot* stage of her life and entering the lukewarm stage, right? Wrong! So very, very wrong.

Lawrence shuffled his way up the driveway and she smiled, adding a little wave. "So, how was doggie day-care today? Looks like Quaid's working you overtime."

"He drove me home." Lawrence reached in his pocket and pulled out folded bills. "*I* got paid," his grin so big there wasn't much room left for nose and eyes. "I'm going to open an account at the bank tomorrow and save for a telescope."

He sat beside her, the stillness of evening falling around them. They spent time together now, enjoyed each other's company instead of her rushing off to the loft: the upside of losing one's job, being home and ditching a conniving husband who wasn't much of a father. "Last time I checked it was a microscope."

"Quaid says there's a place called Stevie's Ridge between here and Memphis out in the middle of flipping nowhere that—"

"Flipping?"

"That's what Quaid says. I think it's a colloquialism, I don't remember hearing it in New York. Anyway, it's a good place to look at the stars because the lights from the city won't interfere. And with my bedroom on the third floor here I can set a telescope by the window. Quaid used to go to the ridge and watch the Perseid meteor showers. They're happening right now, mid-August—and if it's okay with you he'll take me."

Quaid O'Fallon, stargazer? With some cute chickie tucked under each arm, no doubt. Lawrence's eyes sparkled. "I could never look at the stars for real in New York with all the lights. This is so great, Mom. I think I want to be an astronomer or maybe an astronaut. Quaid says I'd be a good astronaut because I'm smart. He's down at the dock. Can you go down and tell him it's all right to take me to the ridge?"

"How about I'll call him tomorrow?"

Lawrence bit his bottom lip, reached into his pocket and held up a key with *O'Fallon* engraved on a pewter towboat. "If you went to see him tonight you could return this. It's the house key and I forgot to give it back. He said it was important not to lose it because some guys were after their baby. Why would someone be after Bonnie?"

"Seems her mom's on the run because she has information on a fraud scheme."

"Holy cow, no kidding. Poor little baby. Maybe I'll be a PI when I grow up and help people like her mom. Since Preston's staying with us I can ask him all about it."

"Do it over cobbler. Your grandmother has some cooling. Go wash up and you can have a piece before you go to bed."

His little face pinched together. "Do I have to have a piece? How about an apple, can I have an apple instead? Or a carrot? I'll eat a carrot."

Cynthia put her finger across her lips in *shhh* fashion, leaned closer and whispered, "You'll hurt your grandmother's feelings. She's really trying to be a good cook, Lawrence. There's ice cream in the freezer. Drown the cobbler in it. You won't taste a thing."

"There's not that much ice cream in the world. Mr. Wright said dinner was delicious. It was like rubber. Quaid's dad was grilling a steak for them for dinner when I left. Tomorrow they're having fried chicken. He gave me steak right off the grill. Oh, Mom, you should have been there. I think Grandma forgot to cook the peas. Is there something wrong with Mr. Wright, how could he not notice? Why would anyone want to pay to stay here and eat this stuff?"

Cynthia considered the steak and real fried chicken and her taste buds wept. "Mr. Wright's just being polite and he seems to like your grandmother. They're the same age and have things in common so they get along."

"He winked at her—I saw him. She laughs at his jokes. They're really bad jokes, Mom."

And that wasn't the only thing bad. She still had the key situation to straighten out and she did not want to see Quaid, after her kissing frenzy. "I could take you to drop off the key."

"I'll miss *Nova*. It's the one on the Hubble telescope and nebula."

"Guess that doesn't have anything to do with Nebula purses. They come in black, tan and gold this season." He laughed. They were closer now than ever. 'Course if she didn't get something going in the employment department she and Lawrence and Mother would be very close and starving. "Okay, it's a shower, cobbler, *Nova*, bed." The towboat medallion felt heavy in her palm.

"Are you okay?"

"Perfect." Except she had to return a flipping key.

But an hour later as she walked down the path that led to the docks the only thing flipping was her stomach. How could she face Quaid? How embarrassing. Should she apologize? *Sorry about the kiss, I had . . .* What? Primal lust overload? Hormonal meltdown? Not been laid in a year? Two? Ugh!

The empty docks stretched before her, two tows roped to pilings. She'd never been to the docks before. She shouldn't be here now. Mercury vapor lights came to life; the last sun rays turned the Arkansas shores red and gold, leaving the Mississippi black and mysterious. "Hello?" she called, trying to sound confident.

A light shone through the office window; Quaid sat at a desk, bent over a clipboard. He was busy, she should go . . . except . . . except he looked so incredibly handsome and she had that darn key. Handsome had already gotten her in trouble. Heck, it had been getting her in trouble for years, Quaid was just the latest installment.

Opening the door she went in, winding her way through the deserted office to the glassed-in one at the end. She tapped on the door and entered as he looked up. She focused on the back wall. One glimpse of those green eyes and she risked another kissing attack. "Here's your key, thanks for hiring Lawrence, he can go to the ridge whenever you want, bye." There, she did it. Done. She turned away.

"Hey." He stood, she walked till he snagged her arm. "I won't bite."

Yeah, but she might and that was the God's honest truth. She was pathetic!

"Is everything okay with Lawrence? Not like him to forget the key."

"He has *Nova* on the brain."

Quaid grinned, making her feel at ease till she looked in his smoldering eyes, and since there was no one else around and they weren't smoldering for the water cooler . . . that left her. Oh, boy. "I really should go."

"Why'd you come?"

"The key . . . your house . . . *Nova*."

"What you brought isn't the key."

She fished in her pocket. "I forgot it." With luck the earth would part and swallow her whole. How could she forget the key? Lawrence had *Nova*-itis, she had Quaid-itus. *Nova*-itis had a cure.

Without letting her go, Quaid rounded the desk and drew up in front of her. "Interesting."

"Absentminded." Lust ate her brain cells. How was she going to get over this man—and she had to do that right now. Men were the bane of her life . . . *remember*.

He hooked his finger under her chin and turned her face to his. "I'm glad you came." He smiled a little. "And I'm glad you forgot the key."

"Why?"

He slowly brushed his lips against hers as if testing her response. "Maybe you're here for another reason?"

"This is not the reason."

He kissed her lightly and she kissed him back, her body doing an August burn even in air conditioning, her lips . . . hungry. "I'm so much older than you."

He smiled and it wasn't the kind that made fun but the kind that appreciated. "It's not the years, it's the mileage. You've had bumps and so have I."

He kissed her again, his mouth lingering. He touched her cheek and she shivered.

"Cold?"

"I wish." His lips claimed hers in a kiss that took her breath away as his arms slid around her back bringing her tight against him. Chest to chest—his firm, hers heavy and wanting. Oh, Lordy, did she want! Quaid O'Fallon sure could kiss, except no tongue. Okay, *where was the tongue?* She really wanted the French kiss and before she could stop herself, she French-kissed him. And he returned the gesture, his palm sliding to her bottom, pressing her into him.

Been a long time since she felt a man hard and ready for action and no matter how much she proclaimed she could live without sex . . . right now it wasn't possible.

"You are so fine," his voice thick and smooth, reminding her of a double latté with extra whipped cream.

"My life is complicated, Quaid."

He backed her to the desk, the edge catching her right under her derriere. He hitched her onto it, her legs dangling, his mouth consuming hers, her legs parting, her body waiting. Hussy!

He didn't seem to mind. He turned out the light on the desk and whispered, "We don't need an audience in case the *Arsenic* cast comes by." He stepped away and she felt abandoned. "You're leaving?"

He took the bell from the desk and put it on the counter, and then the lamp and the clipboard.

"What are you doing?"

He swiped his arm across the desk, sending pencils, books, papers flying to the floor with a crash, leaving the desk bare and her heart beating in her throat. "The maid will clean it up tomorrow."

"You have a maid?"

"Yeah." He scooped her into his arms. "Me." He sat her on the desk, this time her legs there, too. He unbuttoned his jeans.

"This is so not a good idea."

"That's pretty much how I live my life and you didn't come here to return a key, Cynthia."

She leveled him a look. "What makes you so sure?"

"This." He kissed her hard, with lots of tongue, proving himself totally right as he lay her back on the desk, her hair flowing over the edge. She felt incredibly sexy, a little wicked, a lot turned on.

"You are so beautiful, have been all your life. I've wanted you since the first time I lay eyes on you, Cynthia."

"I'm a conquest?"

"You're desired." He pulled a condom from his wallet and she considered protesting except how could she say no to such manly attributes so ready for action—especially when she wanted action too?

She couldn't! She sat up and slid off her panties. He grinned. "I could have done that. Would have been happy to."

She held out her arms. "We have to hurry before I get rational."

"You're not rational?"

She tossed her panties and they landed in a soft heap on the *Bootsy B* bell. "Is that the action of a rational forty-year-old from New York? I think mothers go to hell for doing stuff like this."

"Mothers are women." He eased her back, then hitched himself onto the desk and positioned himself over her, his eyes now black as the darkness surrounding them. "Wrap your legs around me, Cynthia. I need to know you want this as much as I do."

She bit her bottom lip.

"Do you?"

She touched his cheek. The stubble roughness against her fingers and desire humming in her veins made her almost giddy. Without answering, her legs circled his waist. He smiled and the tip of his erection touched her heat. She jumped.

"That hurts?"

"Impatience."

"Me too," he answered in a rough voice. Then he eased himself into her, her body expanding to accommodate him, and it hadn't accommodated in a long time, and had never expanded quite this much.

"You're so . . . tight, sweetheart."

"Out of practice."

He grinned. "Good." Then he eased into her a bit more, then pulled out.

"Quaid?"

"Practicing." He kissed her, his tongue imitating his lovemaking as he entered her again, his erection so hot and hard she nearly combusted from the sensation. She couldn't wait for any more trial runs and she tightened her legs, bringing him into her completely. She climaxed, surprising the hell out of herself. So fast, so intense. She gripped his shoulders as Quaid thrust inside her again then again, his muscles clenching, his body throbbing and pulsing inside her, an incredible experience she didn't want to end, but way too fast. After two years she did not want fast. Drat!

His head sagged forward and she ran her hands under his shirt, his back muscles shuddering and damp with perspiration. He rested his forehead against hers. "Damn, girl. You are something else."

"I just couldn't hold back, I'm sorry I . . . you—"

He kissed her. "I wasn't registering a complaint, Cynthia."

Every ounce of you enjoys sex. Your body was made for it, you're made for it. It was like . . ."

"The first time?"

His gaze met hers and he studied her for a moment. "Yeah," he said in a slow easy voice. "Like the first time."

She licked her lips. "I've never been made love to like this. My ex was a small man, in more ways than one. I didn't realize that till . . . you . . . till . . . He was my first, my only, but I'm forty for God's sake, you'd think I'd know better, have a little more experience but I don't and—"

He kissed her again, stopping her protest, reassuring her and making her feel truly wanted and desirable.

She gasped. "Oh my God, I hear voices."

"Damn, play practice is over early. The night attendant for the office isn't due for another half hour." He rolled off her and disposed of the condom, wrapping it in paper and tossing it in the trash can.

"It's dark," she whispered as she sat. "No one should be able to see us."

He zipped up and dove behind the desk, snagging her along the way as he went. She landed in his lap and he whispered in her ear, "There's a half moon shining in that window like a big old spotlight. We don't want to take chances." He nuzzled her nape and added, "Unless you want to be tomorrow's main topic of gossip around here and have to explain to Lawrence. Just be real still."

Footsteps and laughing approached as he nibbled her neck. How could she be still with him nibbling? And kissing! He slipped his fingers under her blouse, across her ribcage, easing under her bra. "Quaid? You can't do this," she whispered on a quick intake of breath.

"Hmmm?" he replied next to her ear, his other hand sliding up her thigh.

"Quaid!"

"Shh," he cooed, his fingers dipping into her still wet patch. He delved deeper, her legs spreading while his fingers massaged her nipple, his thumb rubbing her clit. Voices and footfalls sounded right in front of the office. He kissed her shoulder and his fingers—one, then two inside her—making her quiver in his arms. If the actors looked inside they'd see a ball of fire behind the desk. How could she be so ready for Quaid *again*?

She bit the back of her hand to stifle her cries as another climax claimed her. Quaid's body cradled her, protecting her. She lay there in his arms, her limbs rubber, sort of like Ida's chicken. Quaid said, "I think they're gone."

"Who?"

"The actors. While we're behind the desk."

She turned her head and studied him through the darkness. "How could you do this to me? What the hell am I doing?"

"I'd consider it a pleasure to remind you."

She untangled herself from his arms, straightened her skirt and scrambled to her feet. "Where are my panties? I need my panties."

He stood beside her. "Are you okay?"

"Bottom line, I'm an idiot." She smacked her palm against her forehead. "Whenever I get a man in my life it goes straight to hell. Oh, it may take a while but eventually, it's all hell. How could I do this? Did I not learn anything from the last disaster?"

"I'm only half of the equation but this didn't feel like a disaster."

"I swore and swore I was going no-male and then you show up with your . . . great equipment and I melt."

"Great equipment? I think I've been used."

"It won't happen again. I can't afford it." She went for the door.

"Cynthia?"

She spun around. "No more sex, I mean it, Quaid. You're incredible, I'm sure you've heard that before, but I have to be strong or something else rotten will befall the Landon women and I can't—"

He tossed her the panties. She caught them and looked at the yellow swatch. "Oh, Lord, I so need therapy. I should go see that Doctor Phil guy." She ran through the deserted offices like some stupid flustered teenager, headed out the door and down the dock, not daring to look back. She stuffed the panties in her purse, fired up the Buick, and made for home. She'd been here four days and already involved with a guy, and guys were trouble . . . always.

She parked in front of the house and plunked her head on the steering wheel. Okay, it was over. She'd had her fling with the local wolf—ohmygod, what a wolf—and now she could go on. A quiet night with bad peach cobbler, she could handle that. She walked up the steps and opened the front door as Ida scurried into the hallway, eyes huge, dripping wet, draped in a towel. "Oh, thank God you're home. I think I killed him."

"A bug?"

"No, Preston Wright."

"The cobbler was that bad?"

Ida looked wounded as a puddle formed around her. "My cobbler's wonderful. I killed Preston with a vase from my bathroom windowsill. He tried to climb into the shower with me, of all things." She put the back of her hand to her forehead and looked ready for a swoon, southern style. "Mercy me, I never dreamed he was that kind of man."

"You seem to be going through your share of vases lately. I wonder what that's all about." Cynthia dropped her purse on the walnut sideboard. "Where's Lawrence?"

"Asleep, I checked."

"Well, thank the Lord for that. Probably scarred him

for life." Cynthia followed Ida into the bathroom; Preston sprawled out naked on the tile floor, was enough to scar her for life. Cynthia covered his backside with a towel, a senior buttock was not a thing of beauty . . . at least to her. "He's breathing."

"I didn't waste him?" Cynthia arched her brow in question and Ida shrugged. "We were watching Magnum reruns together. Guess I got caught up in the lingo." Cynthia ran a glass of water in the bathroom sink and dumped it on Preston.

He sputtered and coughed and opened his eyes. "What happened?"

"What in the world were you doing in the shower with my mother?"

Preston staggered to a sitting position and grabbed the towel tight around him with one hand as he ran his fingers through his hair. He looked at Ida, not quite focusing. "I thought you wanted me."

Ida's eyes nearly popped from her head and Preston continued, "In Rockton there's a house of special pleasures, shall we say, called Lord and Ladies. Kind of a secret place, run by a guy named Landon if you get my drift. I heard about it while working on a case up there."

Ida sagged against the wall. "Holy mother of pearl."

"Then I got here and that Quaid O'Fallon guy said the women at Ivy Acres were Landons and would make me feel right at home. I just assumed—"

"Well, my stars," Ida said, "I imagine I broke my first vase over that poor man's head the other time for this very same reason. He must have heard the Landon name too. I'm ruined."

Preston looked more dazed than ever. "This has happened before?"

The Curse of the Landon Women had come to roost again. *Let a man in your life and this is what happens.*

Cynthia said to Preston, "Are you feeling sick to your stomach, do you see one or two of everything?"

Preston nodded. "One. I'm okay. Magnum got knocked out all the time and I think I was more dazed than anything." He gave a sheepish grin and rubbed his head. "Looks a lot better on TV than it feels in real life."

"I don't think you have a concussion—the vase was thin bone china." Cynthia pointed a stiff finger to the door. "But I think you should leave."

Preston shrugged his pale shoulders, which looked as if they'd never seen sun in Hawaii or anywhere else. "I didn't mean any harm. After teaching thirty years and doing everything by the book, I'm looking for a little adventure outside the books, a bit of . . . action and—"

"You can get adventure somewhere else. Right now I have to go, and when I get back I want you out of our house."

Preston stood, the towel slipping. Cynthia looked away. "The towel please, Preston."

"Oh, right." He grabbed it tight around his hips, and shuffled out of the bathroom mumbling, "And to think that Quaid fellow promised me free dinners at Slim's for as long as I stayed here. Now I have to find a new place and—"

"Q . . . Quaid paid you?"

Preston looked at Cynthia over his shoulder. "He said it was part of the deal as long as I was here. And a nice perk, if you ask me."

Cynthia growled, "This is not the house of perks and is none of Quaid's business."

Ida asked, "Why would Quaid do something like promise dinner? I don't understand."

"I intend to find out what's going on." Cynthia headed for the front door and Ida called, "You're leaving me here alone like this? There's not a speck of brandy in the whole blessed house and my sensibilities have been seriously up-ended over this intrusion."

"Try hot chocolate, Mother."

"Without brandy? Sacrilege."

Cynthia grabbed her purse and made for the Buick. People thought living in New York was stressful and totally out of control. They should live at Ivy Acres. Everything was nuts or maybe it was just her. And to think she expected some R and R when she came home. Ha!

The night attendant had already taken over for Quaid down at the docks by now, so she turned toward the big white rambling frame that the four O'Fallon men called home. A house of all males? Even going near the place with her Landon Women's Curse was risky.

She parked the car in front of the driveway. The night was still too hot and humid to stir. Moonlight slipped through the branches of the big oaks in the front yard as bullfrogs courted, crickets serenaded and a heron barked like a chihuahua with a stomachache—least that's what they always sounded like to her.

With the porch light on she could see Quaid sitting in a wicker chair, feet propped on the railing. She'd recognize his silhouette anywhere, especially since she'd just spent a half hour intimately pressed to it. She still didn't have panties on in case she forgot just how intimate that pressing was.

Well, she'd better have enjoyed it because there'd be no repeat performance of sex on the dicks . . . *docks*! Oh dear God! *She meant docks!*

She was so not up to facing Quaid again tonight and telling him she wanted nothing more to do with him no matter what. Being a complete coward, she backed the car down the road and headed for home, saying a little prayer that Quaid didn't see her, that he was asleep in that chair.

She needed time—a century might be enough but at

least till tomorrow to get herself together, her brain working because one look at Quaid now and she'd cave, tackle
him to the floor of that porch and have a repeat performance of the office situation right out there in front of
God and everyone.

Couldn't the man have a pimple, a big old scar, a gold
front tooth that would turn her off just a little? Those
things wouldn't help. She'd be attracted to the man—gold
tooth, scar and all.

The bottom line was there could not be any more *situa-
tions*. Men were poison to her and tomorrow she'd be
stronger and make that clear to Quaid no matter what it
took.

Chapter 5

The next evening Cynthia drove the Buick into the O'Fallon driveway and parked right in front of the house. It had taken her all day to get up this much nerve, but there'd be no backing out this time and she didn't want to confront Quaid with Lawrence around. She had to get things straight between her and the local hunk and then she'd forget about him. No more night visions of Mr. Hunk on top of her when she was trying to sleep. No more remembering the two of them huddled behind the desk. When he was out of her life for good, all that would go well . . . right?

Walking up the steps she nearly tripped over a big yellow dog sprawled out like some welcome mat. He had a bandana around his neck. Super Dog. This was no doubt Max and she patted his head, his tail wagging in appreciation. Guess she smelled enough like Lawrence not to cause a barking frenzy. She rapped on the front door, remembering when Lawrence was a baby and how she'd contemplated homicide when someone rang a doorbell waking him from a nap.

Quaid answered, surprise slipping across his rugged, incredibly handsome face. "Hi," he said with a smile. "I'm glad you're here."

"Well, you won't be." She folded her arms, trying to add some menace to her words that she didn't feel at all. Hard to be stern with Quaid right in front of her. This was much easier when she practiced in the hall mirror. "I'm here on business, personal business, between-us business."

"Sounds serious." He came outside, closing the screen door quietly behind him, another member of the napping baby club. His familiar unique scent of hot sexy guy filled her head, making her a bit dreamy, until she caught the aroma of . . . "Oh my God." She walked past Quaid and pressed her face to the screen door, not caring that it left little tic-tac-toe marks on her nose. She inhaled deeply. "Fried chicken. Real, honest-to-goodness fried chicken."

"Well it isn't rubber."

"I know, I had that one over at my house last night." She sniffed in another lungful. "Any leftovers?"

"You came here for Dad's chicken?"

"Not exactly." Maybe a little.

"Kitchen's down the hall to the right. Chicken's in the fridge."

She glanced back at Quaid but the lure of fried chicken dragged her onward and she followed the scent to the fridge in the neat yellow and blue kitchen. She pulled a drumstick from the platter covered with plastic wrap and eyed a thigh that somehow found its way into her other hand. She took a bite, euphoria washing over her and she nearly succumbed to one of Ida's swoons.

"Good?" came Quaid's voice from behind her.

"Terrific," she managed around a mouthful while nudging the fridge door shut with her hip. She took another bite. "I'm starved."

"You're not eating over at your place?"

"Ida and I can't cook. Totally suck at it. Pea soup for

dinner, tasted like beebees. Rocks for rolls. Very sad." She licked her thumb.

"Lawrence told you about Dad's chicken, didn't he?"

"He might have mentioned it in passing, right after telling me about steak on the grill, but that's not why I'm here."

With his index finger he wiped a smudge of gravy from her cheek. "Could have fooled me."

He licked the gravy from his finger and for a moment all she could imagine was doing the same thing, then maybe tasting him all over. He had a great all over, she was sure, and she didn't get a chance to lick one single part on the dock, but she'd like to do it now. Except she was preoccupied with the chicken and this was business. *Business, business, business.* She wagged the half-eaten drumstick at him. "You sent Preston to Ivy Acres. And you bribed him to stay by offering him free dinners at Slim's. What in the world were you thinking?"

Quaid propped his hip against the counter. "That you run a bed and breakfast and he needed a place to stay and you could do with a little extra cash? And the dinner wasn't a bribe so much as an incentive. Dad hired Preston, and springing for some food seemed like the right thing to do."

"Well, last night Mr. Wright sprang into the shower with Ida, doing the full Monty, and his head ruined a perfectly fine antique vase that was my great-grandmother's."

"Preston did all that?" Quaid stood straight. "Damn. He doesn't seem like that kind of guy. Rory checked him out. He's a retired teacher, impeccable reputation. Oh, he's got this Magnum thing going on but he's harmless. Is Ida okay?"

"She's fine, but I want you to butt out of our lives. The Landons are not a charity case. We just can't cook." She stiffened her spine, suddenly aware that she probably looked beyond charity and more like something the cat dragged in that happened to be hungry. Landons were proud, they were better than this . . . until lately. She hated lately, but she really loved the chicken. "We may not be the high and mighty O'Fallons, but we can still manage on our own. Lawrence does not need your money and neither do Mother and I and—"

"Hey, hold on. I apologize if Preston didn't work out but leave my family and Lawrence out of this. I wanted to help you out, that's all there is to it."

Oh, no! she thought. *What if he . . .* She jabbed the drumstick in the direction of the docks and lowered her voice. "You didn't . . . I mean *we* didn't . . . because you felt *sorry* for me?"

"Holy hell, Cynthia." He raked his too long black hair. "Did I act like I was feeling sorry for anyone?"

Well, thank heavens for that. She tipped her chin. "So, I owe you a coat and something for this chicken that I just scarfed down and then you and I are through. I told you when a man finagled his way into my life everything went wrong and that's what's happening now. I got you, then we got Preston. Package deal. Who knows what else will turn up next, so I have to get you out of my life right now."

"So that's what this is all about. Not very rational, didn't you say that before?"

The tip of his fingers touched her chin and he tipped her face to his and looked into her eyes as she felt herself getting lost in his. She stepped away, feeling dizzy, a direct result of being near Quaid, the lure of fried chicken suddenly not enough of a distraction. "You're getting a coat if I have to tie it around you with a rope. This debt gets paid off, making us officially uninvolved."

"And you think that will disengage the curse?"

"That's the plan. You are not the first man in my life to activate a bad situation and I intend to cut my losses and get away from you before the roof of our house caves in or there's an earthquake that swallows up Ivy Acres, or whatever else the fates can dream up."

"You know this makes no sense."

"Sense isn't the issue, bad karma is and I have a lifetime of proof that the curse not only exists but is thriving and hereditary."

Quaid's brows rose. "You inherited it?"

"Genes are amazing." She tramped down the hall and elbowed open the screened door since she still had the chicken in her hands.

She wasn't sure what made her madder, Quaid interfering in her business or that she made love to him last night and completely enjoyed it even though she shouldn't have.

Quaid suddenly caught up with her on the porch. "Wait, I'm going to make this easy for you so you don't have to fabricate crap about a curse."

His mouth smiled but there was a hint of hurt deep back in his eyes and the only reason she recognized it was that she'd felt it herself when she realized how Aaron had betrayed her. "You think I'd lie about all this? Trust me, I don't have that good an imagination."

"The real deal is I'm not in your class."

"Okay, that's part of it. I'm older. When you were in the second grade I was in—"

"Not that kind of class. I'm not good enough for you. That garbage before about the high and mighty O'Fallons was just a cover for the high and mighty Landons." He shrugged. "Not a problem, I understand."

She was so tempted to just let him believe that and then he'd stay away from her and all would be well, but she couldn't. "Look at me, Quaid O'Fallon." She held out her arms, chicken in each hand. "I'm broke, pilfered your food, haven't had a decent manicure in months, my hair's all roots, I drive a fourteen-year-old blue Buick, my father's reputation is in the toilet and I have a mother who thinks brandy is the fifth food group. Class? What class?"

He shrugged again. "You live in the big white house on the hill and I'm always going to be the adopted river rat." He lowered his voice. "That you had sex with me is probably not setting too well with your blue blood right now."

"You arrogant creep!" She flung the drumstick and it bounced off his forehead and fell to the porch floor. "Here I am, baring my soul after I bared a lot of other things to you on that dock, and you think I'm telling you about this damn curse because I'm a snob and don't want to associate with you?" She resisted throwing the thigh; he wasn't worth it. "I swear I will never understand men if I live to be a million."

Quaid watched Cynthia stomp her way to the car. That was one damn ugly ride and she may be broke but the Landons would always be the Landons and he would always be the badass. Rory strolled out onto the porch, Bonnie in one arm, diaper bag in the other, the screen door slamming shut behind him. "What's that baloney about some kind of curse?"

"Eavesdropping?"

"Hell, yes. Every chance I get. How do you expect me to find out what's going around here with you kids? I missed the part about what happened on the docks, but what's with you not thinking you're good enough for the likes of Ms. Cynthia Landon?"

"Caught that too, did you?"

"You're good as anybody, boy, and better than most. Though you could do without the gravy smear on your head."

"Thanks." Quaid grinned, took a tissue from the diaper bag and wiped off the gravy.

"You don't need to thank me, just believe it."

Taking Bonnie from Rory, Quaid held her up and blew raspberries on her soft tummy. Nothing in the world sounded as happy as baby giggles. Rory gave him a long look, the kind dads give their sons, making them squirm no matter how old the son or how old the dad. "You're an O'Fallon through and through, you know that."

Quaid kissed Bonnie's head, her curls soft against his cheek. What a gift. "I know."

"Your brain does, but what about in your gut?"

"My gut's just fine." He nodded at the diaper bag. "You and Bonnie off for a night on the town?"

"Hastings House. More plumbing problems."

Quaid cradled Bonnie, the warmth of her little body next to his incredible. He'd never felt more protective of anyone in his life. "That plumbing's been acting up for a while. You spent the whole day up there. Want me to take a look? Maybe a fresh eye—"

"I'll take care of it. Conrad's in New Orleans and I don't mind helping Thelma with a few things now and then. Since I got you here to mind the docks and take care of the business I can do that much for her. She's family. You can always trust family and that's mighty important."

"Want me to watch squirt here?"

"To tell you the truth, you look like a man who could do with a drink. Tell Slim I said the pie's in the oven and he can stop around for a piece if he has a hankering. Always good to catch up on what's going on around town. These are troubled times."

"What pie?"

"Up at Hastings House, of course. You just tell Slim, he'll know. Don't forget."

Weird request. Rory's gaze met Quaid's. The baby stirred in his arms and Rory's brow arched a fraction. Rory spent more time at Hastings House than in his own house. He always had Bonnie with him when he went there, and always seemed in a hurry to get back. Interesting. Quaid said, "Plumbing problems, huh?"

"Yeah." Rory winked and gave a little smile—the action safer than a conversation, the message the same. In the age of electronics Rory wasn't the only one who could eavesdrop around this house.

"Take Max with you. He likes to run the fields up at Hastings House." And there wasn't a better watchdog anywhere. Quaid followed Rory down the steps to the Suburban and strapped in Bonnie as Rory lowered the tailgate for Max. Rory started the engine and Quaid leaned into the rolled-down window and whispered under the hum of the engine, "Watch your back, Dad. Is that why you hired Preston?"

"He's Magnum, attracts all the attention and we get none, leaving us to do our own thing, like take care of plumbing problems." Rory gave a little salute then drove off, leaving the peace of night in his wake. Only the sounds of nature and the rumble of tows out in the river broke the stillness.

Quaid's survival senses went on full alert. Three desperate men wanted Mimi out of their lives permanently, and the link to finding Mimi was through Rory and Bonnie. The bad guys had already kidnapped the baby and would not stop with one foiled attempt. Millions were involved, not to mention years in prison. Being Bruno's prison bitch was not how the presidents of River Environs intended to spend their golden years.

Quaid turned on a light in the house, set the alarm and headed on down to Slim's. Rory was right about keeping up on the latest talk around town, new folks coming and going, and the way to do that was to make everything seem normal as . . . pie.

He crossed the deserted road and made for the red neon Budweiser sign in Slim's window. The old shack had been perched above the Mississippi as long as Quaid could re-member. In contrast a load of fresh-cut lumber in the side parking lot hinted things were about to change. Sally said something about adding outside seating. Sounded stuffy . . . like Cynthia Landon.

What the hell was he thinking, getting involved with her? That woman was so far out of his league he couldn't touch her with a ten-foot pole. Except he did touch her and she touched him, and not just physically. If that's all there was to it he'd be contented to love her and leave her. But dammit all, he liked her.

He liked the way she smiled and the way she smelled, and he really liked the way her eyes sparkled when she talked about Lawrence. He admired the way she handled all the mess that had hit her right upside the head. The only thing he hated was her making up that lie about being cursed. Why the hell didn't she just stay away from him? He would have gotten the message that sophisticated gals didn't mess with badasses from the wrong side of the tracks. Rory O'Fallon may have dragged him over to the right side but that didn't erase the past, his roots. Never would.

Even with the door closed the mellow beat of BB King reverberated outside of the bar. From the corner of his eye he caught movement in the shadows behind the lumber pile. Two people making out. He smiled, then stopped dead. Demar? Quaid recognized his profile, and the gal was tall and lanky and definitely not Sally.

Fuck! How could Demar two-time Sally? She said there was another woman and she was right. Keeping his anger in check, Quaid opened the bar door without ripping it off its hinges—a major feat. Sally was a friend, had been since the days before he had any. Smuggled him sandwiches when he was hiding from Pete, gave him a blanket and let him sleep in the storage room when things were tough. Four cases of beer shoved together and a rolled-up apron for a pillow made a pretty damn good bed.

A slow night, the bar only half full. Sally served a platter of barbecue to a couple in the back and gave Quaid a friendly wave. "Hey, good looking," she said as she came up to him and kissed him on the lips. "Where have you been all my life, sweet cakes?"

Taking grief from Cynthia, watching your man cheat on you. But he said, "Loafing and proud of it."

Sally went around the bar, cracked open a Bud and handed it to him. "On the house."

He took a long drink and leaned across the polished wood. "Meaning you want something. I know that innocent look that isn't so innocent."

Sally laughed. "That's what happens when you grow up together. We know each other too well, Quaid O'Fallon." They exchanged looks that underlined what she'd just said. Then she nodded to the corner. "Preston needs cheering up. Something happened over at Ivy Acres and I don't know what. Not a word of gossip on the subject and Preston's not telling, but he sure is down in the dumps about it."

"And I'm your cheering committee?"

"You walked in the door, you got the job. I got a bar to tend to, Dad's watching the game upstairs and Demar's minding the grills."

Wanna bet? "Tell Slim there's pie waiting for him over at Hastings House. Dad's there on a plumbing problem and wants company."

"I'm surprised that old house hasn't floated away with all the plumbing problems going on over there. Personally I think it's a cover for something else."

Quaid nearly choked but kept his cool. "Like what?" He took another casual swig.

"Haven't figured that out yet. Let me know if you hear anything."

"I better see to Preston. I feel responsible, since Rory hired him." Quaid wove his way through the tables toward the corner one. If the plumbing at Hastings House had Sally suspicious, others wouldn't be far behind. And if Sally found out, everyone would know. Sally Donaldson, Harvard MBA, was also a BMA—biggest mouth around. If you wanted to know something—ask Sally.

Quaid sat down at the table as Scrapper Blackwell's "Bad Liquor Blues" trilled from the jukebox. "Heard there was a situation over at Ivy Acres and you got caught in the middle of things."

Preston frowned, not looking up from his beer. "Bad news travels fast."

"Not as fast as you think. The only reason I know what happened is because Cynthia gave me hell for sending you to Ivy Acres in the first place. Did you really get in the shower with Ida?"

Preston turned as red as his Hawaiian print shirt. Like Rory said, Preston drew the attention. Flamboyance was a good thing. They needed him to stay at the Landing and for people to think he was the one gathering information on Mimi.

Preston said, "Over in Rockton there's an escort service, Lord and Ladies. Real hush-hush, but run by a guy named Landon, a regular sex machine."

Quaid nearly slid out of the chair. "Edward Landon?"

"Never knew the first name but when you told me about Ivy Acres . . ."

"You thought Ida Landon was the . . . sex machine?" He could barely get the words out.

"Seemed to fit . . . the *house,* the name, maybe a franchise. But she's not that way at all." Preston took a swallow of his beer. "I screwed things up big and the real trouble is I like Ida, I sincerely do." Preston gave a sad smile. "We watched Magnum together. She likes it." His smile collapsed. "But now she thinks I'm the scum of the earth. I'm in such a funk I can't keep my mind on the case. I came here to maybe talk to some people, see if anyone's seen anything suspicious." He leaned closer. "It's my professional opinion that the bad guys will come here hoping Mimi will contact Rory."

Quaid gave a casual shrug. "I think she's smarter than that."

"There's Bonnie. A mother can't stay away from her baby, everyone knows that." Preston's hunch deepened. "But I can't help you and Rory anymore. I don't want to be here if I don't have a chance with Ida. I've never felt this way about a woman before. Been single all my life and then I met my little magnolia blossom and I don't want to be single a minute longer. I even made breakfast for us the other morning. Ida can't cook for beans but I don't care, I'm a great cook. We ate in the garden, talked about visiting Hawaii. It was truly heaven."

Think, man, think! He had to find some way to keep Preston here. "What if I can help you win Ida back?" Except he hadn't a clue how.

"She hates me, it's too late." And as if to prove his point Ida strolled in, eyed Preston and strutted on over. "My stars, are you still here, Preston Wright? You have some nerve being in my town. I thought you'd have the decency to leave and not bother decent folks."

"I apologize, my pet."

"I am not your pet, Preston. I am a church-going decent woman. A pillar of the community."

"Can you give me another chance?"

"And why ever would I do a thing like that?" She stuck her nose a little higher in the air.

Quaid said, "Because Preston wants to make it up to you." *If he could just think of how in the hell to do that.* Ivy Acres could use the money, that was for sure, but Ida wouldn't take kindly if he blurted that to the world. "Preston can cook . . . for you . . . for the other guests. He likes to and you need a cook." *Was he brilliant or what!*

"We don't have other guests."

"But you will if Preston helps out. Bet he can cook rings around Thelma, and the word will get out and you'll have more guests than you know what to do with." *If Thelma ever got wind of this he was dead meat.*

Preston brightened. *I can do breakfast and dinner, and that leaves time for my private eye work during the day. Like Magnum. He lived at the estate and worked security, and took on other jobs."* Preston gazed adoringly at Ida. "It would be my total pleasure to cook for you."

She harrumphed. "Well, the only reason I'll let you do such a thing is because you scared the living daylights out of me, Preston, and this is . . . penance." She leaned closer to him and wagged her finger. "But you should know right here and now there will never be anything between us. There simply never could be." She turned in a huff and strutted back to the bar.

"See," Quaid said as he patted Preston on the back. "You're in."

"But she said there will never be anything between us." Preston nodded at the bar. "And look, that guy in the white jacket and gray hair is making eyes at my magnolia blossom and she's making eyes right back. What's the use? My goose is cooked."

"Hey, would Magnum quit? Would he let the other guy win the girl?" Quaid clinked his longneck to Preston's. "You have to fight for what you want."

Preston sat straight in his chair, his eyes clearing.

"You're right. I never thought of that. I had a little setback is all. Magnum had setbacks all the time, never got the girl till the second part of the show."

"Well there you go. This is your second act." And Quaid hoped Preston did succeed and not just for hanging around to help out the O'Fallons, but because he was a nice guy. Though Quaid wasn't all that sure about Ida Landon being a nice woman, but that was Preston's choice.

Sally scurried over, panic on her face. "You got to get Ida out of here fast. She's ordering brandy."

Quaid held up his beer. "This is a bar, that should work okay."

"Not when one drink leads to another and then another. Cynthia can't come get her because she can't leave Lawrence, and he's sleeping. I promised I'd look out for Ida. She must have gotten a ride here with someone because Cynthia hid her car keys. That means you have to take her home before she gets sloshed."

Quaid put down his beer. "Since when are you and Cynthia Landon buddies?"

"Since she did me a favor. Now are you going to help me or do I have to beat you up?"

Preston said, "My little magnolia likes brandy?"

"Is the bear Catholic?" Sally shook her head. "Or whatever that saying is. Hurry."

Quaid stood. "I'll see what I can do. But right now I'm thinking the Landon women are considerably more trouble than they're worth."

Sally sucker-punched his arm. "And you really expect me to believe that line of malarkey? I know how Cynthia looks when she talks about you and I know that look in your eyes when you talk about her, and that look has nothing to do with trouble and a whole lot to do with mischief."

"Looks don't mean squat. She told me today she wanted me out of her life."

"And since when has what someone else wanted ever gotten in your way, Quaid O'Fallon? It just makes you more determined than ever and you know it."

"All of a sudden you're on Cynthia's side?"

"Like I said, she did me a favor. Can you get a move on?"

Quaid grinned. "Must have been a humdinger of a favor." He gave Sally a quick kiss and approached Ida sitting at a table by the bar. "Mrs. Landon, Cynthia needs you back at the house."

Keeping a protective hand on her brandy, Ida looked up at him, her gray eyes glassy. Seems that Ida was a lightweight in the booze department. No wonder Cynthia was concerned. Ida said, "Why would she call you, Quaid O'Fallon? Is there something wrong with Lawrence? Last time I checked there wasn't a soul at our bed and breakfast so why would she need me this very minute?"

"Lawrence is fine. Sally got the call and I can take you home if—"

The gray-haired man with a neatly trimmed beard and dressed in a white sport coat, sitting at the bar, sprang to his feet. He stepped in front of Quaid and faced Ida. "Well now, this is indeed my good fortune." He did a low bow to Ida. "My name is Beau Fontaine of the Charleston, South Carolina, Fontaines, and I find myself in desperate need of a place to stay while setting up a new restaurant establishment here in town."

He took Ida's hand and kissed the back of it as she fluttered her eyelashes. "And lo and behold it turns out this pretty lady right here in front of me has such a place at her disposal. It was meant to be, my dear." He offered the crook of his arm to Ida. "If you would permit me the honor of taking you home to your daughter and grandson. And I will be forever in your debt if you would allow me to stay at your charming bed and breakfast. I would consider it a great and personal favor."

Ida held her hands to her breast. "Why my dear Mr. Fontaine, how you do go on." She stood, smiled and slipped her arm through his. "I am thrilled to meet you, a fine southern gentleman." She glanced Preston's way as if to say *So there, you oaf.* Then she and Beau Fontaine of the Charleston Fontaines strolled out of the bar.

Preston came over and Quaid said to Sally, "Didn't go exactly like I planned, but it worked."

Preston looked totally forlorn. "For you, maybe. Ida now has a boyfriend. I don't think she knows I exist."

"Magnum? Second half hour, remember?"

Preston shook his head and sighed. "Maybe I should forget about staying on here. I'm from Milwaukee and no match for some smooth-talking Southerner."

"Hey, you're a private investigator, you don't give up on your case. You're *the man.*"

"The invisible man."

"I'll walk you to your car. Go back to Ivy Acres and see what happens there. Maybe this Beau guy's not as suave as he seems."

"Maybe the earth is flat," Sally said to Quaid as he headed for the door. "While you're out there, tell Demar he can shut down the grills. I think we're done for the night. And it's a darn good thing too. He burned that last batch of ribs. I think the man's losing his touch."

That depended on what he was touching, the gal in his arms seemed to be happy with it. Quaid followed Preston to the red VW.

"Just be yourself. You're a great guy, and if Ida's too

thickheaded to see that, another woman will snap you right up."

"But I don't want another woman. I'm smitten." Preston drove down the street.

The question now was, should Quaid say something to Demar about seeing him with that other woman or butt out? The *real* question was, could he say something without decking him on the spot? Maybe it was just a one-time thing for Demar, a lapse in good judgment, and it wouldn't happen again. The best approach was to clear the air between him and Demar—let Demar know Sally was a friend, and no one mistreated Quaid's friends. Except when Quaid got to the back porch Demar was already playing tonsil hockey with Miss Long and Lean.

Quaid caught Demar's eye and he took a step away from the girl. "Want something, O'Fallon?"

"Like breaking your fucking neck. Sally could come out here any minute and find you like this."

"What's it to you?"

"Go to hell, Thacker." Quaid opened the back door and stormed his way to the front of the bar, anger eating at his gut. What was he going to do now? Tell Sally? Not tell her? Shit!

He felt a big hand on his shoulder and Demar said, "If you got something to say, say it, O'Fallon."

Quaid turned. "How about you're a fucking asshole, that clear enough for you?"

Chapter 6

Blind Boy Fuller's "Lost Lover Blues" blared as Demar narrowed his eyes, anger pumping through his body. So Sally was Quaid's friend, big fucking whoop. This wasn't his business. Jett was Demar Thacker's gal and everybody better damn well get used to it, starting now.

Demar swung hard, Quaid ducked the blow and leveled one at Demar's ribs. He grunted from the impact, sailing into a table, scattering beer and patrons. A woman screamed as he scrambled to his feet, fury making him mean and fast. He leaped at Quaid, knocking them both hard against the bar as he sent a blow to Quaid's jaw and Quaid's fist connected with Demar's eye. Demar caught a jab to his gut, then the corner of his mouth, leaving the metallic taste of blood. He hit Quaid's shoulder, then his nose.

Longnecks and glasses crashed to the floor, stools toppled and Sally slammed a baseball bat against the top of the bar, yelling, "What the hell are you two doing!"

Slim appeared in the kitchen doorway, shotgun in his arms, looking more grizzly bear than man. "By God, that's enough or I'll blast you both with buckshot."

Demar staggered back and Quaid did the same, Slim

bellowing, "Take it outside and don't either of you set foot in this here establishment again till I get an apology."

Breathing hard, Demar wiped the blood from the corner of his mouth, pulled a fistful of bills from his wallet and threw them on the bar as Quaid did the same to cover damages. Demar headed for the door, and when he got outside he felt Quaid's presence behind him. Demar spun around and threw a blow that Quaid blocked with his forearm, bringing them face-to-face, breaths hot and fast, gazes locked. Quaid said, "I don't give a shit about you fucking up your life, but you're fucking up Sally's too. She loves you, dammit. She loves you a lot." He dropped his arm. "Ah, screw it! You're too stupid to understand, you're thinking with your dick."

Quaid turned away, heading for the O'Fallon house. Demar watched his retreating back then made for the back porch to check on Jett. He'd left her in a rush and wanted to make sure she was okay . . . except there was no Jett. Insects circled the porch light over the smoldering grills, an owl hooted in the trees, August humidity closed around him and he was alone—again.

He tore off his apron and dropped it on the steps where it landed in a soft white heap. He must be out of his everlovin' fucking-proud mind. He banged his head against one of the wood uprights supporting the roof. *Stupid, stupid, stupid!*

Jamming his hands in his pockets, he cut behind the pile of new lumber then crossed the street to the O'Fallon house. He needed some answers and his brain felt too fractured to find them. Besides, Quaid would be more than happy to knock some sense into him.

The driveway curved up to the house, making a circle. Quaid sat on a white wicker chair, head back, ice bag on his face, another covering his knuckles. Demar felt his right eye swelling shut. "Least I'm not the only one in pain."

"I think you busted my damn nose."

"Just for the record, you're right about me fucking up my life." Demar took the ice pack from Quaid's knuckles, plopped down on the settee and applied the pack to his eye. "Don't suppose you have any whiskey handy."

Without looking up, Quaid passed over a bottle of Jack Daniels Black Label. Demar took a swig, the alcohol burning the shit out of his mouth; then again, he had it coming. "A year-and-a-half ago Jett dumped me for my best friend. She shows up here sweet as you please with *Demar you're the greatest and I can't live without you* on her lips, and I bought it."

He paused, letting that much sink in as he figured out what the hell was going on. "I'm not in love with her, I'm in love with the idea that she came back to me strutting her stuff. It's one hell of an ego trip."

"And you're confessing all this, looking for absolution from screwing around on Sally?"

"Never got to the screwing stage." *Thank God!* "The question is, what's Jett's game? I'm a cop, here looking for Mimi and the guys after her. Jett's a cop and all of a sudden she's here too."

Quaid pried open his eyes as Demar added, "Suddenly she's paying one hell of a lot more attention to me than ever before. That's a lot of coincidence in my book."

"Probably your imagination." Quaid slowly sat up. "Let's take a walk down by the docks. I got to check on some tows and you can help me load cable." Quaid slid his feet from the table and stood. "Come on, move your ass."

"I'm in pain here, man. You damn-near killed me." Then he felt Quaid's eyes staring at him hard, his right brow arcing a fraction. This was not about a damn walk or cable. "Right, a tug. Be still my heart." Demar got up, every muscle in his body screaming in protest. Quaid chuckled. "Too much barbecue, not enough running?"

Neither said a word as he followed Quaid down the steps toward the dim light coming from below the bluff that marked the docks. Demar finally said, "What the hell's this all about and I know it's not a boat."

Quaid slowed as they reached the gravel road that dropped to the river. "There's no way of knowing if the house is bugged or not. If you got something going on with Jett and it includes finding Mimi, we need to keep it quiet, not tip our hand."

"Your house is bugged?"

"They stole Bonnie from right under our roof. Anything's possible."

Demar stopped under a big maple at a bend and gazed out at the water, black as ink in the darkness. He could hear the gentle swells lapping the shore, the frogs having one hell of a party. "Jett's not only giving me the rush act, she's wanting to meet my new friends, especially the O'Fallon clan. Either she's here to find out what I know, because the police figure I'm not leveling with them, or . . ."

"Or she's working for someone else who wants to know what's going on."

"As a cop, Jett always played by the book in Nashville. I have no reason to think she's changed, but I got a bad feeling like I'm being used. No matter who she's working for, I can play her game and get information from her like she wants from me. We're not even close to finding the bad guys and Mimi's not coming out of hiding until we do. We wind this up soon or the case gets dropped. We're desperate . . . but then so are the bad guys. It's crunch time."

Quaid leaned against the tree trunk and raked his hair. "So the deal is, you keep your connection with Jett till we figure out what she knows?"

"And somehow work it around Sally." He gave Quaid a long look. "I don't want to lose her, I know that now. And I sure as hell can't tell gossip central what we're up to. The girl's great, and I love her, but keeping things to herself is not Sally's strong suit."

"Meaning you get to juggle two women at once," Quaid chuckled. "I can't even keep up with one female in my life. You're going to need one hell of a lot of luck to pull this off."

"More like a damn miracle. And there's another wrinkle. Jett's staying at Hastings House." He paused, gauging Quaid's reaction.

"Oh damn."

"I see you've been talking to your dad. If there's a slip up and Jett's one of the bad guys, Mimi could be in real danger. I'll pay Jett a visit tonight, see what I can find out. I've got an apartment over the old carriage house there, and can keep an eye on things." He nodded at the road. "I'll leave now, you follow later. We shouldn't be seen together. If we suddenly get too chummy after our little altercation it'll look suspicious. Since there are more strangers in town with the building going on, we don't know who's watching who."

Demar headed up the road and got his car from the parking lot at Slim's and drove to Hastings House. With luck, Thelma left him a few scones and a fresh pot of tea. He could do with some tea, ease some of his aches and pains. But first he had to connect with Jett.

He parked by the carriage house that he'd helped Thelma and Conrad renovate, then trudged across the back lawn and brick patio lined with planters overflowing with red and white flowers. He went inside the main house, the back halls empty at this hour, guests enjoying music and cards in the drawing room. Thelma had made cookies instead of the scones tonight, the scent of vanilla and cinnamon making his mouth water. He took the back steps to the second floor—if Rory was here tonight on a plumbing run, he and Bonnie would be on the third floor, which Thelma kept closed off.

Demar treaded softly and listened at Jett's door before knocking. Voices . . . Jett's. A phone call. Something about scones; guess Jett didn't realize that tonight's snack was cookies. Nothing but an innocent conversation. He knocked and heard the phone drop into the cradle. She opened the door. Eyes bright, hair shimmering, jeans two sizes too small showing off delicious curves.

"Why here you are," she said as he came in. "I was getting ready to call the sheriff. I was worried, sweetheart."

But not worried enough to hang around and see if I was okay.

She threw her arms around him and nudged the door shut with her bare toes complete with pink polish. She touched his eye. "Does that hurt?"

What hurt the most was that he nearly ruined things between him and Sally.

"Did you and Quaid come to some kind of understanding? I don't want you to get enemies over me, especially the O'Fallons. You like them a lot."

"You know guys overreact but we're okay now. I told him you and I were friends and just hanging out on Slim's back porch."

"Friends?" She giggled and tossed her hair. It hung loose and free tonight, swirling around her shoulders, sexy as hell. "Friends don't kiss the way we do, Demar." She ground her soft mound against his dick, her eyes turned sultry and she kissed his chin.

Things were about to get sticky and he had to slow the relationship down. He needed information, not a roll in the hay. He took her arms from around his neck and stepped away. "I want to take it slower this time, Jett. I want us to get to know each other before we jump in the sack."

"But, baby," she sulked. "You are so good in the sack." She pressed her chest to his, her lush breasts nearly pushing out of the vee-cut of her blouse. She walked her fingers up his front to his lips and traced the soft pad of her thumb across his bruised mouth. She gently kissed the split in his lip where Quaid's fist did its work. "I want you, Demar," she hummed. "I told you I was sorry for leaving you, and I so want us to be the way we were. We were happy, sugar. We had a lot of good times together. I want that for us again, and I want the good times to never end."

He kissed her because if he didn't she'd start to smell a rat, and at the moment that's what he felt like. He was kissing one woman and in love with another. He was getting too old for this undercover crap.

"Okay," he said, breaking the kiss, searching for a diversion. "Let's go for a walk."

"A walk? I don't want to walk, I want to run my hands all over you." She pushed him backwards. The bed caught him in the knees and he fell backwards, sprawling out across the top. Jett put her hands on her hips. "Oh, Demar, now that's just the way I like you—all to myself for the whole night, me on top, you on the bottom, so I can do all kinds of delicious things to you."

Holy crap! He started to get up but wasn't moving as fast as usual and Jett dove on top of him, her face to his, every muscle in his body hurting.

She smiled wickedly. "I want to feel you getting hard just for me, sugar. I want to watch every inch of your big dick keep getting bigger. Then I want to lick you and suck you and—"

He rolled over, taking her with him and trapping her under him. Sweat beaded across his lip. His ribs ached, his head pounded. "I can't do this, Jett." Now he had to think of a reason other than *I love Sally and I'm playing you and I'm not screwing you no matter what.* "You hurt me really bad last time and I can't go through that again. I want this to be the real thing between us."

She slid her hand between them and cupped his erection. "Sure feels like the real thing to me and we don't have to wait at all. You're the one for me, Demar. I know that. It took me time and a lot of soul-searching to realize how much I love you. And I do, baby, I really do. Take me, Demar. Do it right now. It'll feel so good, I promise."

She looked into his eyes and he felt as if she were assessing the situation. "I can't, Jett. Not yet."

Something flashed in her eyes and it wasn't hurt, but closer to anger. "I understand," she managed in a convincing voice. "And if taking a walk is what you want, then that's what we'll do." She kissed him gently, like kissing a rose. "Thelma has a plate of macaroons downstairs. The aroma's been driving me crazy all evening. We can grab a handful and go outside and watch the moon and talk. You can tell me all about what you've been doing here."

Not exactly. The plan was to wheedle information from Jett. He'd worked undercover; he knew the game, he knew how to get what he wanted. The big problem was, so did Jett.

Sally swept up the last of the broken bottles as "Goin' Down Slow" filled the room, and Cynthia Landon swayed into the bar. This was not the Cynthia of twenty years ago. That Cynthia . . . pranced like she had a stick up her butt. "What brings you here?"

"Is it always this crowded on a Wednesday night? You have some business."

"Only when we have a fight. Everyone wants a front

row seat if another breaks out or at least rehash the last one over a few beers." Cynthia claimed a stool and Sally dumped the last of the broken glass into the trash. "You just missed my main man and yours duking it out in the middle of this place. I am so pissed at those two idiots!"

She stashed the broom and dustpan behind the bar. "They could have totally wrecked everything, and I don't even know why they were fighting in the first place. Scared folks in here half to death. What the heck were they thinking, going at each other like two tomcats?"

Cynthia's eyes were huge. "Quaid? Demar? How? Why? Anybody hurt? And Quaid is not my man."

"Oh, really." Sally gave a sassy look. "You telling me you think of him as what—your brother?"

Cynthia blushed and Sally laughed as she handed a tray of longnecks to Slim. Nothing like a big ornery man who tipped the scales at about two-fifty to make folks behave. "To set your mind at ease, both of the town idiots got a little bloody but they left under their own steam. Could have gotten ugly if Dad didn't break things up. They were well matched, with Demar being a cop and everybody knows Quaid's been fighting all his life."

Cynthia nibbled a pretzel, trying to look not all that interested but failing miserably. "Not everybody."

Sally refilled baskets with pretzels and chips and put them on the bar. "I keep forgetting you were off to college when Rory adopted Quaid."

"Hey, don't rub it in. I'm starting to get a forty complex."

"No rubbing intended," Sally said, amazed she and Cynthia Landon James were sitting here discussing men and bar fights, as if they'd done it their whole lives.

Cynthia leaned closer. "Well, are you going to tell me or not?"

"About . . . ?"

"Quaid," she ground out. "You just had to make me say his name, didn't you?"

Sally gave a devil grin and put a beer in front of Cynthia. "He used to always be in trouble, stealing, fighting, you name it, getting picked up by the sheriff. One time he came across Keefe and Ryan. They were about ten, and getting beat up because Keefe was more interested in school plays than pitching knothole. The three of them kicked some major butt and were friends from then on. Quaid's grandfather raised him and used to come home drunk and knock him around regularly. Quaid would run away, always looked like hell, came here sometimes, but then Pete would promise to change, and the sheriff would drag Quaid home. The talk is, Rory found Quaid shivering and cold and a bloody mess, hiding out on one of his tugs. He got fed up, paid off Pete and adopted Quaid."

"Rory bought Quaid!"

"More or less. School was never Quaid's thing and Rory put him to work on the tows. Youngest captain on the Mississippi, had his pick of any girl in town. When he turned twenty-two Rory made him join the Coast Guard to get a fresh start."

"And now Rory's got a problem."

"And Quaid's back—bigger, better and more handsome than ever, in case you didn't notice—which I'm sure you have." Sally handed off another tray of beers to Slim.

"There is nothing with me and Quaid." Cynthia took a swig of beer, pinky extended as if in Le Cirque. New York wasn't that far away after all.

"So what brings you into town tonight?"

"Quaid."

Sally laughed outright and Cynthia gave a sheepish grin. "I just wanted to thank him for persuading Mother to come home, and really thank him for sending us Preston-

the-cook." She let out a blissful sigh. "He made scones . . .
I have a real thing for scones, and so do Mother and our
new boarder. Preston whipped up a spinach omelet and I
nearly had an orgasm."

"I think that's where Quaid comes in."

"So, how are things with you and Demar?"

"Changing the subject will not save you from my prying
questions, but as for Demar . . . ever since Boobs came to
town he's . . . distracted."

"I thought you were un-distracting him. Making a play
for him."

"We played in the closet, but now what? What do I do
for an encore? I'm not exactly into boy and girl fun and
games, I'm a business major. If he wanted advice on his
401K I could wow his socks off."

Cynthia propped her chin in her hand and twirled a
pretzel around in circles on the bar top. "Let's see, you
want the wow factor. There's Carmen Electra's Aerobic
Striptease DVD, you can learn a lot from that, and Satori
Oil of Love potion that gets warm, and it's edible, more
like lickable. There's a Prisoner-of-Love Kit, that's a real
hoot, and Daring Dice, it has body parts and . . ." Cynthia's
gaze came back to Sally's. She knew her eyes were huge.
She couldn't have stopped them from bulging if she'd
wanted to.

Cynthia said, "What?"

"Okay, a minute ago you were sipping beer with your
pinky out and now you're rattling off sex games? What
exactly did you design in New York, girl?"

"My loft was above an adult toy store, very refined and
tasteful. Two gay guys ran it, Eddy and Freddy, and they
were totally darling and great friends. Don't tell anyone,
but I asked their opinions on more than one design I created. They had marvelous taste. They ran Simple Pleasures.
We met every morning for coffee."

"I was on Wall Street, dealt with obnoxious over-testosteroned men in ugly suits with gross ties, who hated women, and you got Eddy and Freddy. I totally chose the wrong profession."

"I also got Aaron." She chomped the pretzel hard. "He had a mean, vicious side I never knew about until it was too late. I should have come in here years ago. I probably wouldn't have wound up with Aaron the ass." She studied Sally. "Don't wait too long to make your move with Demar. He's a keeper and Jett is on the prowl."

"You know, you are absolutely right, time's a-wastin'. I've been thinking about it all day and I need to do something now."

Chapter 7

Sally took off her apron and slid it over Cynthia's head. "I'm going after my main squeeze. Something calm, because Demar just got beaten up ... unless ... unless I can think of some way to make him feel better, and we all know what makes men feel better."

Cynthia held up the apron. "I can't tend bar."

"I'll play nurse. Nurse Sally." She giggled. If I had time I'd get you to make me a uniform."

"No wonder you worked on Wall Street, you're steam-rolling right over me."

"I'll check Demar out, top to bottom and everything in between." She handed Cynthia a towel. "Open a beer, serve a beer. Slim will help. Piece of cake. Besides, this was your idea."

"Remind me to have my tongue removed," she yelled after Sally, who headed for the back stairs.

Sally ran upstairs to the quaint apartment—quaint except for Slim's wide-screen TV in the living room, which her mother would have had a stroke over, God rest her soul. She pulled white short-shorts and a halter top from the dresser in her bedroom, and drew red crosses on them with a Sharpie pen. She folded a hat out of paper, added another cross, and found an old pair of white heels. Nurse Sally needed heels! She grabbed a bottle of Rémy Martin Louis XIII from Slim's private stash and the rest of the mocha almond fudge Häagen Dazs she'd been saving for a special occasion. Ta-da, special occasion on the way!

She dressed, applied double eyeliner, cherry-red lipstick and squirts of Obsession, then headed for the truck out back and made for Hastings House. Through the breaks in the trees along the river, she caught sight of moonlight on the Mississippi. The thought of Demar naked in that same moonlight made her hit the accelerator harder than usual, until a flash of something darted across the road.

Oh, damn! On reflex, she stomped the brakes, the truck fishtailing then taking a nosedive into a ditch, the airbag deploying. "Grant!" she grumbled as the bag deflated. "Damn that man!" Hadn't he harassed the South enough already?

She smacked the steering wheel and yelled out the window. "It is not raining and I am not a new Southerner. It's me, you stupid Yankee. Why don't you go back where you came from."

She closed her eyes. "Dear God, I'm yelling at a ghost." She snapped her eyes open. "And I'm talking to myself." She considered cutting her losses and walking home—except she was dressed like a hooker. The gossips would love it.

She stepped from the truck, teetering on her heels in the dirt. She snagged the bag of brandy and ice cream from the front seat and crossed the road, fading into the woods leading up to Hastings House so as not to be seen in this getup. Enough moonlight broke through the trees, letting her find the path that she hadn't used since she was little. All the kids played in the woods around Hastings House . . .

until it got dark. Then the woods belonged to Grant, and she'd already had that encounter.

Mosquitoes bit in obscene places, no sense of decency in the insect world. She swatted at one crawling up her right butt cheek, tripped over a rock, fell with a hard thud and twisted her ankle. She lay flat on the dirt catching her breath. This kind of stuff never happened to those girls in *Sex and the City*. They always looked great, met terrific guys and never gained an ounce, no matter how many times they went out to eat, and they always ate out.

She sniffled, feeling a pity party coming on. This was so not fair. Sitting, she glimpsed the silhouette of Hastings House just beyond the tree line, except the only way she'd get there was to crawl. What happened to her night of seduction, her inspecting Demar head to toe, him slurping seventy-year-old brandy from her navel? Ruined! She pried the lid off the Häagen Dazs, dug her finger into the starting-to-melt goodness and scooped it into her mouth. Normally it would be about two-hundred calories per finger full and Fat Fighters would flip out . . . except everyone knew ice cream eaten in the woods at night when you tripped and fell didn't have calories.

After the fourth scoop she heard voices at the top of the ridge. Saved! Until she realized one of the voices was Boobs and she was talking to a man. They stood just inside the woods. The good news was the guy wasn't Demar. The bad news was she'd rather eat worms than be saved by Demar's ex.

Sally strained to hear. She got nothing from the man in his low guy voice that was more North than South, but Jett's voice carried. She mentioned a baby, then Mimi. Holy crap! Mimi? Jett was connected to Mimi? This was huge. It also meant Boobs was not on the up and up about just being here to win back Demar. In fact, she was probably using Demar. Sally did a mental happy dance. Boobs was up to something sinister, and now all Sally had to do was tell Demar, he'd see her for the user she was, and Boobs was history. All would be back to normal—providing she got out of the woods.

The pair parted, Jett going to the main house, the man keeping to the woods. She could follow him, if she could walk, but since that was out the next best thing was to keep her presence a secret so Boobs and Mr. X didn't know she was on to them. To kill time she finished off the ice cream—spy calories didn't count either—found a stick and struggled to her feet, wobbling on one high heel. She retrieved the shoe that wouldn't fit on her swollen foot, put it in the bag with the brandy and empty container, then hobbled off, keeping to the edge of the woods so as not to be seen.

Using the stick-hop method she made her way to the carriage house. Did Demar have to be on the second floor? Holding on to the railing, she clamped the bag in her mouth and jumped onto the first step. Demar opened the door, looked, looked again and blinked—least his one good eye did; the other was swollen shut.

"What are you doing? What's with the crosses? You joining a cult or something?" He was barefoot in loose cotton pants, the kind tied with a drawstring, and a gray T-shirt. One delicious man except for his banged-up face.

She tried to talk but the bag didn't help. She stopped on the fifth step. "I'm a nurse, dammit, and you really do look like hell."

"Very scary nurse, babe."

"I came to minister to you, make you feel good. and then Grant made an appearance and ruined everything." She leaned against the railing. "Let's see, so far the truck's in the ditch, I screwed up my ankle and I ruined my outfit."

He came down the steps. "Have you been drinking?" He sniffed. "Nope, I smell ice cream. Mocha almond fudge?" He kissed her, his tongue sliding to meet hers. "Oh yeah, mocha fudge."

She touched his cheek, hating that it was bruised. "I had the ice cream to share, except I fell and needed consoling. Mocha almond fudge consoles great."

He brushed a strand of hair from her forehead and kissed that place. "Bet I can do a lot better."

She held up the bag. "Medicine."

He reached in. "One empty container, one very sexy shoe." His mouth covered hers. "Love the shoes but your dad's going to skin you alive for the brandy. This is his good stuff."

He scooped her up in his arms and she yelped and laughed. "Then we should drink it. If I'm going to get skinned let's make it worthwhile."

He headed up the stairs, grunting as he went. "I can walk, Demar."

He nudged open the door. "Your ankle's swelling."

He smiled, parting the split on his lip. She wiped the blood away with the pad of her thumb. "Why were you fighting with Quaid? I thought you two got along. In fact you sort of remind me of each other."

Demar walked past the bedroom and into the bathroom. "Difference of opinion."

"Men should learn to get over it. Shop, have lunch, compliment each other's hairstyle."

He set her down on one end of the vanity top, propping her foot up on a towel on the other end. "I think we need to get you cleaned up."

"I came to look after you." She touched his eye. "Did you have a doctor check that out? It looks bad."

"I've had worse. And you have a million bug bites. What happened?"

"I cut through the woods, didn't want anyone to see me in this getup. Can you imagine the gossip? Obsession is a mosquito magnet."

"I think I need to see what's so special." He nuzzled her neck, nipped her earlobe, his hot breath on her skin making her mind blank, except for Demar. "Damn smart mosquitoes. You smell like heaven."

"And you feel like heaven." She ran her hands under his T-shirt, his smooth, hard muscles making her weak. His fingers crept under her top and he massaged her left nipple, then the right, into hard beads. "I'm so glad I came."

"Ditto." He eased the top over her head and looked his fill. "You are a feast for my eyes." He cupped her breasts and planted a soft kiss on one, then the other. She nearly slid off the vanity. "Oh, Demar."

"Every time I see you, you take my breath away."

His eyes went smoky, he unzipped her shorts. "Wiggle for me, babe, so I can get these things off you."

"I think that's just an excuse for me to bounce around."

He grinned. "Maybe a little." She put her hands on his shoulders and moved her bottom side to side as he tugged the material free. "No panties. I'm one lucky guy."

"Except this tile is freezing my behind."

"Can't have a frozen behind. Only a hot one."

"Maybe this will help to warm me up." She tugged at the thin string of his pants, the waistband loosening, the bulge underneath growing. "These are so much easier than jeans." She kissed him. "And a lot more fun."

The soft cotton slid from his hips but didn't fall off. "I do believe your jammies are caught on something. I should take a peek and see what's holding things up." She pulled the pants free and they dropped to the floor. "My, my, what have we here? You are one well-hung stud." He blushed and she added, "Bet that's what all the girls say."

"You're my only girl." He stepped out of his pants then pulled off his shirt.

"And now you're wearing my favorite outfit, your birthday suit. And it looks like you're all ready for fun. And just so you know, I've been thinking about this fun all day."

He laughed and swept her into his arms. "Have you now." He kissed her. "Me too." He sat on the edge of the tub with her across his lap, her breast nuzzled against his broad chest, her arms around his shoulders, his erection pressing between her legs, suggesting what was to come. "I think I like sitting on your lap."

He turned on the tap, the warm water splashing against the white porcelain. "Naked. Naked is definitely an added bonus."

She swallowed hard, her insides on fire as he lowered her into the tub. "Lean back. Let me get a look at you. Some beautiful water nymph."

She did as he asked, and he took her left foot and propped it on the edge of the tub by the soap dish, then put a towel under her heel. "Keeping your foot elevated will help the swelling."

She eyed him. "And what are we going to do about your swelling?" I look like a porn star. One leg up, leaning back in a tub, showing everything I own."

"And you own some pretty fine stuff there." He gazed at her as water crept up around her.

"You don't have any bubble bath, by some miracle?"

"And bubble over this fine view? No way. Oh, honey, you are so sweet."

"And you're sitting there like King Tut when there's work to be done." She pointed to herself. "That means you get to work on me." She winked. "And then I get to work on you. It'll be fun."

"I'm observing."

She pulled the hair on his leg and he yelped, "Hey."

"Now that I got your attention, you can observe from in here. Or maybe I should come out there and take you right on the tile floor," she whined, "you're driving me crazy."

"Why, I think that's an invitation." He laughed as he climbed into the tub then knelt between her legs and kissed her knee.

"You have really bad aim for a cop." She pointed to her lips. "Do that here."

"Such an impatient woman." He kissed the inside of her other knee as his fingers trailed up her thigh, pausing at the apex of her legs, tormenting her, teasing her, making her want him. He added more kisses as his fingers tangled into her wet curls then gently grazed her clit. Good thing the drain was closed or she would have slid right down.

He looked at her, his eyes dark, his voice husky as he said, "Do you like this?"

He turned off the water and his fingers began to massage her, slow and easy, and she thought she'd lose consciousness from the sheer ecstasy of it. "Demar," she panted, her hips arching hungrily against his hand, begging for more. "You are incredible."

"H'mm." He applied a bit more pressure, lingering, then started his seduction again, barely giving her time to recover . . . to breathe.

Remembering—somehow—where she saw the soap, she retrieved it and lathered her hands, then stroked his penis in slow, sudsy strokes, watching it swell, her fingers tightening just a bit. His whole body quivered and his fingers suddenly slid into her, giving her more pleasure than she could ever imagine. "Oh, baby," he hissed.

His fingers delved deeper into her, making every cell of her body scream for more . . . more, her legs widening in response. Her heart pounding She stroked him faster, his erection swelling, his response to her the biggest turn on of all.

"Demar!" She yelled his name as she climaxed and felt his penis pulsate with release that seemed to go on and on, matching her own.

He eased his fingers from her and leaned against the side of the tub. "Dear God, Sally girl. I think you ruined me. I'll never be able to perform again."

"That better not be true," she said on a laugh that took more energy than she had at the moment.

"I'm nuts about you, Sally, and not just in the tub or storeroom or wherever we make love. I want you to know I care about you no matter what."

"Well, you're sounding awful serious."

"Life has a way of spinning out of control, getting crazy, and I want you to believe that I care for you more than anything in this world." He closed his eyes for a second. "I'm so glad you're here. Being with you is the best thing that's ever happened to me."

"I'm not going anywhere, baby." Something was wrong, she could feel it, see it in his eyes, hear it in his voice. But what? Jett! Things had gone straight to hell since that other woman strutted into the bar.

"You know," she said as she smiled at him, making things light again, "we didn't get very clean in this tub. We need to try again. I think we got distracted. And it was a great distraction." Using her big toe, she flipped the lever, letting out the cooling water. He turned on the tap, this time running the shower, which sent a soft warm spray over them. He swept the curtain closed, shutting out the harsh light, filtering it into a glow.

"This is very nice. I think I could live here with you forever."

"We'd be in a permanent state of prune, get really bad

skin, and we'd get really, really hungry." He snagged a bottle of shampoo. "Now I get to wash you, but I'm afraid you're going to smell like a guy."

"Then whenever I take a sniff I'll think of you." She looked at her foot, propped up and smeared with mud. "I really did get dirty in the woods."

"You could have spent the whole night there. Unless Grant came along again."

Steam billowed, the water soothing. "Actually, there was someone besides me and Ulysses hanging around. Jett made an appearance."

"Jett was in the woods?" His eyes widened a fraction and he stiffened for a split second. No one else would have caught it, but after just making incredible love to the man she still felt that intimate connection, an inner sense about him. Something was off and she needed to know what, since . . . since she was flat-out, totally in love with Demar Thacker. "She was there with another man."

Demar's gaze met hers, a spark of interest in his eyes. "Did you see who? Any idea at all?"

Was he jealous? Her heart squeezed tight at the possibility. "Couldn't tell, but she mentioned a baby and Mimi. I don't trust her, Demar. I . . . I don't trust her in this town and I really don't trust her with you. She wants something, I can feel it."

"Jett and I are friends, that's all she wants." The simple answer that he gave so often came quick—too quick, as if automatic and trying to hide something deeper. "She's a cop, and the job can get to you. She's here for a rest and to kick back," Demar continued.

He shrugged, trying for a casual response. "If you saw her in the woods it was probably with a new friend she met here, and they were talking about what everyone else is, missing Mimi and baby Bonnie."

"Hiding in the woods?"

"Maybe it wasn't hiding so much as a walk in the moonlight. It is a lovely night and there are new guests at Hastings House she's gotten to know." He kissed Sally. "Let's forget about Jett."

Demar was different when he talked about that woman, as if fighting to find the right words or offer excuses for her or . . . or explain away her actions or something. He worked the suds into her hair, the bubbles tickling down over her skin. Right now everything was perfect and she wanted to focus on that.

She kissed Demar through the suds as she closed her eyes, avoiding the sting of the soap and the sting of the other woman in his life. But no matter how hard Sally tried to forget, deep down inside she knew something was going on with Demar and Jett, and it wasn't one bit good for Sally Donaldson.

Chapter 8

Cynthia glanced at her watch as she left the bar. One A.M.! She kicked the front tire of her station wagon. She smelled like smoke and stale beer from spilling as many orders as she served. She was a clothes designer, not a barmaid, and anyone at Slim's tonight would applaud that statement.

"What are you doing here so late?" came Quaid's voice from behind her.

She spun around, hands to her chest. "You scared the heck out of me."

"Residual effect from living in New York?"

"Pickled brain from inhaling barbecue sauce fumes." She nodded at Max by a tree. "Dog walking?"

"Dog sniffing. Max takes doing his business in just the right place real serious." He nodded at the Buick. "Car trouble?"

"Sally trouble. She conned me into helping out so she can seduce Demar." Which was exactly what she wanted to do to Quaid right now.

"Hell, that should take about ten minutes."

About as long as she'd last with Quaid. He grinned and hitched his hip onto the fender. She licked her bottom lip and tried not to drool. "She's worried Demar's falling for Jett, his ex-girlfriend who came to town a few days ago. Somehow I opened my big mouth and got roped into the problem. You missed that conversation since it happened after your brawl. What was that all about anyway? No one seems to know for sure, but everyone at the bar sure had an opinion. My personal favorite was that you and Demar are gay and had a lovers' spat."

He laughed, the rich sound floating off into the stillness of the night. "We had a little disagreement."

"Translated that means it's about a girl. My bet is Demar's paying too much attention to the new girl in town and you don't like that he's two-timing a friend. End result is you beat the stuffing out of him, or at least tried to. How's your nose?"

"About as good as Demar's eye." He assumed an innocent look that he'd probably perfected when he was a street kid talking his way out of trouble. "What Demar and Sally and Jett do is up to them and nothing to do with me."

She grinned. "Right. Like I'm going to believe that."

He took her arm and tugged her closer, her hip against his thigh. He tucked a strand of hair behind her ear, sending chills down her spine and setting fire to her gut. "Think you know me pretty well, don't you?"

"I know you're loyal to your friends and family. That's why you're here and not in Alaska." She captured his chin between her thumb and forefinger. She wanted him to know that what she had to say was more than idle conversation. "And I know Lawrence thinks you hang the stars each night and make the tides roll in and out each day."

"Are you kidding? That kid knows exactly what causes those things."

She laughed, but not the happy kind that made her feel good inside. It was one of those crappy laughs, when she wished things were different but they weren't. "Aaron wanted Lawrence to be a pitcher for the Yankees, or a quarterback for . . . for one of those teams that use quarterbacks. Being the second Einstein was not on Aaron's radar and Lawrence knows that. It didn't do much for Lawrence's self-esteem. You help—you help a lot. He likes you, and that you like him and respect him is more important than you can imagine right now. Thank you."

He took her fingers and kissed the tips. "Lawrence is a great kid."

"Except he doesn't have a kid brain."

"His brain is only one part of him, Cynthia. He's still a little boy."

His mouth covered hers as his arm slipped easily around her middle, drawing her between his legs. His hand went under her blouse, then her bra, and cupped her breast. "What are you doing?" she asked against his lips.

"If you don't want this say the word."

"We're out here in the open."

"We're in Slim's parking lot in the middle of the night behind a row of trees. Even gossips sleep sometime."

She rested her forehead against his chin. "You make things so hard."

"That's my line."

She pulled in a deep breath. "Here's the deal." His thumb stroked her nipple and her insides pulsed with wanting him. "That is so *not* part of the deal."

He kissed her forehead. "I like being with you and when I'm not, all I do is think of you. You're special to me. Always have been. When I was sixteen, I took one look at you and wanted you right there on Main Street in front of everyone."

"At sixteen you had a permanent hard-on and as long as I was female you would have wanted me on Main Street or anywhere else."

"I want you now more than ever."

"And that's the part that can't happen." She pulled his hand from her blouse and stepped away, missing his touch, his lips, the warmth of his body moving against hers. "The reason I came to the bar tonight was to find you."

"Mission accomplished." He held out his hands inviting her back.

She clasped her hands behind her back. "I really want to touch you," she said on a whisper, then let out an audible sigh. "Oh, who am I kidding, I don't just want to touch you, I want to have wild uninterrupted sixteen-year-old sex with you more than I want to breathe."

"Ah, babe, you can breathe and have sex and do anything else you want."

"I can't and that's the problem. I came into town tonight to tell you how great things are now that we're not together anymore."

"I feel another 'the curse' lecture coming on."

"Here's the deal. Things are so good in my life since we parted, and if we don't stay parted things will fall apart like they always do and my life will revisit the toilet. I'm tired of living in the toilet, Quaid. I know there is no logic behind it. Maybe it's because I'm distracted when there's a man in my life, or it's hormonal . . . too much testosterone interferes with my estrogen-originated brainwaves. I don't know. But whatever it is, it's not good. Think about it. Right now we have Preston at the house, the cook to die for, and Beau Fontaine of the Charleston Fontaines. He's a perfect gentleman and a paying customer. Mother is still on the wagon, thank God, and Lawrence is happy, and we even have two nuns who have come to stay for a while."

"Nuns?"

"And they're helping with painting and repairs and getting the place in shape."

"Nuns?"

"They said it was their calling to assist where needed. I don't get it either, and Ivy Acres is not exactly missionary work, but they insist and are a huge help. But the bottom line is, all's well because there are no men in my life." She poked him in the chest because she suddenly wanted to touch him. "And that would include you."

She went around the other side of the Buick and took the sport coat from the back. She held it out to him, suspended on a hanger covered in plastic. "Summer wool. Navy."

He wasn't going to take the jacket, she could tell. She held his hand and wrapped his fingers around the hanger. "There you go. This now makes it official. We are now even and uninvolved."

"I never felt you owed me anything."

"It's not about you so much as paying off the fates."

"At least you didn't have to throw yourself into a volcano." He laid the coat carefully across the hood of the car then snagged her waist and lifted her onto the fender beside the jacket. "I want us to be eye-to-eye, Cynthia Landon. I want you to remember what I'm going to tell you. Screw the fates. You and I are not done, not even close."

She tipped her nose, hoping for an air of authority and determination. "But what if I want us done?"

Before she could draw another breath he took her in his arms and kissed her, his mouth devouring hers, her lips opening to him no matter how much they should stay tight together. His tongue tempted hers, and won. Then her traitorous legs—which obviously missed the whole fates speech—wound tight around his hips.

He whispered against her lips, "No curse is going to keep us apart. I want you to remember that and think about that when you sleep tonight."

"I'm supposed to go home and sleep after this?"

He grinned. "Why do you think *I'm* walking the streets at one in the morning?" He unwound her arms and legs then lifted her down, gave her one more kiss, snagged his jacket and flipped it over his shoulder. He strolled off toward his house, Max following, the moon low and mellow, her head spinning.

"Oh, damn," she murmured. She was hotter than ever for Quaid O'Fallon and she had no idea how to put the fire out.

Quaid fed Bonnie her morning bottle and stifled a yawn. "That woman's killing me. I can't sleep and I can't even eat. When you grow up try and be a little easier with the guys, okay? Just cut them a little slack once in a while."

There was a knock at the door and Quaid put down the bottle and tucked Bonnie in his arm like a football. He wouldn't be able to tuck much longer—she was growing like mad. He opened the back door and Lawrence shuffled in, head lowered, looking more ragged than usual. "Did you sleep in those clothes, buddy?" Hell, at least he slept!

When Lawrence didn't answer, Quaid tipped his head back and looked into a swelling-shut right eye and bloodied lip. "Well dang. I'd hate to see what the other guy looks like."

"They look just fine."

"They?"

"I don't exactly fit in around here. I'm not good at sports or stuff like that so . . ." He shrugged. "It's no big deal and they leave me alone when I have Max, but when I don't . . . Don't tell my mom, okay? She'll freak out. She thinks I'm doing okay." He looked at Quaid and his good eye widened. "Wow, what happened to your jaw and nose?"

He shrugged back at Lawrence. "I don't fit in around

here, not all the guys like me, but don't tell my dad, he'll freak out."

Lawrence laughed and followed Quaid to the kitchen table. "Sit down. You feed Bonnie and I'll get some ice. We can tell each other how much we hurt."

"You want me to feed a baby? I've never even held a baby before."

"Bonnie's hungry, Rory's taking a tow to Rockton today and I'm getting ice. That puts you on baby duty for a few minutes." Giving Lawrence something to do would help get his mind off his own troubles. "Support her head in the crook of your arm, holding her up a little, and then put the bottle in her mouth. She'll do the rest."

Lawrence took Bonnie and the bottle. A slow smile broke over his face as Bonnie gobbled breakfast. Quaid said, "See, you're a natural."

"Did you know that suckling is the only behavior common among mammals?"

Keeping an eye on the feeding situation, Quaid got a plastic baggie and filled it with ice. "Did you get in any good punches?"

"The only punch I know is that red Hawaiian stuff that comes in a can and is totally bad for you but tastes great." He was quiet for a moment, then his smile dropped. "Dad calls me Ms. Sissy or sometimes he calls me 'worm' because I'm a bookworm." Lawrence looked up quickly, his eyes big. "But you can't tell Mom that either. It would make her mad and she's mad enough at Dad already." He looked back to Bonnie. "Boy, this baby is really hungry."

Quaid never been more pissed off at another man in his life, and that included Pete and he hated Pete's guts. He hunkered down in front of Lawrence. "Until Rory adopted me I was raised by my grandfather, who was a lot like your dad. He told me I was useless and would never amount to anything and—" *that I was a no-good bastard kid* but Lawrence didn't need to hear all the details. "Pete will always be my grandfather but that doesn't mean he knows everything, and I certainly don't have to like him. You just listen to your mom. You are a terrific boy, Lawrence. You're honorable and caring and loyal and compassionate. That's what makes a man. And you're intelligent, so you can do things better than most."

"Except fight." He looked Quaid dead in the eyes. "Will you teach me how, please? You were just in a fight and I bet you didn't lose. I'll take care of Max for free for a year if you teach me."

Quaid stood. "If I teach you to fight your mother will wring my neck for a year."

"So we won't tell her. Just between us, man to man."

Quaid took Bonnie from Lawrence and set her on his knee for a burp, as Lawrence went on, "I have to learn how to be a guy around here or I'm going to get beat up till I go off to college."

"Which could be next year."

Lawrence cracked a smile. "I did some boxing in prep school but there was all this protective gear and a referee. That's not exactly how it is in the real world."

Lawrence needed some confidence. He had the mental part aced but now there was the guy part to deal with. "Tell you what, we'll go in the living room and move some of the furniture out of the way so we don't break something and give Rory a fit. I can teach you a few things that will keep you out of trouble. But you're going to have to tell your mother what's going on. You got your eye to consider."

"I'll wear sunglasses, and if I hang around here all day and we do the meteor showers tonight like we planned, she won't see me."

"Sport, that shiner's not going to go away in a day, more

like two weeks. After you walk Max, go level with your mom. But I will pick you up tonight around nine and we'll drive up to Stevie's Ridge and take a look at the Perseids."

Lawrence patted Bonnie's head. "And when she gets older we'll take her with us."

"You should think about being a pediatrician. You have a way with babies."

Lawrence carried Bonnie into the living room and strapped her in the swing. "No way. I'm going to learn to fight and join the army and do special ops."

Quaid groaned as he pulled the overstuffed chair to the side of the room. "Now your mother is definitely going to kill me."

And later that night as Quaid lay on his back in the field of grass, staring up at meteors tearing through the sky, with Lawrence beside him and Max chasing critters, Quaid decided that Cynthia was killing him without even trying. Heck, she didn't even have to be around him to do that. The problem was he wanted her, she didn't want him, and she was winning—and he had to figure out what to do about it.

Quaid checked his watch. "It's one A.M., champ." He considered where he was last night at this time . . . his arms around Cynthia and her legs around him. Great place to be. "We better get back home."

Lawrence yawned and sat up. They collected the blankets and water bottles, put Max in the back and got into the Jeep. They bounced over the rutted gravel road that led to the two-lane beyond. Quaid said, "We'll come back when there's a new moon and bring a camera. We can take time exposures."

Lawrence nodded at an old rundown house behind them. "We can take shots from that roof. Doesn't look like anyone lives there anymore."

"That's Stevie Valentine's old place. He was a riverboat

captain. The attic has a trapdoor. His wife refused to have alcohol in the house so he smuggled it in that way. When she'd go visit her sister in St. Louis he'd throw one heck of a party. We made a few runs to New Orleans together. He was a good captain, a good friend. We used to go fishing off his dock on the other side of the road."

They cleared the last rut, then Quaid turned for Ivy Acres. Lights of a tow moved out in the channel, a sliver of moon perched on the horizon. He glanced over at Lawrence, already asleep, not able to stay awake for the fifteen-minute ride home. When Quaid pulled into the drive he spotted Cynthia on the top step, leaning against a column. A moonbeam fell across her face, and he was sure he'd never seen a more beautiful sight or a more beautiful woman.

Too bad *seeing* was as close as he'd get. Damn that curse! Hers might have ended when she kicked him to the curb but his just started, and had every indication of getting worse.

He went to the passenger side, unclipped Lawrence and gathered him into his arms. Cynthia came up beside him and he inhaled her sweet feminine scent of . . . "Brandy? Thought you got rid of it because of Ida?"

"Not the apricot—that would be a sin. I hid it and was sharing some with the nuns." She nodded at the front of the house. "They painted the shutters today. God is smiling on my no-man decision."

"Except it's translating into a no-woman decision for me. Why are nuns doing all this, again?"

"They said that's what he would have wanted them to do." Cynthia pointed to the sky. "I'm guessing the *he* is the one up there. God works in mysterious ways."

Quaid followed Cynthia inside to the black-and-white marble floor in the entrance, antique lamps on antique tables in the living room, along with a flowery sofa and delicate matching chairs. Not a La-Z-Boy or remote in sight.

They took the winding staircase to Lawrence's room. Cynthia pulled off his shoes and Quaid slid him under the covers. "Thanks for taking him stargazing tonight," Cynthia whispered as they came back into the hall, dimly lit with some stained-glass fixtures. "He was really looking forward to this."

"So I guess he's okay?"

"Except for the bruises from when Max chased that raccoon and dragged Lawrence into that fence post. Poor Lawrence, he looks like he was in a fight."

Blast that kid. Quaid leaned against the wall and fiddled with the collar on Cynthia's blouse. Maybe that would distract her from what he had to say, because she wasn't going to like it. "Uh, there wasn't any raccoon or fence post. I'm sort of teaching Lawrence to . . . to throw a left hook."

Cynthia's pretty mouth opened in surprise—and he'd so much rather it opened to kiss him. "What? Why? Are you out of your mind?"

"Some kids beat him up because he's—"

"A brain." Cynthia let out a long breath. "We ran into this in New York so I put him in another private school. I suppose I'll have to send him away to boarding school with other kids like himself. He'll fit in there and he'll be happy. I have no idea how I'll afford that but somehow—"

"Running away from a problem doesn't solve it, Cynthia."

"Oh that's crap. Of course it does. You go one place, leave the problem behind, works pretty good."

"What about letting Lawrence work things out here where he has support? He has to live with all kinds of people, not just the brainy ones."

"No, the brainy ones will be just fine." She folded her arms. "And I sure as heck am not going to let my son get beat to a pulp because he's smart. Lawrence is a timid creature by nature."

"Last time I checked he wanted to join the army."

"What have you done?" Her eyes narrowed. "You and your macho ways have ruined him."

"Oh for God's sake, Cynthia, let him be a boy. You can't protect him all the time."

Her spine stiffened and her snooty nose jutted into the air. "I can try. I'm his mother. It's my duty." She pulled herself up tall. "You know nothing about children, Quaid O'Fallon."

He didn't want to argue with her, he wanted to take her to bed. Damn. "When I was a kid no one tangled with me, but school was a nightmare. Rory made me get my GED and go on to college for two years. Sort of an academic left hook. It was good for me, defending himself is good for Lawrence."

He gave her a quick kiss, then made for the front door. He stood outside for a moment, the quiet of night surrounding him, his brain in high gear. Sending Lawrence off to some snobby school was not a good idea. Academics were just one part of his life, there was more, lots more. Quaid mentally kicked himself in the butt for not telling Cynthia that. He should have.

Preston's VW rumbled up the drive. He parked to the side, then got out, baseball cap low on his head, blue Hawaiian shirt flapping in the light night breeze. "Out on a hot date?" Quaid asked.

Preston frowned. "Ida's the only date I want and she won't have anything to do with me. She only has eyes for Beau Fontaine of the Charleston Fontaines, unless it involves food. His cooking is as bad as hers. I asked a friend of mine in Charleston about the Fontaines. He never heard of them."

"Old money likes to keep a low profile."

"Well, why can't this guy take his low profile and smooth manners somewhere else?" Preston sighed. "I was out on the case tonight and handed out pictures of the two presidents of River Environs, but no one's seen them. 'Course if those guys dyed their hair, put on a mustache and let their hair grow they could blend in anywhere. Mimi's somewhere close by, I'm sure of it, and if I know that, the bad guys do too. They'll show up sooner or later, and with time running out my bet's on soon. I checked out the contractors in town, and new workers, but they all seem legit. No one suspicious except for Sister Ginger and Sister Candy. Now there's a duo for you."

"The visiting nuns. Cynthia sure thinks they're a godsend."

"From the order of Fervent Penance in Rockton. They wear little black bandanas on their heads along with short-shorts, halter tops and blue mascara. They drive a red Mustang convertible, this year's model. Sure don't look like the nuns who taught me in grade school. And there's . . . spillage." He made a rounded gesture across his chest that indicated big-breasted women.

"Guess they have a lot to be fervently penitent about?"

"Beats the hell out of me, but I have to admit I'd sure like to see the rest of that order. Dang." Preston said good night and went inside as a light came on upstairs. Cynthia no doubt. He should try harder to make his case for Lawrence staying at the Landing. Besides, what else would he do tonight, take Max on another sniffing tour?

Quaid zeroed in on a trellis at the side of the house. Familiar territory. He'd climbed one of these things to give Sarabeth Carmichael a sweet-sixteen kiss, least that was his great plan. Too much testosterone; too little common sense—and here he was with too little sense all over again. Age did not necessarily bring on wisdom.

Quaid took hold of one of the slats supporting a carpet of ivy against the house, put his foot onto a cross section and levered himself up. Seemed sturdy enough. He got past the first floor, and suddenly the front door creaked open and a man he didn't know stepped out, followed by a woman in a black bandana and a baby doll nighty. She wagged her finger at him and whispered, "Do not come here again."

"But honey . . ."

"Shhh, no honey. I've got work to do here. Go away and do not sneak back in here, do you understand?" She closed the door, leaving the man pouting. He slinked his way down the driveway, keeping to the shadows. A car started in the distance, then faded away. What the hell was that all about? Who was that guy and what was he doing in the house so late? A friend of the sisters? Ministry work nuns in skimpy pjs?

This was another reason why he needed to talk to Cynthia tonight. But the main reason, the most painful one, was right between his legs and hard as stone—which made climbing a real bitch. He continued on to the second floor till . . . till he heard an ominous cracking sound and this time it wasn't Sarabeth's father cocking a shotgun aimed at his butt, but it was definitely an *oh shit* moment.

The slat under his right foot sagged, then cracked clear through. He struggled to get his foot onto another slat but it snapped too. He grabbed tight to steady himself, but pulled the next board clean off the side of the house. He teetered backwards, swallowed a string of curse words, fought the air, lost, then fell back, landing in the bushes. *Ouch!*

The window flew open, followed by the screen, and Cynthia stuck her head out, his gaze meeting hers. "What in the world are you doing, O'Fallon?"

"Convincing you that Lawrence needs to stay here?"

She closed her eyes for a moment and pinched the bridge of her nose. "Did you break anything?"

"I think I killed your rhododendron."

"Not that, I mean . . . Oh, for heaven's sake. Don't move, I'll be right down."

He sat up, waiting for all the bones in his spine to shift back into place and for his head to reposition itself straight on his neck. Cynthia stood over him, the faint light from inside shining through her nightgown, giving him a terrific silhouetted view of underneath. It made nearly breaking his damn-fool neck worth it.

"You could have broken your damn-fool neck."

Great minds think alike. "Did you know there was a strange man in your house?"

"You'll have to be more specific. It's getting kind of crowded." She peered at him. "And I'm not up to arguing about Lawrence at two A.M."

"Fine, no arguing, but do you really think uprooting him again is the answer?"

"Getting the heck beat out of him is?" She sat down beside him and pulled her legs up under her gown, resting her chin on her knees. She let out a big sigh.

"Hey, are you okay?"

"To tell you the truth, sometimes I don't know if I'm doing anything right. Raising kids is not easy. No directions on the heel."

He draped his arm around her. "Honey, Lawrence is a really great kid, and he's going to continue to be that way no matter where he is. Just think what it was like to try and raise someone like me."

She gave him a soft smile and touched his cheek, the simple gesture unexpected and warming him clear through. "Rory O'Fallon did have his hands full. Three sons . . . how does anyone handle three sons? The man deserves a medal."

Quaid leaned back on is elbows and studied her. "Damn, I like looking at you."

"I think you fell on your head. I'm in my ratty nightgown, no makeup, and my hair still needs a dye job. Joan Rivers would not approve. We need to get out of the bushes, we're giving the place a bad name." She held out her hand and he took it, then snagged her around the waist, fell back and tumbled her on top of him. "I like this even more than looking at you."

With no bra to get in the way, the soft mounds of her breasts swelled against his chest.

"No sex, remember?" she said against his lips, her voice barely a murmur. Her eyes shifted from one side to the other as if suddenly aware of her surroundings. "Dear Lord, what are we doing?"

"Hiding so the fates won't see us. Hell, no one can see us. Makes the curse null and void. Can't curse what can't be seen, right? I got an idea."

"And why do I have the feeling it involves me and sex?"

"Because it's a really good idea and both of those things would be in any really good idea of mine. So, we fool around and find out what happens. If things go right to hell, we got our answer."

"And if they don't, we can continue to fool around in hiding places and we're okay?"

"There is that."

She punched his arm. "We already got involved at your office on the docks and my life started a new downward spiral. We broke it off and things straightened out. There, we have our answer."

"But we need to make absolutely sure it's not coincidence." He winked. "Whaddaya say?"

She closed her eyes and put her face to his, eye to eye, nose to nose, lips to lips. "I say I want you so bad I can't sleep."

"This is a good start."

She licked her lips and in the process licked his lips as well. "Maybe . . . maybe fooling around *is* the answer. What I mean is, that way we're simply into mutual gratification, period. No getting involved."

"Too late. I'm crazy about you, Cynthia Landon, and it's not diminishing because of some curse or disagreement over Lawrence, or that I'm the street kid or you're the local princess, or anything else you can throw in the mix."

"Shh." She put her finger to his lips, her eyes dark and lovely and full of passion. God, he loved her eyes like that. "Too much talk," she whispered as she sat up, a sliver of moonlight falling into her hair, making it shimmer like spun glass. She slipped up his shirt and looked her fill, then gently rubbed her sweet hands over his abs and across his chest, her touch making his muscles quiver and his brain melt. "You are a banquet of pure maleness." She grinned. "I heard that on a commercial somewhere and always wanted to use it but never had the chance. You are definitely the chance I've been waiting for."

She planted a row of kisses from his navel to his chin, each touch of her lips searing his skin. "You are one delicious man. Are you comfy?"

"If I was any harder for you I'd rupture something. But damn, girl, I can't imagine a better place on earth right now."

"I mean, are there sticks jabbing your back? Bugs? I hate bugs. Crickets are great to listen to, but I do not want to look at one. Yuck. So, are you okay where you are?"

He took two handfuls of her nightgown. "I will be real soon."

"Wait." She bit her bottom lip and held the gown down. "I'm . . . forty, you have to remember that."

"This is another birthday warning, isn't it? Between the birthdays and the curse you've got a regular litany going. I don't care how old you are, and I got to tell you, this is really strange foreplay. We can do a whole lot better. Just give me a chance."

"I'm starting to . . . to sag a bit."

"I can tell this is an issue and we're never getting to the good stuff till it's resolved. Okay, so let me see, strictly a clinical analysis, I swear. I'll give you my most honest opinion."

"Oh that is such a line of crap, you just want my gown off. But the thing is, maybe I should have a boob job."

"You already did, you got rid of Aaron." She laughed and he used the opportunity to lift the nightgown, revealing the gentle indent of her navel, her smooth midriff, then the lush roundness of her sweet perfect breasts. He dropped the gown beside him then cradled one breast in each palm, looking his fill, because he was supposed to and this was a great opportunity. "I pronounce you perfect."

"Spoken like a man with a naked woman sitting in front of him."

"Shhh." This time he put his finger across her lips. "You really are perfect, Cynthia. I said I'd give you an honest opinion and I am. But the direction of your breasts doesn't matter."

"You can say that because they're not your breasts. Just wait, you'll be forty some day and . . . and you'll still be handsome as ever. Men do forty so much better than women and that bites. How could Mother Nature do that to one of her own kind?"

"Forty's just a number. What matters is that you love Lawrence, take care of Ida, are willing to help Sally, and that you drive a really ugly car but it doesn't bother you. I admire you, and not just the part I can see . . . though that's pretty damn good."

He trailed his index finger up her middle and she took his hand, looked at it for a moment, then placed a soft kiss in his palm. Her eyes went black as a Mississippi squall. "This is just sex, Quaid, nothing more."

"Your words, sweetheart, not mine."

"That will have to do because I don't think I can leave right now, no matter how many curses are after me." Then she unbuckled and unzipped his jeans.

Chapter 9

Cynthia smiled down at him, a wicked sexy glint in her eyes. She took his erection in her hand, then let out an erotic breath as she traced her finger up one side of him, pausing at the tip to drive him insane, then slowly down the other side. "I love feeling you all hard for me."

"When you're around that's the condition I'm usually in."

"Really?"

"Damn uncomfortable and potentially embarrassing as hell." He smiled. "You should be ashamed of yourself." He fondled her breast, appreciating her warm naked flesh against his palm, her areolas dark, and nipples taut with desire . . . desire for him. Her thumb stroked his arousal, his blood pumping harder and faster.

"You are so much a man," she whispered into the still night. Then she leaned over and took his erection deep into her mouth.

For a second he couldn't see, the intimate unexpected connection catching him off guard. His brain fried as her tongue licked the path her fingers had taken before. Her warm moist mouth took him deeper and he curled his fingers into her thick flowing hair that spilled down around his groin. Every cell of his body screamed to have her right now. His control ebbed; excitement twisted his gut. "I can't keep this up."

She straightened and glanced down at his dick. "Doesn't look to me like you're having any trouble keeping it up."

"I'm dying here and I have a naked comedian on my lap." He shifted to one side and slid his wallet from his back pocket, pulling out a condom.

She snapped the package from his fingers. "You're mine, all mine right now, Quaid," she growled, then tore open the package with her teeth. She unrolled the latex, her fingers on him in exquisite torture. She winked. "Now you're dressed for success, I think. It's hard to see."

"Got the hard part right." He snagged her hips and pulled her forward, her wet heat now over his rock-hard cock, her legs wide and straddling him.

"Oh, I think I like this," she said on a ragged breath as she ran her fingers through her hair, scattering it in all directions, free and sassy and sexy. "You do make me feel like a woman, more than I've felt in my entire life. No fancy clothes or makeup or strappy shoes make me feel the way you do."

She leaned forward and braced her hands on either side of his head, her breasts suspended close to his mouth, her face right over his, her hair tumbling around them, shutting out the rest of the world. "I think I like being a little naughty in the bushes with you. And I really like being in control."

"I'll remember that." He took a nipple into his mouth and she pulled in a deep breath then lifted her hips, freeing his dick from the warm cocoon. She lowered her wet open sex onto him. The sensation of sliding into Cynthia nearly reduced him to ashes.

She panted, her hot breath fast and shallow against his forehead. "Every time we do this I swear it won't happen again . . . except . . . except you feel so good, Quaid," she said on a groan of pure pleasure then arched her hips, taking him all the way in, then out.

He looked up, her eyes liquid, her rhythm increasing, hard even strokes fast and deep. His heart pounded, his chest too tight. Then she gasped, her muscles clenching around his dick. He brought her face to his and took her cries of climax into his mouth while pumping into her again and again, reaching his own climax, his insides on fire, his head reeling, obliterating any thoughts but being with Cynthia.

She collapsed on top of him, knocking what air was left in his lungs right out. "Oh, Quaid," she said in one long breath of resignation. "I am so going to get it now."

He kissed her damp hair. "Okay, but you have to give me a few minutes to recoup."

Her teeth nipped his chest and he suddenly wanted her again no matter how exhausted he was at the moment. He always wanted her again.

"Not that, the curse. If this little rendezvous doesn't bring on bad karma nothing will."

"And if it does I'll take care of whatever it is."

She shook her head, her soft cheek rubbing against his heated skin. "No way. I need to stand on my own this time, do things my own way. The sex is great and I thank you for that but—"

"You're thanking me for having sex with you? Like in servicing your needs?"

"Try and understand, I have to straighten out my own life. Maybe I'll hang garlic around my neck for the next few days and ward off any bad stuff lurking about."

He tucked his finger under her chin to make her look at him. "I'm better at handling problems than garlic, Cynthia. Trust me."

She pushed herself up and retrieved her gown, sliding it

on. "You think you have to save the world, especially me, but you don't. I'm doing okay, for the moment."

"I know. And I respect that. But if things go south—call me."

"And who do you call when things go south, Quaid O'Fallon? Me? I'll believe that when it happens."

She sat up. "Things are good right now. I'm designing a mother-of-the bride dress for Lydia Clampton—her daughter's getting married in November. Seems there's an abundance of really dumpy mother-of-the-bride and mother-of-the-groom dresses out there. Maybe this is my niche?"

"I can invest in your company and—"

"No. I'm doing this on my own—whatever this turns out to be." She rolled off him. "Good night, Quaid." She gazed down at him. "Sleep tight . . . but not in my bushes."

Quaid brushed his teeth with enough force to strip enamel. Sleep tight? Wasn't that what Cynthia said to him last night? She was the most hard-headed female he'd ever met. He could help her, dammit. Make things easier for her. But would she let him? Hell no! He cared for her, blast it all, so how was he supposed to sit back and let her fend for herself?

He stopped brushing. Then again, maybe all this independent talk about doing things herself was just a trumped up excuse to distance herself from him. They never really resolved that issue, and the only times they got together were for sex.

That was it. All this crap about a curse really was a front for fooling around and not getting involved. She enjoyed the sex, just not him. It had to be, no one believed in curses—did they? Well, fine. He'd gotten over women before, he'd damn well get over her. No more sex, no more Cynthia.

She'd have to deal and so would he. He yanked on his jeans and T-shirt, opened the bathroom door and faced . . . "Ryan? Holy hell, man! When did you get home?" He grabbed his younger brother in a bear hug, nearly lifting him off the floor. "Damn, it's good to see you."

"We got in about an hour ago."

"We?"

Ryan grinned. "Effie, the Wilson part of O'Fallon and Wilson, Architects L.L.C. Effie's already out looking at the sites for the new homes going up along the river's edge overlooking the Mississippi. I think she's really picking out one for us."

"I can't believe you're really moving back from San Diego. At one time all you wanted was to get the hell out of here."

"Things change, like you giving up the Coast Guard." They exchanged looks that said they both understood why they were here. "Have you found out anything on Mimi? The longer this goes on the more dangerous for her and Rory, and especially for Bonnie. Is Mimi—"

"Let's take a walk down by the docks."

"But—"

"I've got some paperwork that needs to get done. And you can look it over." He started down the stairs. "I could use your advice." Ryan followed him out the front door, Max trotting beside them, till Quaid stopped under the oaks. A morning breeze stirred, an egret swooped low over the river, and Max plopped down in the cool grass, doing a doggie roll. Ryan said, "Okay, what the hell's going on? My advice on the tow business? That's your baby."

"Rory thinks the house could be bugged. The guys after Mimi are desperate to find her. Anything important we take outside. Some things we don't discuss at all, too risky. Listening devices are small and powerful these days. I think it's all getting to Rory. He's . . . gone a lot."

"Is Thelma still having . . . plumbing problems? I heard about that."

"It keeps Rory occupied. You should visit Thelma. See what's changed since you were last here." Quaid grinned. "I'm damn glad you showed up. You can help me keep an eye on things."

Ryan stuffed his hands in his jeans pockets and leaned back on his heels. "And who's keeping an eye on you? Looks like you've been in one fight recently and then there's Cynthia Landon. Rory thinks she's going to break your heart and stomp it flat."

"Don't know who gossips more around here, Dad or Sally, but there's nothing to worry about, no broken hearts or bones. Cynthia's made it clear she wants no men in her life, but I think that mostly means me and my reputation. She is Cynthia Landon and . . ."

"And you're an O'Fallon clear through, and screw the reputation thing. We're a family, a terrific family, and Cynthia's got nothing on you. If you like her, go after her, but if she's still the stuck-up snob from years ago that I remember, you can do much better."

"I don't know about the better part, but we sure aren't a match made in heaven. She's a New York designer, reads *Vogue* and drinks beer with her little finger extended. I do T-shirts, jeans and read *Field and Stream* and—"

"Cynthia Landon drinks beer?" Ryan arched his brow. "Well, I'll be damned." He put his hand on Quaid's shoulder. "The Cynthia Landon of back when would never have done that. Guess there's still hope for her. Here's the way it is. You two are the most mismatched couple on the planet, next to me and Effie, of course, or maybe Keefe and Callie. How'd a soap star and a reporter ever get together? Then there's the real champs of total opposites, Dad and Mimi— fifty-two and thirty-eight and they have a baby to really complicate the hell out of life. In my opinion, this opposite thing runs in the family."

"I'll get over Cynthia, she's just another woman."

Ryan laughed and slapped Quaid on the back. "Yeah, you keep telling yourself that. I better find the woman I swore to get over before she wolfs down all the barbecue at Slim's without me. Keefe and Callie are due in from New York. He's got *Arsenic and Old Lace* to put on. If his star performer doesn't measure up, Keefe gets to build the high school a new baseball field. And you know what that means?"

"That *we* get to build the high school a new baseball field. I got a feeling that's going to happen no matter how good that play is. Damn glad you're back, the four of us together again. I'm taking a tow to Memphis to drop off a propeller and engine parts to a friend of Dad's, but I'll be back tonight."

Ryan headed for Slim's. Quaid turned for the docks, then eyed the two-lane leading to Ivy Acres. He should fix the trellis and then he'd tell Cynthia he wouldn't bother her anymore. He got it now, Cynthia Landon might like to screw around with him but that's all he'd ever be to her, a hot roll in the hay. She admitted that last night.

He was done with Cynthia, now he just had to convince his heart. Hell, he'd survived worse, a lot worse . . . probably. Maybe. Quaid followed Max down the two-lane, feeling a little like Opie on a hot summer day, and a whole lot like a lovesick jackass who couldn't get a woman off his mind. Sounded like a bad country-western song.

The road dipped, then rose, the red brick of Hastings House looming beyond the woods to the left and Grant's favorite haunt to the right. The white stucco of Ivy Acres came into view, and Quaid followed Max up the path, cutting through the back yard, around the garden, and passing under the open side window. He heard Cynthia's voice, low and shaky, and that made him stop dead. Even when he met up with her that first night when her car slid into the ditch she didn't sound like this.

She said, "Aaron, why are you doing this to our son? You don't want custody of Lawrence."

"Like hell I don't, and I bet I can get it too. I'm still in New York, and that's where Lawrence grew up and where he went to school. And you know how I can sweet-talk the women. If I get a woman judge I can make her believe anything, and make you out as an insensitive, uncaring bitch who yanked my son from my loving arms and moved away. Sounds pretty damn convincing doesn't it?"

"You said you didn't care what I did, where I went after my loft paid off your loans. Actually you said you didn't care *if* I gave you that antique necklace I got from my grandmother."

"Yeah, well I pawned that last week and the money's gone. If I get custody you pay me child support. I figure that'll go a lot further than some necklace. Look at this place, it's got to be worth a damn fortune. I'm thinking I want my share."

"Ivy Acres is already mortgaged."

"So mortgage it again, sell it, I don't give a rat's butt what you do. You're going to pay me child support, wifey dear. Get used to it."

He laughed low and mean and Quaid felt his blood go to ice. He rounded the corner of the house and took the front steps two at a time, tore open the front door, and made for the living room, Max in his wake, his claws tapping on the marble floor. Cynthia wasn't there now but Aaron was, and he had his fist around Lawrence's arm.

"Did you hear what I just said to your mother? You're coming to live with me, worm." Lawrence tried to step away but Aaron held him in place and shook him. "No more mommy to hide behind. Just you and me, kid."

For a split second a million memories flooded into Quaid's brain, taking him back to the worst time of his life. He could feel a mean hand on his arm, getting shaken and smacked and . . . Max growled, snapping Quaid back to the moment, and in a flash he came up behind Aaron, twisting his arm up behind his back where Lawrence couldn't see. "Let the boy go," Quaid said, amazed he hadn't torn Aaron in two.

The guy sucked in a quick breath. "What the hell do you think you're doing? Who are you? This is my damn son, I can do whatever the hell I want to do with him."

Quaid twisted harder. Aaron stood on his toes to lessen the pressure. Max bared his teeth, growled and Aaron released Lawrence. Quaid said to him, "I bet it's breakfast time, sport."

"I already ate."

"Eat again."

Lawrence nodded, turned, glanced back, then ran through the dining room, his little footfalls retreating across the hardwood, Max right behind him.

Quaid waited till the two were out of sight, then let go of Aaron's arm. He spun around, swung at Quaid, missed, stumbled and knocked over a chair. Quaid slammed Aaron in the gut, then jammed his forearm into his neck, flattening him against the wall, knocking a picture of Stonewall Jackson off its perch, crashing to the floor, glass scattering. "You ever touch that kid again," Quaid seethed, "I'll break off both your arms and jam them so far up your butt you'll be scratching your eyes from the inside. Got me?"

"You threatening me?"

"The name's Quaid O'Fallon. I have two brothers and a father who are gentlemen, men of honor. You happened to meet up with the asshole of the family. Let me make something perfectly clear—you're never coming here again. You're calling Lawrence on his birthday and Christmas and you're sending a gift, something nice. If you don't I'll hunt you down and make you wish you had."

"Fuck you."

Quaid shoved his knee into Aaron's side, against his bottom rib, feeling it give under the pressure. Aaron's eyes bulged with pain and he grunted.

"Got me?"

Aaron nodded, his face red with rage. Quaid continued, "You'll never call Cynthia again or make contact with her in any way. You do, and the next thing you'll contact is the bottom of the Mississippi with a cement block at your neck."

Quaid stepped back and Aaron slumped to the floor, panting hard. "You can't get away with this."

"I just did. Get out of here."

Aaron staggered upright, started to flick Quaid off, thought better of it, then stumbled his way into the hall and out the door. Quaid looked around and spotted Cynthia standing in the dining room entrance, eyes wide, not breathing. Two women wearing black bandanas stood beside her, grinned and suddenly applauded. The blonde said, "Well hot damn, boy . . . I mean God bless you my son!"

The redhead added, "Amen and praise the Lord. That was one damn-fine piece of work, my man." The nuns strutted to the main hall, the front door closing behind them. Cynthia still didn't move, staring straight ahead.

"It's okay, babe," he said in a soothing voice. He put Stonewall back on the wall, kicked the broken glass under the couch and set the chair upright. "See, all's well. Antiques saved for another few generations." Bees hummed in the hollyhocks outside the window; the nuns chattered on the porch. An engine started then faded down the drive.

He took Cynthia's elbow and led her toward the couch. She looked fragile, like something had snapped inside. Maybe he should call a doctor. "Gee, I'm starved and Lawrence is having breakfast. Bet Preston left something good. He probably made coffee. I could really use some—"

"Thank you." She stopped dead, he still didn't know if she was breathing. "I don't know what I was going to do if Aaron tried to take . . . I don't have money for lawyers and—" She swallowed, her eyes narrowed, her spine stiffened. "He was going to take Lawrence away from me." She started to shake. "If I had a gun I would have shot the son of a bitch dead as a mackerel and buried his putrid hide in the garden."

"Excuse me?"

"The little prick caught me off guard. I knew I hated his guts but now . . ." Cynthia threw back her shoulders, jutted her chin, her eyes cleared. "I need a gun."

"What?"

"You can teach me how to shoot. You're military, they shoot things all the time. Now I got a thing that needs shooting. I need something with major firepower. Something with . . . cahoonies."

"Cah . . . cah . . . It's over with, Cynthia. I swear it is. No one's taking Lawrence anywhere, least of all—"

She paced. "I'm thinking one of those AK-forty-somethings they talk about on TV."

"AK-47. It's an assault rifle, and you just can't go into a store and buy one and—"

"Quaid." She looked him dead in the eyes, hers unforgiving, determined. "I'm from New York. Give me ten minutes and I can buy anything."

Holy shit! "Cynthia. This is really not a good idea."

"He tried to take my son!"

"Okay, it *is* a good idea. But there's a problem, jail could be involved. You would not like jail, really ugly clothes. No designer anything. Cheap material. Let me handle it."

Her eyes went beadier still. "And what if you're not around next time, huh? I'm getting a gun, this is Tennessee, I'm entitled. Birthright and all that."

"Mom?" Lawrence's voice came from the dining room. "You're going to buy a gun?"

"For . . . rats," Quaid chimed in. "Just to scare them." He was no psychiatrist, but knowing that your mother was gunning for your dad—no matter how rotten he was—might cause some scarring, even in Tennessee.

"Big fat rats," Cynthia added. She turned to Quaid. "What are you doing today?"

"Taking a tow downriver. A short run, but—"

"Lawrence is going with you."

"And so are you. There's no way I'm leaving you here with a rat problem."

"I'm good at rat problems, getting better all the time. I'm not into boats."

"You'll get better at that too." Though with that pissed off look on her face he wasn't sure about anything. He said to Lawrence, "Get on shorts and gym shoes, sport. Grab the sunblock, it's a blast furnace on the river."

"Yes!" Lawrence grinned, pumping his arm in triumph. "A towboat, I'm going on the river!" He darted for the stairs. As soon as his feet hit the bare wood Cynthia said, "I am not going with you."

"Lawrence needs a diversion right now. In case you missed something, this has been a rather tedious morning even by New York standards. Besides, if I leave you here you'll go gun shopping. Christ almighty, woman, I should just call you . . . Cyn."

She gave him a lopsided grin. "I think I like it."

"Cynthia!"

"All right, all right, I'll go and forget about guns. I'm not happy about either decision but you're right that Lawrence needs something else on his mind besides his dad, and if I don't go with him, he'll be thinking about me."

"Now take your hands from behind your back so I know you're not crossing fingers, making your words null and void so you won't show up."

She held out her hands, wiggled her digits and huffed, "There, happy?"

He felt a bit better, but not completely. Miss-Priss-does-Annie Oakley was something he didn't know how to reckon with. "Meet me at the docks in twenty minutes and we'll shove off. When we come back tonight we'll talk about Aaron and what to do with him that doesn't involve ... cahoonies."

She folded her arms. "You know, when it comes to dealing with that man and protecting my son, I think I've grown a nice big set all my own."

Chapter 10

Cynthia stood on the top step of the porch and watched Quaid and Max head down the road. Quaid turned back and waved, giving her one of those you-better-not-be-messing-with-me-looks, like Ida did when Cynthia was little. Well, Cynthia Landon, once-upon-a-time James, wasn't little any more.

Ginger stood beside her, white brush from painting the side of the house in hand. She said in a low voice, "Honey, if you're needing some help, Sister Candy here and I can lend a hand. We have connections."

"You're right, prayer always helps."

The nuns exchanged looks and Sister Ginger added, "Our order is one of those God-helps-those-who-help-her-selves kind of orders, and no one needs protection like a woman doing woman's work, no matter what that happens to be. You got your baby to take care of, and we're going to help you do it. That's what he would have wanted."

"God is caring and—"

"Not exactly the *he* we were talking about, though this *he* did let out an *Oh my God* when he got real excited. I guess that's close enough."

"Damn straight . . . I mean darn straight." Sister Candy

added, "Sister Ginger and I will be back in a few hours. If you're feeling the need for some artillery to keep you and your offspring safe, we'll get it for you. All of us women need to work together to make things happen."

Cynthia helped the sisters gather up the drop cloths. "You two are so accommodating."

Sister Candy giggled. "We hear that all the time."

They stored the paint on the side of the porch, and the sisters got in their metallic red Mustang convertible and headed down the dive.

Cynthia sat on the front porch and tried to unwind. At least Ida didn't have to witness this little altercation with Aaron, since she and Beau had gone into Memphis. Beau needed to take care of family business while Ida shopped, and Cynthia hoped it was more window shopping than buying shopping.

She looked around, everything quiet and peaceful, a perfect summer day—except for the shiver snaking up her spine. See, this is what happened when testosterone invaded her life. She kicked off her sandals and studied her crossed toes. She'd promised Quaid she'd show up, but this was her fight. What if the nuns came back empty-handed? Lawrence came outside and stuffed his hands in his pockets, looking much older than his eight years. "Is Dad really gone for good? He doesn't love me, does he." It was a statement, not a question.

"Your dad doesn't love anyone but himself. I think you've known it for quite a while now. There are people like that, and there's no changing them. What you have to remember is: you don't want to be that way."

"Some people luck out and have two good parents, like you, some get one, like me, and some get none, like Quaid till Rory came along. Quaid turned out okay so I'll be okay too."

"You use your head and your heart and you'll be fine."

Cynthia mentally called her piss-ant ex every name she could think of for terrorizing Lawrence, and she was building quite a list of adjectives. "Your dad will not hurt you, Lawrence, and he will definitely not take you away from me. You are perfectly safe, I swear it." And she meant every single syllable, no matter what it took. "Now I'll drop you off at the dock with Quaid, and I'll run up to Slim's and get us something loaded with calories to eat on the boat."

His face morphed into a slow grin. "I think it's going to be a good day after all. We're going to ride on a tow. This is great! Aren't you excited?"

She kissed his cheek. "Exciting is the début of spring fashions in Paris, but this will definitely be an experience."

"Ah, Mom, you are such a girl." She kissed him again then grabbed her gym shoes from the hallway. They got into the Buick and she pumped the gas pedal, smacked the dash and cranked over the engine. "Good car." A complimented car was a smooth-running car.

She dropped off Lawrence then headed for Slim's, except this was not just about things barbecued and lunch. The sun hid behind a puff of clouds as she parked the car and went into the bar, door open with the heat of the day not yet at full blast on the Landing.

"Well if it isn't Cyn," Sally yelled, then waved from behind the bar.

"I need lunch for three and how'd you hear about my new name already?"

"It's been a half hour. That's a coon's age around here for good gossip. Besides, your visiting nuns stopped by to make sure I kept an eye on you in case a certain cretin of an ex reappeared. Those are my kind of gals—helpful, smart, take no crap from anyone. In fact, the way things are going with me and Demar, I'm giving serious consideration to signing up and getting my own black bandana.

The man's driving me bonkers. He's with me, all sweet and nice, then he's not with me and I bet he's with Jett, being all sweet and nice." She fluffed her spiraled curls. "I'd look real good in a black bandana, don't you think? And the Mustang is superb."

A young woman sitting on a barstool started to laugh. She spluttered, "You, a nun?"

Sally parked her hand to her hip, trying for the indignant look and not succeeding. "I'd be a good one."

"Except for the no-sex rule," the woman added. "You are so not into no sex."

Sally loaded chicken, fruit and cake into a bag as she nodded to the woman. "Cynthia Landon, meet smart-ass Effie Wilson, fiancée of one Ryan O'Fallon. And she can sit there now and be hooting her head off at me, but I remember not too many weeks ago when Ryan was pushing all her buttons and making her loony as a bird, too."

"Oh, he still does," Effie said, wiping tears from her face. "But he is worth it. Lord knows I never thought I'd say such a thing, but the man is."

Sally folded her arms, looking a little dangerous, as she said to Cynthia, "Heard your ex paid you a nasty visit and you're searching for a little protection."

"I'm thinking semiautomatic protection . . . though I'm not all that sure what semiautomatic means, but it sounds edgy."

"Actually it sounds like Quaid. Anything happens to someone he cares about and he's automatically protecting them with everything he's got. I hear he showed up and saved the day."

Cynthia pursed her lips. "He did, and I'm grateful, but I need to be able to take care of myself and it's turning out to be tougher than I thought. I never considered the possibility of seeing Aaron again. I really thought we were through."

Sally nodded. "Well, if you ever need any help you know I'm here."

Effie added, "Hey, count me in. I've dated the scum of the earth, and know just how ruthless some guys are to get what they want. They'll lie and cheat and feed you any line in the book that suits them."

Cynthia took the bag of food. "Thanks for the support, I just might take you both up on it. Right now I'm off for a day with Quaid and Lawrence. We probably won't be back till late. Can you tell Ida? She and Beau are headed here for an early lunch. I forgot to leave her a note."

"Note for what?" Preston asked as he strolled in.

Cynthia turned for the door. "Sally will fill you in. If I don't get a move on Quaid will be after me big time."

"I better go too," Effie said. "Ryan and I are trying to find a little office in Memphis so we can meet clients there."

Cynthia wished her luck, then made for the docks. She parked in the lot, the sun baking the earth as it always did in August. She changed her sandals for gym shoes, took the bag and headed the rest of the way down the gravel road. The Mississippi stretched far and wide, like a big piece of glass, the blue sky dotted with clouds, humidity high enough to curl the straightest hair and smear the best makeup.

Lawrence waved from up in the pilothouse. She spotted an orange splash of life vest over his chest and around his shoulders, making her feel a bit better about an outing on the Mississippi. Quaid was busy with boat stuff on the main deck, hoisting ropes and cables. She slowed, taking in the man in his element—a very handsome man with raven-black hair, incredible green eyes and a butt tight enough to bounce quarters on—though she'd rather be doing the bouncing herself.

When it came to Quaid and sex, she had no conscience, just plain old lust.

"Can I help you?" said a boy in his late teens, coming out of the dock office.

She nodded at the tow. "I'm going for a ride on that thing. Say a little prayer."

The boy grinned. "You'll be with Quaid, he's the best."

"And you are . . ."

"Hank. Quaid hired me on a few days ago. Gave me a place to stay down here. I . . . I appreciate it."

Max barked, catching Quaid's attention. He spied her and one of his too-male grins covered his face. "Hey," he yelled, then came over as Hank trotted off to help another tow pulling in. Quaid helped her on board, the gentle swells supplying a pleasant little rock. Pleasant rocks were good, those she could deal with, pretend she was at a big sale at Bloomingdale's and getting jostled about.

Quaid said, "What took so long? Anything I need to be concerned about, like the Bureau of Alcohol, Tobacco and Firearms showing up any minute?"

"Only if they're looking for a stashed bottle of apricot brandy back at the Acres. I'm perfectly innocent."

"Before the AK-47 conversation I would have believed that, but now—"

"Since you're not too happy with me over the gun issue, you might as well get your boxers in a bind all at one time. I've definitely decided to send Lawrence away to school no matter what it costs. He needs to be in a place where he feels safe, now more than ever."

"I don't wear boxers, as you already know, and I agree that Lawrence needs to feel safe. We differ on the locale. He can feel that way right here on the Landing, where people care about him and he can learn to care about them." Quaid shook his head. "But you've made up your mind, haven't you?" He nodded to the pilothouse perched up in the air. "I'm going up there and we'll shove off."

"Uh . . . There's something else you should know. I'm not too good with boats, especially ones that go up and down a lot. I was on the Staten Island Ferry once in rough weather and . . . and it wasn't pretty."

"Well, Admiral Nelson, you're in luck. There's not a cloud in the sky, except for a few white puffs."

At least that was true when Quaid said it, Cynthia consoled herself hours later, but now rain hammered the little pilothouse, perched much too high above the water, as it pitched and rolled in the waves. Lightning cut the sky and Lawrence, Quaid and Max were having the time of their lives watching monitors and talking weather reports.

"What happened to our cloudless sky?" She swallowed back nausea and held onto the arms of the elevated captain's chair where she sat.

"Sorry about this, Cynthia," Quaid said, staring out the window. "Bad weather blows up quick this time of year with all the humidity."

"Don't worry, Mom," Lawrence chirped, watching the radar and looking like a kid at Disneyland. "We're fine as long as we steer clear of other boats and landmasses. We don't even have to see to do it."

He pointed to the screen. "The radar gives us range and relative direction. We place the cursor over a target with the trackball and convert that position relative to the *Annabelle Lee*. We get the actual bearing by adding our ship's compass heading to the bearing of the boat or object and adjust that number for compass error. If the number is over 360° we just subtract 360 and the remainder is the boat's true bearing from our position. Piece of cake."

Quaid grinned and patted Lawrence on the back. Cynthia

considered throwing them both overboard for being so damn cheerful. "How'd you learn all this, Lawrence?"

"Read the manual while we were waiting for you."

"And I can't even program my darn cell phone," she moaned, as another wave rolled over the front of the boat. The scent of barbecue, which usually smelled like heaven, was now hell. Her mouth tasted like a dirty dish towel as her stomach rolled and her eyes crossed. She prayed for a quick death.

Quaid glanced over to her. "Are you okay?"

"Peachy."

He said to Lawrence, "I don't think your mom's enjoying this as much as we are, sport. She's turning a little green. We should put in at the Memphis terminal dock till this weather eases up."

Lawrence gave Quaid a salute. "You're the captain. Maybe someday I can be a captain. Since you're training Hank, you can train me too." He glanced at the chart book on the console and pointed. "The dock's two nautical miles off port side. At our present speed we should be there in—"

"Mayday, mayday," blared over the mike gizmo thing hanging by Quaid. "This is *Moneymaker II*, a mile due north of Memphis, with failed starboard engine, sporadic port engine, taking on water, requesting immediate assistance."

Quaid and Lawrence exchanged looks, and the mike beeped to life again with, "*Moneymaker,* this is Coast Guard four-niner-six at mile marker one-fifty-two, putting us thirty minutes from you. Requesting any craft in the area to lend assistance."

Quaid gave Cynthia a sympathetic look. "Honey, we have to help."

"It's the rules of the high seas." Lawrence grinned, looking happier than ever as he jumped up and down and pointed to the radar screen. "That's them right there. Cool!"

"This is the Mississippi, not the seas," Cynthia whined, knowing it would do no good but feeling the need to vent. "Can't they just go to shore?"

Quaid arched his brow, and she caved. "Right, they can't get to shore. I think I've had enough of this fun afternoon and I'll walk home now, if you all don't mind."

Quaid snagged the mike and pressed the side button. "Coast Guard four-niner-six, this is the *Annabelle Lee*. We're approximately one mile from *Moneymaker* and will lend assistance. ETA ten minutes."

"Ohmygosh, ohmygosh," squealed Lawrence, then threw his arms around Quaid's waist, squeezing hard. "We're going to help a sinking boat. This is so intense."

"That's one way of putting it," Cynthia groaned. She slid from the seat, tore open the pilothouse door, instantly got soaked to the skin, then lost her breakfast over the side railing.

Quaid watched Cynthia stagger back into the pilothouse as the *Annabelle Lee* took another plunge into a wave. "Feeling better?"

As he passed her a towel, she gave him a look that said *eat dirt and die,* and Lawrence handed her a cracker. "Eat this, Mom. It helps."

She reclaimed her perch on the chair and Lawrence pointed out the starboard window. "There's the *Moneymaker*, Quaid. She's off the bow."

Quaid directed a spotlight in that direction and turned the boat, slowing the engines. "Okay, now it gets dicey."

"Now? Now?" Cynthia's eyes covered half her face. "What was all that stuff from the last two hours?"

He glanced at Cynthia. "I need you to take the controls."

She laughed. He added, "All you have to do is hold the

stick steady and ease back the engine when I give you the signal."

"Quaid, I can barely stand. I'm not that great at driving a car. This is way beyond a car."

"We don't have a choice here, babe." Lawrence added, "I'll help you, Mom." Quaid's gaze met Cynthia's. She was scared and sick and really did want to walk home. "You can do this. I know you."

She let out a big sigh and scooted off the chair. "New York was never like this. I could hail a taxi, I'm really good at that." He wrapped her fingers around the brass controls. Quaid said, "Keep it on this heading."

"Heading?"

Lawrence pointed to the compass. "Keep the line right there by pushing or pulling a little on the stick in your hand. The engine throttle is here, and when Quaid gives the word cut it back."

"To here," Quaid said, showing her the marking. "Got it?"

"*Annabelle Lee*, this is *Moneymaker*. We need some help down here real quick."

Quaid replied on the mike, "*Moneymaker*, approach down wind." He gave Cynthia a kiss on the cheek. "I have to go." He handed the mike to Lawrence. "If something goes wrong, call the Coast Guard."

Her knuckles blanched white with her death grip on the stick. "Do not even mention things going wrong, Quaid O'Fallon. You save those guys' fannies and then get yourself right back up here."

He shrugged into a life vest. "You got it, captain." He winked at Lawrence then opened the pilothouse door. The tug pitched in the waves, the rain horizontal, the river tearing hell out of everything. He'd been in worse trouble, much worse, but he didn't have a terrified but very heroic woman and her son riding shotgun. He hated putting

Cynthia and Lawrence in any sort of danger, or even near danger. The one consolation was that the *Lee* was built like a battleship and safe as any boat could possibly be. Cynthia and Lawrence were safe where they were. Completely out of harm's way.

He zipped his jacket and sprinted down the metal-grate steps to the main deck. He called Cynthia to cut the engines as *Moneymaker* approached from port. Looked like a thirty-four foot *Sea Ray*, mega bucks. One of the men tossed the rope like some damn city boy who didn't know squat about the river except how to buy a big boat. Quaid swore. He was out here risking Lawrence and Cynthia for two stupid asses who had no business being out on the river in this storm in the first place.

The guy missed with the third throw, and Quaid took a line and tossed it to *Moneymaker*. One of the men grabbed it, nearly lost his balance, but managed to tie it to a side cleat. The *Sea Ray* limped closer to the *Lee*, bobbing and twisting and crashing against the *Lee*.

Quaid reached for one of the men as he climbed on board, the man nearly pulling Quaid over the shallow freeboard and into the river. Quaid reached for the other man and suddenly realized Lawrence was beside him. *What the hell!*

He yelled to Lawrence over the driving rain, "Go back to the pilothouse."

"You need me. Max is with Mom. They're doing fine." Lawrence took one of the men's arms and helped him gain his balance, but then stopped dead for a moment, as if confused. Quaid helped the other guy fight the swells to get a foothold on the *Lee*, and when Quaid looked back to the deck there was no Lawrence. For a split calm second, Quaid thought Lawrence went back up to the pilothouse.

Until he looked to starboard and spotted an orange life-jacket bobbing in the water.

Chapter 11

Demar draped his arm around Jett as they stood on one of the upstairs porches of Hastings House and watched the storm blow in across the Mississippi. The big trees swayed with the erratic wind and clouds gathered, shutting out the afternoon sunlight. Jett snuggled closer. "Oh, sugar, this is so romantic. A big old southern mansion and you and me huddled together like we used to be."

Her hair twisted in the breeze and her breast nestled against his arm. The heat from her skin penetrated into his, and her eyes shown, dark and hungry. She was every man's sexual fantasy, every man's sexual desire—except his. He wanted Sally. In fact he wanted her more than ever. Each time he was with Jett, knowing she was playing him, using him, he appreciated Sally that much more.

Trouble was, he couldn't do one diddly-damn thing about it. He had to lull Jett into feeling secure about him and their relationship. Then she just might let down her guard and give him some information that would break this River Environs case wide open. He needed that. Rory needed a break.

"You're awfully quiet, Demar," she purred. "Let's go back to my room. There's a big window with a view of the

Mississippi. We can open it wide and let the storm blow over us and we can make our own kind of storm."

She circled in front of him and slid her arms around his neck, gaping her blouse in front and giving him an eyeful of her really nice rack as he looked down at her. The view should make him harder than a gun barrel, but it didn't. All he could think about was holding Sally, being here with her, having her in his arms and then making love to her all day long. He unwound Jett's arms from his neck and stepped away.

"Demar, did I do something to upset you? Are you mad at me?"

Oh, crap, now what was he going to say? Out of the corner of his eye he caught sight of someone on the other porch. Mimi! Holy shit! If Jett saw Mimi she'd contact the person she was working for, placing Mimi in immediate danger. *Think, dammit, think!* Do something!

He snapped Jett into his arms and kissed her as Mimi dashed back into the house. Demar breathed a sigh of relief until Thelma and Ryan stepped out on the brick patio below, looked up at the storm, and connected with him and Jett intertwined, playing kissy-face.

Well fuck a duck! There was no justice in the world. He saved Mimi and just ruined everything with Sally. There was no way Ryan wouldn't tell Sally her boyfriend was cheating on her. Folks looked out for each other on the Landing. His only hope was to get to Ryan and Thelma before they got to Sally, and set them straight on what he and Quaid had cooked up.

Jett broke the kiss and smiled up at Demar, her cheeks pink, her lips wet and full from his kiss. Damn. "Oh, sugar, now that's more like it."

"I should go."

She twisted her fingers into his shirt and held tight. "I want to make love to you, Demar."

Oh, double damn!

"I want you in my bed right now. I want to stroke that big cock of yours and feel it sliding deep inside me for the rest of the day and into the night. You are my big stud, Demar. I want you now."

"Let's eat. Have lunch. I'm hungry, aren't you hungry? Storms make me really, really hungry." He couldn't get away from her without causing suspicion, but he could stay out of her bed . . . he hoped!

Her fingers wound tighter and she pulled her face to his, "And you make me hungry. I want you for lunch, sugar. Every thick inch of you."

He swallowed. His Adam's apple felt like the size of a baseball. "I'm not ready for that, Jett, not yet." *Not ever!* "I know a great place in Memphis, fine food, a bottle of Rémy Extra, you and me and the rain." Just mentioning Rémy reminded him of the last time he had it—with Sally in the tub. Damn, he wanted to be in that tub with her again.

"Memphis? Why there, sugar?" Jett ground her hot mound against his dick, which responded as if it needed a good dose of the little-blue-pill. She frowned, a wrinkle furrowing her brow, but there was a spark of wariness in her eyes. "Something's bothering you, Demar. You are so not yourself."

If he didn't get with the program he'd blow his cover to hell and back. He forced a grin, "I've been without you so long, baby, and missed you so much, and now you're here. Takes a little getting used to, is all."

He kissed her again because he had to, then he slid from her arms and hooked her around the waist and led her into the house. "Get into something pretty for me and we'll go into town. I want to show you off, let everyone know I have the prettiest girl east of the Mississippi on my arm. I'll get Slim to cover for me today and we can take our sweet time." This would give him a chance to find Ryan and straighten things out . . . he hoped!

She slipped her fingers in the waistband of his jeans and held him tight. "I'm ready now, and after we eat in Memphis I'm having you . . . all of you . . . for dessert. You know how I like my . . . chocolate, thick and creamy."

She hooked her arm into his and ushered him down the hall. He said, "I should call Slim and—"

"Thelma can call for you. We have plans. You promised."

Now what the hell was he going to do? He called himself every name for stupid, for not being an accountant like his mother wanted him to. Oh no, he just had to be a damn cop and get himself embroiled in a real mess that could cause him to lose the woman he loved.

And he did love Sally Donaldson, every lush inch of her. From her curly hair to her beautiful smile to the tips of her cute hot-pink toenails. For a second he grinned like a lovesick teen, then it was gone, because he couldn't level with her about that or about Jett. What he had to do was take Jett to lunch, get her relaxed, and then get her to talk and spill why she was really here and who she was working for, and then bring his damn investigation to a close. Then he'd get his Sally back in his arms, where she belonged, for good.

Rain beat on the metal roof of the bar as Preston sat on a stool and Sally served him a plate of ribs and a cold longneck. Since the racket overhead nearly drowned out Clarence Carter's "Stroking," she saw fit to help him along. "I stroke it to the north. I stroke it to the south."

Preston grinned as another clap of thunder rattled the building. "A girl could get in big trouble singing a song like that."

She laughed and glanced around. "Thanks to the rain

no one's here but you and me and a few of my regulars. I think I'm safe."

Preston bobbed with the music. "If you didn't already belong to Demar Thacker I'd make a play for you myself."

Sally laughed, "And what about your Ida? You just going to forget about her?"

Preston pulled off a section of rib. "She's got Beau, and I don't think there's much I can do about that. He's one smooth operator and not quite what you think. I've heard him talking on the phone, and that southern accent you can cut with a knife sure fades away real fast when he thinks no one around here's listening."

"I bet he's using it to charm Ida. He knows how she likes all things southern. She prides herself on being a true-blue southern belle."

"I think maybe he's trying to sweet talk her into selling Ivy Acres to him for his restaurant. But if I warn her she'll think I'm jealous and trumping up trouble."

Sally put her hand on Preston's arm. "I'm sorry about Ida, Preston, I really am, and I know how you feel about things not going right. They aren't all that terrific with Demar and me either."

She tore off a chunk of meat from his plate and nibbled. Eating under stress was calorie-free, everyone knew that, and when it came to Demar there was enough stress to last three lifetimes. Ryan strolled in and took a seat beside Preston and she said, "You look like you've been ridden hard and put away wet. What's wrong?"

"I'll have a shot of Black Jack and a beer."

"Honey, it's only three in the afternoon. I know it's raining and you're used to all that San Diego sun but you'll adjust, it's not that bad."

He leveled her a long look that said this was not about lack of sunshine. She'd known Ryan all her life, they grew up together, read *Playboys* that she snuck from her dad's secret hiding place, figured out the facts of life together, and then lost their virginity to each other one hot summer night on the banks of the Mississippi. Something special about your first time, and there'd always be something special between her and Ryan O'Fallon. Whatever he had to tell her, he didn't want to. "Spill it. What's going on?"

He cut his eyes to Preston, and Sally said, "Preston's okay, just say what you have to say and get it over with before I jump out of my skin."

He ran his fingers through his hair. "Look, I have no right to tell you this, in fact it's putting my nose where it doesn't belong and it's none of my damn business, and I hate busybodies who go around and cause trouble where they think—"

Sally grabbed the front of Ryan's shirt and pulled him across the bar and peered deep into his eyes. "Whatever it is, it's got to be better than this blabbering, you're driving me nuts."

"Dammit to hell, it's Demar, okay? I was at Hastings House and he was . . . he and Jett were . . . he . . . Ah, hell, Sally, he was kissing her and she was kissing him back like she meant it. There, I said it and I feel like shit." Ryan swiped Preston's beer and downed the contents in one long gulp. He banged the empty on the countertop and swiped his hand across his lips. "Fuck," he muttered under his breath.

"You saw him do that too?"

"Good God, no!"

"Well thank heavens for big favors. Least he's not screwing around on me."

Ryan went behind the bar and got his own beer and another for Preston, and gave Sally the shot of Black Jack. She pushed it aside and perched her elbow on the bar then rested her chin in her palm. "What am I going to do now?"

"Running him over with Quaid's Jeep is looking pretty good."

"I don't want to lose Demar, least not without one more crack at him, and that just might be my bat over his head, but at least I'll go down fighting. The question is, what does Jett have that I don't?" She glanced down at her chest. "For openers, a nice set of womanly attributes up top, and less rounded womanly attributes below. Bet she's a card-carrying member of Fat Fighters. I think I hate Fat Fighters." Sally stole another rib from Preston's plate and wolfed it down.

Ryan took a swig of beer while lightning zigzagged outside the window. "Want me to talk to him?"

Sally arched one brow. "Oh, I can just imagine what that conversation would be like. Quaid already had a run in with Demar and I'm betting it was over this very thing." She kissed Ryan gently on the lips. "You are the sweetest man, and that includes your whole family. But this is between me and Demar and we have to figure it out on our own."

"Which means . . . ?" Preston asked.

Sally took off her apron, hooked it over Ryan's head, and draped the bar towel across Preston's shoulder. "It means I'm going to figure out why Demar's cattin' around with someone besides me, and then I'm going to fix it, if I can."

She started for the door and Ryan snagged her arm. "You're too good for him, Sally."

"But I love him, I really do, and I've got to give us one more shot or I'll never forgive myself." She pulled a letter from the back pocket of her shorts. "I just got a terrific offer from a first-rate investment firm in Seattle. Dad's recouped from his heart attack, and if Demar and I aren't meant to be then . . ."

"Good God, you're taking the job? We all finally get back here and now you want to leave again?"

"Every song, every sunset, every plate of barbecue will remind me of Demar and I'll lose my mind if I stay." She kissed Ryan on the cheek this time, then did the same to Preston. "Take care of my bar for a while, boys. I've got a hot date to tend to."

Sally headed upstairs to the apartment and her room, and sat on a window seat, staring out at the storm. Demar was like a . . . stock, going down in price when it should be going up. Why? She needed a stronger product. She needed . . . Google. Now there was a good stock—new, edgy, innovative, flashy, hip and trendy. So what made a woman all those things? Sure wasn't being a barmaid.

She caught her reflection in the next flash of lightning. She needed to do something more than just tend bar. She loved it, no doubt about that, but it was a waste of an education and her dad had paid dearly for that education. "Face it, sweet cakes, you're hiding out." She'd been licking her wounds after getting roughed up on Wall Street. "Coward."

Well, her coward days were over, starting tonight. She was going after what she wanted—and that was Demar Thacker in her bed keeping her warm and satisfied. And if he wanted new, flashy, innovative, edgy . . . she'd give it to him.

Demar stifled a yawn as he climbed the stairs to his apartment. The day from hell was over. The only reason it hadn't slipped over into the night from hell is that he told Jett he had a migraine. Really bad excuse, but the best he could come up with, getting out of dates wasn't his usual practice. Then again, since he'd met Sally dating was the last thing on his mind . . . unless it was her. He opened the door to his apartment, went inside, and something struck him in the back.

"Put your hands up high."

"Sally? Why are you jabbing a . . . carrot into my back?"

"It's a gun."

"Sweet thing, you hate guns."

The carrot jabbed again. "Into the bedroom and lay face down."

"What are you doing? What are we doing? Have you been reading porn? I think I like it."

"I have not been reading porn, a carrot is the only gun-like thing I have around. Think innovation."

Except it had been a day of innovation, mostly on his part, to stay at arm's length from Jett and for sure out of her bed. Right now he wanted basic existence: a beer, the blues, his babe Sally. God he wanted her, but if she wanted carrots he'd go along with it.

He stumbled into the bedroom lit with candles. "Nice décor." He sniffed. "Spice?"

"Glade Plug Ins. Best I could do for the Landing. We so need a Target out here."

He collapsed facedown on the mattress and she sat on his butt. "Good start, but I'd rather you'd be sitting on what's on the other side."

"Tonight belongs to me."

"Because you have the carrot?" He started to laugh, and suddenly felt something close over his wrists, both of them. "What the hell?" He tried to free himself. "Where'd you get handcuffs?"

"Your sock drawer, of course. One on each arm and hooked together in the middle looked really uncomfortable, being so tight across your back, so being the nice girl that I am I gave you more room."

He turned his head to the side. "Girl, I got to tell you that I am in no mood for—"

"*You're* in no mood?" Her voice rose an octave and she slid off him; he could feel the heat from her sex slide across him making him, instantly hard in spite of being handcuffed with his own equipment.

She added, "I get to hear how you're playing smash mouth with your ex-partner and now you're not in the mood for me?"

Could this day get any worse? "Look, that kiss was a . . . mistake."

"Yeah, and you made it. Well, it's my turn and I'm going to seduce you, Demar Thacker, if it takes all night."

It was so not going to take all night after he'd thought about her all damn day. "Look, I have no problem with seduction but can we just ditch the preliminaries and get to the good stuff?"

"Namely, you boinking me then going to sleep? No way. I want you to remember more than just a good piece of ass."

"I know you're more than that, I swear. Give me a break, Sally. I'm really beat."

"Tough, because I'm going to screw your brains out."

There were worse things, and he suddenly didn't feel so tired. "I probably shouldn't ask this but . . . why?"

"To win you over to my side."

"I'm yours, babe, all yours, I swear it. You got to trust me on this. I know things feel off, but they aren't. They're on, just you and me."

She rolled him onto his back and tossed the carrot, which landed on his chest with a soft plop. He'd rather Sally landed there with a soft plop. The sultry beat of "Tennessee Stripper" vibrated the room, and Sally sang along with the lyrics, *"Take a look but you can't touch, I*

can tease you till it's too much." And he believed every
word.

A spotlight flashed on, highlighting Sally with her arm
bowed around a horizontal pole—where'd she get that
pole? She wore a fringy red dress, white boa, long white
gloves and a rope of pearls that hung the length of the
dress.

"Dang, you *have* been reading porn."

"For God's sake, Demar, I'm an MBA from Harvard,
this is Google."

"Google? What the hell does Google have to do with
this?" Then she started to sway with the music and he didn't
care about Google or anything else. She smiled and rolled
her shoulders with the music, as she pushed one glove
down her arm and then, with her teeth, suggestively pulled
the cloth from each fingertip. Taking the long white swatch,
she swung it around her head and sent it sailing, landing
on top of the carrot.

She danced around the pole and sang, *"Peek at this and
peek at that."* Then she slid off the other glove and sent it
his way. She peeled the dress down, bit by bit, revealing
one lovely naked breast then the other, except that damn
boa kept getting in the way, ruining his view. "Take off the
boa!"

"You are so damn demanding. Always the cop. Be pa-
tient."

"No."

"Bet Mae West never had these problems," she groused.

She slid the dress off, leaving her in thigh-high hose,
heels, beads and the boa. If he had his way he'd keep her
like this for the rest of her life. She leaned one way on the
pole, lifting one breast as if offering it to him, making his
mouth dry. She leaned the other way and offered the other
breast, making his mouth drier still. He'd kill for a beer,
even drink it through a straw, since his hands were tied.

Then she did a little swing around the pole twitching her great hips, her fanny—till the pole moved, then completely gave way.

"Yikes!" she yelled as she stumbled and the pole crashed to the floor. She spun across the floor, bounced against his nightstand, then tripped onto the floor.

He tried to stand to help her but couldn't because his damn hands were behind his damn back, throwing him off balance. "That's it," he said as he fought the cuffs. "Get me out of these things."

One of Sally's hands crept over the edge of the bed beside him, then the other, then her head appeared. Hair hung in her face and she blew it out of the way, but it just fell back. "Are you okay? Get me out of these things."

She plucked a key from the nightstand, he rolled over and she undid the cuffs. He rolled back and pulled her off the floor and onto his chest. He laid her back; heavily made-up eyes complete with glitter and sequins looked into his, her mouth touching his. "What the hell is this all about? First you get me in the storage room and entice the hell out of me, then the cognac, now this? I'm not complaining, mind you, but I'm just curious. Besides, I'm worried you may not live through another episode."

Her index finger trailed a line from his forehead to his lips. "I wanted tonight to be something special but it didn't work out . . . again." She kissed him. "Using one of those spring-mounted shower curtain bars for a dance pole wasn't a great idea but it's all I could get, had to bring it from my bathroom at home. I can never seem to get it right. I thought you'd like a striptease. Everybody does."

"Really. Do you?"

"Trust me, Demar, a woman taking off her clothes does nothing for me, unless it's a dress on sale that she doesn't want but I do."

"What about a man?"

"If he wants the dress he has to fight for it like the rest of us. Gay rights don't count for squat in a sale."

He rolled to the side of the bed and kicked off his shoes, and she whined, "Don't go away."

"Not a chance." He stood in the spotlight, gave her a devil look, then pulled up a corner of his T-shirt to give her a peek at his abs that he worked hard to keep in shape. He let the blue cotton slide back down, as he did a side step and quick turn that he had used as tight end playing football at the University of Tennessee.

Sally laughed and giggled then slid her two little fingers to the corners of her mouth and let out a terrific wolf whistle worthy of any man. "Bring it to mama, baby. Let me see it all. Shake it, shake it."

He laughed and peeled off his shirt, then did a few more steps, trying to imitate a Gregory Hines move he'd seen. He thrust his hips, unzipped his jeans, rezipped, then finally peeled them off over his hips and down his legs . . . which must look really awkward. Had to respect those Chippendale guys. This left only his briefs, as she called, "Take it off, all off, Demar. I wanna see what I'm going to get."

He grinned, slid out of his briefs, and kicked them into the air. Sally caught them, cheered and hooted, "Oh, baby. You are my man. And you better be watching how you move or you'll break something and I so do not want *that* something broken."

He shuffled her way and lifted her in his arms, one under her knees, the other across her smooth back, her arms around his neck. He danced, swaying to the music, then collapsed with her onto the bed, both laughing.

"I never knew this side of you, Demar."

Reaching into the nightstand, he took out a condom. He grinned down at her, "Oh, babe, you are fun. What would I ever do without you?"

"I hope you never find out." She took the condom from his fingers and tore it open. "You are one sweet dancer, Demar." She sat up, gazing at his hard dick. "And you sure got the stuff to strut."

She rolled the latex on, massaging as she covered him with excruciating slowness, driving him nuts. She sat back on his thighs and studied his shaft, kneading his testicles now, rendering him speechless. She peered into his eyes, hers hot with desire. "I love feeling you inside me." Her fingers held him tighter. "You being so much a part of me."

He cupped her breasts, appreciating the tight pink nubs at the tips, the satin softness of her warm dark skin resting in his palm. "You are so smooth, so perfect. I've never wanted a woman like I want you. Hold on to me tight, baby. Love me all the way."

He rolled them over, bracing himself on top of her. "Wrap your legs around me. I want to take you so deep you'll never forget. I want to fill every sweet inch of you, make you mine with all I have."

His heart slammed his ribs, his arms quivered as her velvety thighs rubbed across his waist, bringing her wet hot sex against his dick, making his head swim and his vision blur. He arched his hips and entered her, just a bit at first, his insides screaming for more . . . all . . . now. But he wanted to make this last. "You are so fine, girl. Everything about you is perfection."

He eased into her a fraction more, watching her pupils dilate with need, her breath quicken, feel her fingertips dig into his shoulder muscles, exciting him all the more. He pushed again in one fluid movement, this time giving her all, the sensation of burying himself in her sweet slick passage more intoxicating than anything he'd ever experienced. Her lips formed a perfect O, her hips arched to him, taking him in.

"Demar," she moaned, her head falling back, her lovely chest arched and curving up as she surrendered her body totally to him.

His insides screamed for release this very second, but his mind wanted the memory that went beyond the physical. He eased himself out, deliberately slow, her tight muscles not ready for his absence and holding firmer. "Demar?"

"Patience, baby, patience." He pumped into her again, this time a fraction faster, increasing the rhythm as he spread her again, increasing the intense pleasure of making love to Sally. She sucked in a quick long breath. "I can't hold on, Demar. I want you now."

"A little more. Just a little longer. I don't want this to end." He filled her once more, his testicles tight to her body, her heat surrounding him. The scent of raw sex mixed with the spice, the aroma decadent, indulgent. He withdrew, almost completely, knowing he'd then get to replenish her again. Her legs held him tighter, the first shudders of climax claiming her as he sank into her hard.

"Now, Demar, please . . ."

His muscles clenched in a furious climax, the pulsing waves fueled by hers, driving him into her again and again. She yelled his name as he ground into her one last time, reveling in the incredible moment, the sensation that went beyond the act of possessing the woman he loved, cherishing her more than life itself.

He gasped for air, fire sizzling through his limbs, then lessening bit by bit. He collapsed onto her, his arms cushioning his weight from her, heartbeats still pounding in his head. "Damn, girl."

"Me too," her words barely audible, her hair damp with perspiration. "I can't move."

"If you wanted me to get up right now you'd need a crane." He pulled in a few more breaths. "What you do to me is sinful. You make me lose my mind."

"Well, you kept part of it because you in the sack is an experience and a half." Her arms folded across his back. "I care for you, Demar, and not just because of the incredible sex. I like being with you all the time." Her warm palm cupped his chin and she brought his face to hers. "I have to know how you feel too. You told me but do you mean it—really mean it?"

"I swear I do, Sally. There's no one but you. Trust me on this, trust in what we have. Promise me you will, no matter what."

"I—"

"Fuck."

"Good grief, I didn't say anything yet. Give me a chance here."

"Someone's knocking at the damn door. It could be important."

Her eyes widened. "And this isn't?"

He kissed her. "Yeah, it is but . . . Damn, there's always a but." He slid from her, disposed of the condom, pulled the curtain and peeked outside. "It's Jett. I have to see what she wants. Stay here and keep quiet."

Sally bolted upright. "Excuse me?"

Candlelight gave her breasts a warm glow that beckoned him to return to her right now . . . except Mimi and Bonnie depended on him. "Just sit there for a moment and—"

"And you can go fuck yourself and the horse you rode in on, Demar Thacker." She threw a pillow at him, then a handcuff, grazing his forehead.

"Ah, babe, I—"

"Damn you to hell!" She yanked off the covers and stood naked and mad and completely glorious. "I hope your dick rots and falls off."

Ouch! "Sally?"

She grabbed her coat. "There's a back stairway and I'll

find it and then you can screw around with your old partner till you drop dead."

"That's not going to happen but I can't tell you what's
going on and—"

"Like I can't see for myself? If that woman was carrying
a sign that said *Come screw me Demar* she couldn't be any
more obvious."

Sally slipped on one heel, hopped on it as she slipped on
the other.

Naked and high heels suited her—hell, everything suited
her, thought Demar. She tromped for the back entrance.

Jett called, "Demar? Are you all right in there, sugar?"
More knocking. "Is your headache better? I brought
soup."

Sally mimicked in a high squeaky voice, "Oh, Demar,
you big hunk of man, I brought soup." She said, "Your
woman's calling."

He snagged Sally's arm, turning her back to him. Their
bodies tight together, he could feel the anger pouring off
her in waves, and he hated it. "My woman's right here in
front of me."

"I wouldn't count on that, big boy!" She yanked her
arm away and thundered down the stairs.

Chapter 12

Quaid felt every cell in his body freeze in total fear as he zeroed in on Lawrence, bobbing in the waves. Quaid grabbed a buoy ring, tied the rope end to the railing, threw it overboard, then jumped into the water. A faint afternoon sun penetrated the thick clouds, and Quaid caught sight of Lawrence's jacket and the self-activated flashing light attached to his vest. *Thank God for that.*

Quaid swam for all he was worth, and Lawrence must have spied Quaid, too, and fought his way toward him. Swells broke over his head, the current pull in the wrong direction, taking Lawrence further away. *Shit, damn, fuck!* Quaid gritted his teeth and pulled harder, Lawrence seeming to do the same, till Quaid reached out, snagged the jacket and hauled Lawrence to him.

"Grab my neck."

"Broke my arm."

Quaid put Lawrence in front of him, face to face, cradling his arm between their bodies. "Hold onto me with your good arm." This way Lawrence couldn't slip away from him.

Quaid took off for the white buoy in a breaststroke; he kept losing the ring in the swells till a spotlight landed on it, picking it out of the darkness. Cynthia! God bless this woman!

He swam toward the disk rolling in the waves, and finally hooked his arm into the buoy. At least now they wouldn't be separated from the tow, his biggest fear. He looped Lawrence's good arm through the ring too, then pushed them to the side of the tow. He snagged Lawrence around the thighs. "I'm going to hoist you up. Grab hold with your good arm and I'll push you from behind."

Lawrence nodded and Quaid held onto the buoy for leverage and lifted Lawrence. "You can do it, champ. Step on my leg." He raised his knee and felt Lawrence's foot come down on it. Quaid grabbed the leg and heaved Lawrence up; with his other hand on Lawrence's butt he gave one last boost up.

Lawrence disappeared over the top and Quaid went weak with relief. He stretched as far as he could, the tow dipping down cracking him in the side, but allowing him to snag the bottom of the railing. He pulled himself up the rest of the way, Lawrence tugging at his jacket, trying to help. Great kid. Quaid sat down and braced his legs against the railing to keep from falling back into the water. He lifted Lawrence into his lap, realizing he'd never felt anything more reassuring in his life. He took off his life jacket then stripped off his shirt. He laid Lawrence's arm across the middle. "Does it hurt?"

"A little." Lawrence touched Quaid's forehead. "You're bleeding."

"A scratch." He tied the arms of the shirt together around Lawrence's neck, making a sling. "You are one brave-ass kid."

Lawrence gave him a weak smile. "You are one brave-ass swimmer."

Quaid laughed, then held Lawrence close for a moment because he had the overwhelming need to. He wasn't a praying kind of guy but some God somewhere had a hand in this and Quaid would be thankful till the day he died. He helped Lawrence up, then lifted him into his arms. "Let's go find your mom. Every hair on her head must be gray by now."

"Yeah, and she's going to be pissed."

Quaid thought of Cynthia and the gun. If she planned on shooting Aaron for threatening to take Lawrence, what did she have in store for Quaid for losing Lawrence in the Mississippi? Christ in a sidecar!

Quaid rounded the bow. A light in the bottom quarters indicated the rescued men were obviously there. A part of him wanted to beat the crap out of them for not helping with Lawrence, but they were stupid beyond words. "Hold on to me with your good arm and I'll get you up to your mom."

Lawrence was shaking, even though he smiled. Hypothermia was a real possibility. Quaid tore up the steps and yanked open the door. Cynthia's face was white, her hand still grabbing the stick. "Okay?" Her voice was low but steady and it seemed to take all her energy to get out that one word.

"One broken arm."

She nodded. "Okay." But she still didn't move, as if frozen in place. He set Lawrence on the captain's chair and took the stick from Cynthia. He looked into her eyes, which weren't focusing. "Get Lawrence out of those clothes, there're dry shirts and towels in the cabinet. I'm going to get us to shore."

"Okay." It seemed to be her word of choice at the moment, but then she grabbed Lawrence in a mama-bear hug and Quaid was sure she'd be fine. They would all be fine. The age of miracles was not dead.

He checked in with the Coast Guard, giving them an update on the situation, then radioed the Memphis terminal dock that he was headed their way with a boat in tow. He requested assistance in docking it, and an ambulance to be waiting for Lawrence.

"An ambulance?" Lawrence said, his voice stronger than before. "Wait till I tell the kids back home about all this."

Cynthia added, "That you lived to tell about it is the important part."

She sounded stronger too, beyond monosyllables. A towel hit his head and a shirt landed on his shoulder. He dried off his face and draped the towel around his neck. "Thanks."

"That's just a hint of what's to come."

He glanced back but Cynthia was busy taking care of Lawrence. Quaid turned to port and revved the engine, the abandoned *Sea Ray* bobbing at the side but riding lower now, as she had obviously taken on more water. He entered the channel to the terminal, slowing his speed to no-wake, keeping red channel markers to starboard. He came about to port, killed the engine and glided neatly into position at the dock like he'd done a thousand times before.

Two men jumped on board, securing lines. The ambulance strobe lights gave the rain-soaked docks an eerie quality. Two paramedics hustled onto the deck. Quaid opened the door for the EMS people, then stepped outside. The rain wasn't as bad in the terminal, the building cutting the wind shears.

He clambered down the steps and went into the cabin on the main deck, but no one was there. He asked at the dock, and all anyone had seen was two guys hurrying off into the terminal. He didn't even know who the boat belonged to. Why would someone leave an expensive boat like the *Sea Ray* without taking care of it?

Quaid watched the paramedics bundle Lawrence and Cynthia into the ambulance and drive off. He called Rory to let him know the *Annabelle Lee* wasn't at the bottom of the Mississippi. He squared things with the dock master, made arrangements to tow the *Sea Ray* back to the Landing, since no one else knew what to do with it, went back on board the *Lee* and secured everything, changed into dry clothes, then he and Max hitched a ride in a police cruiser to the hospital. Rough day, but he knew it was nothing compared to the grief Cynthia Landon would heap on him once they met up.

Leaving Max under the covered receiving area, Quaid went in the emergency entrance. He spotted Cynthia pacing in front of the double doors marked *No Admittance*. She looked up at him, furor in her eyes. He slowed. "I'm sorry, I really am. I had no—"

"He threw me out."

"The doctor threw you out? What did you do?"

"Not the doctor, Lawrence. He said I was . . . hovering."

Quaid folded his arms and rocked back on his heels. "No! You?"

She leveled him a hard look through squinty eyes. "And you are on very thin ice. Do not push your luck, O'Fallon."

"It's not like I planned that storm."

"I know that but . . ." Her voice trailed off as Lawrence came into view, camouflage-patterned cast on his arm, the doctor trailing behind looking a little frazzled. Lawrence beamed. "I think I want to be an orthopedic surgeon." He looked to Quaid. "That's during the week. On weekends I want to be a tow captain." He pointed to a technician with *phlebotomist* on her ID tag. "I'm going to go talk to her."

Lawrence walked off and the doctor raised a brow. "He made me tell him everything I did. If he doesn't do med school he'll make one hell of a lawyer." He looked at Quaid. "I think the captain part's a *for sure*. He thinks you're God." He studied Quaid closer. "Nasty cut, son. You need stitches. Why are you holding your side?" He touched Quaid's rib and he flinched. "Looks like you broke a rib or two, or at least bruised it. I should take a look."

"I'm fine, I'm fine. Hospitals aren't really my thing. I'll be okay."

The doctor added, "Word has it that you pulled two people off a sinking boat and saved Lawrence, who the Coast Guard has nicknamed Lucky since you found him in the storm from hell and you both made it out alive. I should check you over."

"I'm going home now." He turned and ran smack into Cynthia, arms folded, eyes glaring. "Go with the doctor."

"No way."

She took a step toward him and he took a step back. He never stepped back. "Yes."

"Fuck," he muttered under his breath.

"Later," she whispered back, knocking the air right out of his lungs and looking as if she surprised herself as much as him.

The doctor laughed. "I'll take that as a yes. You're coming with me. You two can work out the conditions later." He said to Cynthia, "It'll be a few minutes, why don't you grab a bite to eat."

By the time Quaid was finished getting stitched up he was edgier than ever over this whole situation. Some things didn't fit, like the owners of the boat not hanging around, and then there was Cynthia's comment about later that completely undid him. Did she mean it? Why wasn't she furious at him? If he lived to be a million he'd never figure out women and their thought processes. Then again did they really have a thought process? He wasn't sure but he wasn't about to bring up the subject any time soon, he was in enough hot water.

In the waiting room, Quaid found Rory sitting next to Cynthia. He walked over, shaking his head, relief in his eyes, a grin on his face. "I ask you to take one little propeller and engine parts downriver while I take a run upriver, and what happens? You wind up fishing folks out of the drink again. I think the story even made the newspapers."

"Ryan and Keefe are never going to let me hear the end of this."

"Needling is what brothers do best. Publicity hound comes to mind."

Cynthia tore Lawrence away from the technician, who looked bleary eyed from answering questions. The rain had slacked off to a drizzle as they drove home, Max in back, Cynthia in the second seat of the Suburban, Lawrence asleep, his head on her lap, Quaid in the front with his dad. They pulled into Ivy Acres and Rory said to Cynthia, "I'll carry Lawrence upstairs for you. He's getting to be a big boy, and Quaid should give that cracked rib a rest."

Quaid rolled his eyes, knowing Rory was teasing him but also knowing it was true. Truth be told, he was tired to the bone. All he wanted was a hot shower, food and bed. He turned in the seat to face Cynthia and she gave him a tired smile and a little nod that suggested she wasn't about to shoot him dead just yet. No matter what happened between them in the future, they knew they could always count on each other. She was a lot stronger, braver, tougher than most people realized . . . including him.

He closed his eyes and waited for Rory to return, even dozed off for a moment. What was taking Rory so long? Quaid was ready to go into the house when Rory came through the door and got into the car.

Instead of turning the ignition he turned to Quaid, looking serious as hell. Quaid rubbed his sore side. "You got that look, what the hell's going on now?"

"You better spend the night here. There's been a development. Lawrence wants me to tell you that he recognized those guys who you took off the *Sea Ray*."

Quaid was instantly awake. "He knew them?"

"Seems they're the guys in the pictures Preston's been showing around, the two missing presidents from River Environs."

Quaid bolted upright. "Holy shit. I didn't get a good look at them in the storm. Is Lawrence sure?" He gave a half smile. "Stupid question."

"That kid's got a memory that won't quit. He's sure about everything. And he didn't fall off that tow, one of the guys pushed him in when he realized Lawrence recognized him. He shoved him into the railing first and that's how Lawrence broke his arm."

Rory shook his head. "He's scared. Guess his dad showed up today and that didn't go well, then he runs into all this. Hell of a day for an eight-year-old kid."

"Hell of a day for anybody. Bottom line is, I just risked Cynthia and Lawrence to rescue the two men who would like nothing more than to wipe your fiancée off the face of the earth. Christ in a side car!"

"That's my expression, you'll have to find your own."

Quaid slammed his hand against the dashboard. "I don't fucking believe this."

"My guess is they knew we were watching for them on the roads and they were coming to the Landing—"

"By boat."

"Do you think they know where Mimi is?"

"I think they know she's around here somewhere."

"They used the storm as cover to get here. Then it got worse than they expected, the *Sea Ray* broke down and I was making that delivery and our paths crossed."

Rory shook his head. "I thought about that, too much

of a coincidence that they happened to be coming to the Landing while we were all three away."

"Ryan too?"

"In Memphis scoping out an office. Somebody knew and tipped off those guys that today was a good one to come poke around."

"Who?"

"That's the sixty-four dollar question, isn't it?"

"Cynthia stopped at Slim's for food before we shoved off. If she told Sally . . ."

"Everyone would have known we were all gone."

"Now we get to find these guys all over again and figure out who's the leak." Quaid rubbed his ribs. "To think I had them right there." He pointed to the middle of his hand.

"But we know they are definitely headed here, we just have to figure out where they are now. And, I'm suspecting the third member of their little party, that finance guy, is already at the Landing."

Quaid's gaze met Rory's. "That's who tipped them off."

"And Ida has that new boyfriend, Beau Fontaine. Preston said he couldn't find anything on him in Charleston. We'll keep an eye on him but we don't want to give ourselves away that we're on to him. We need all three of the guys or Mimi will never be safe."

Quaid raked his hair. "They have to know Lawrence already told someone who they were. Too bad he didn't tell me before we docked."

"He was in shock with all that happened and it was probably good that you didn't know. If you confronted them it could have gotten ugly on the *Annabelle Lee* and you had Lawrence and Cynthia to worry about. Probably best it happened the way it did. We'll find these guys, we're getting closer."

"If Lawrence wants me to spend the night, I will."

Rory grinned. "He really likes the name Lucky. His mom's not crazy about it but she'll adjust." He raised his brows. "Cynthia Landon's got more moxie in her than I realized. She's changed and I can see that you got a thing for her now more than ever. Go for it, boy. If she's the one for you, then that's what you got to do."

Quaid stepped from the car, his side hurting more than he thought it would. He'd forgotten just how damn inconvenient bruised ribs could be. Rory drove off and Quaid turned for the door, Cynthia waiting for him in the doorway. She looked lovely, a little beat up, but lovely. Before, this woman got under his skin he didn't realize the word lovely existed, sounded kind of mushy and he wasn't a mushy kind of guy . . . till now. He took the steps but she didn't move to let him in. "Do you think those guys are after Lawrence?"

"They know he's already told everyone who they are. There's no reason to come after him."

He gave her a soft reassuring kiss. "I'll sleep on your couch tonight in case Lucky wakes up. Might make him feel better knowing I'm here."

Cynthia rested her forehead against his. "When I went to New York all I heard was be careful, it's not safe, you could get hurt, there are crazy people out there, it is New York after all. And now I come home and this place is like an episode of *The Sopranos.*"

Quaid draped his arm around Cynthia's shoulders and together they went inside. They stood at the entrance to the living room and Cynthia sighed. "Duncan Phyfe is more for sitting around and sipping tea or a mint julep, not so much for sleeping on. You're not going to fit, and we're kind of a full house upstairs." She pulled him close and gazed into his eyes, instantly melting every bone in his body. "I'd share my bed but . . ."

"Your mother and son are here and there's the no-man-in-my-life curse to consider." He kissed her forehead. "Throw me down a blanket and I'll be fine."

"There's a shower in the bathroom in the back." Her lips slid across his, stirring his blood, making him want her in spite of how tired he was. Her body pressed close and he folded his arms around her. "You did good out there today, Cynthia Landon. We wouldn't have made it without you. I'm more sorry than you know that Lawrence wound up in the middle of all this. Somehow a simple rescue operation got a lot more complicated."

"But you saved the day. I got a feeling you're used to doing that."

"We saved the day."

She headed up the steps and he watched till she disappeared around the next landing then gazed back to the dainty furniture. "Damn," he muttered into the darkness. Rotten sleeping arrangements, but Preston lived here too, and that meant food. Suddenly he was starving. He headed for the kitchen and pulled open the fridge. If Ida didn't marry Preston he'd consider it himself just for the great eats. "The man sure knows how to cook."

Quaid made a ham sandwich, added potato salad and chocolate cake and drank a quart of milk. When he came back into the living room, a pillow and towels sat on the sofa. He spread the blanket on the floor and tossed down the pillow. Ida really did need to take a serious look at a La-Z-boy catalogue. Bet Beau Fontaine and Preston would appreciate a La-Z-boy. Both big guys. Beau a little more gray than Preston, a bit older, seemed to be used to having money and smooth talking, except he always seemed preoccupied. Then again, business did that to a guy and he was here on business, not just to woo Ida. Or maybe he was the finance guy. Like Rory said, best not to tip their hand till they had all three and knew who was who for sure.

Quaid took a quick shower. He'd changed clothes on the *Lee* so at least he wasn't crawling back into scummy jeans and shirt. He peeked out the bay window overlooking the front of the house, then went around to the kitchen windows with a view of the garden. The half-moon slipped in and out of the remaining clouds as the earth did a drip-dry.

Lying down on the floor, he curled the pillow under his head, thanked God for saving his ass today and most of all for saving Lucky. If anything had happened to that kid . . . He couldn't think about that or he'd never sleep, and with his ribs against the hard floor and his head pounding, sleep wouldn't be all that easy, period.

He closed his eyes and saw Lawrence in the water, afraid, helpless, alone. And then suddenly he was the boy, helpless and afraid and alone, with Pete beating the hell out of him.

Quaid jerked instantly awake, knocking over the little chair Aaron had toppled earlier. A drop of sweat trickled down the side of his face, his stomach churned, every muscle in his body tight with fear, as if he were back to being that kid again, before Rory found him.

"Quaid?" Cynthia asked from the hall.

He raked back his damp hair and fought to get himself under control, drawing in long quiet breaths. He hadn't had the nightmare in years, but the look on Lawrence's face today triggered it, he was sure. Quaid knew that innate feeling of total helplessness and it nearly made him sick that Lawrence had to experience it at all. No child should have to live that way. He righted the chair. "Hey, everything's fine, go back to bed."

She came up to him, shafts of moonlight falling between them, settling in her eyes. She touched him and he calmed.

"You're not all right, Quaid. I can feel it. Did you hear something? Is someone out there?"

She sat on the couch and tugged him down with her, and he didn't have the strength to resist—or maybe he just didn't want to. "Dicey day is all."

"No," she said in a whisper. "That's not all. I saw your face and for a moment you looked terrified. As bad as things got today you didn't look like that, ever. You're always in control of the situation. Talk to me."

He shoved the past of that little boy who lived in the shack and wore grimy clothes out of his mind. "It's my ribs, they hurt and I can't get comfortable. That's all there is to it."

"Bull hockey."

The comment jerked him all the way back to the present and to where he was, and that was with the most gorgeous woman on earth. How'd he get so damn lucky? He raised his brow and couldn't keep from smiling. "What kind of talk is that for a New York gal."

"Except I'm really a Tennessee gal." She took his face in her palms and looked into his eyes. "You can talk to me, you know. It won't get blabbed all over town. And no matter how big and brave and invincible you are, you need someone to talk to, everyone does."

"You know what I'd really like to talk about?" He gave her a suggestive look because sex with Cynthia was one hell of a substitute for a nightmare. He could get lost in Cynthia, concentrate on giving her pleasure and making her happy. He really liked doing that.

"You're trying to distract me."

"What makes you think that?" He eased back the collar of her silky robe and placed a kiss on her warm, sweet neck that smelled better than a million flower gardens and chased away the last of the bad memories. Her head tipped forward, exposing her nape, and her soft sensual sigh filled the room. "Oh, you feel so good," she said in a husky voice. "But . . . but there are people upstairs."

"All asleep. Now am I going to get the lecture on curses or being forty?"

She cuddled into his arms. "If we can survive today, Quaid, we can survive anything, including a curse and me being forty. Besides, forty is feeling really good right now."

Chapter 13

And, Cynthia realized, she meant it. Forty was good, everything was good, especially when compared to what might have been. Quaid's lips touched her nape then her shoulder. She closed her eyes, the stress of the day fading.

"I want more," he breathed against her ear.

"Good grief, we just started this."

"When it comes to you I'm one greedy bastard." He slid her robe from her arms, letting it pool at her waist. His hands roamed her back, the only covering the thin gown. "I really care about you and Lawrence."

Her hands swept over his cotton T-shirt, damp from fighting whatever demons haunted him in the middle of the night, as he added, "I have feelings for you that go way beyond fooling around, Cynthia."

He nipped the tip of her nose and looked deep into her eyes. "If we never had sex again, I'd still feel this way. But I have to admit it wouldn't be as much fun."

Then his lips found their way to hers as he threaded his fingers into her hair and coaxed her gently back against the . . . most uncomfortable couch on God's green earth.

No wonder they used these things in Victorian times: no one could get laid here and think sex was good.

He braced his hands on either side of her, one on the armrest, one across the back of the wooden frame, golden moonbeams flooding the room. He said, "You are a classic painting lying here all soft and gorgeous." He tugged on the bow at her neckline, freeing the material, letting it fall open.

"Drat. I can't do this." She sat up and rubbed her shoulder. "This is the worst couch ever. And you shouldn't be moving around all that much anyway with your ribs. And you know if we get buck naked someone's sure to come down here."

He sat back. "You know if you had a reclining sofa we wouldn't be having this bad couch problem."

"But we'd still have the packed house and the rib problem."

"There is that. I was just getting ready to admire your cleavage. You really do have great cleavage." He closed his eyes.

She chuckled. "Tonight I thought I'd tell you that you're really well hung."

His eyes flew open and he laughed. "That is one thing I never expected to hear from Cynthia Landon."

"Just wanted to see if you were asleep."

"Well, you sure got my attention now." He draped his arm around her and drew her back against him and she snuggled close. "This is nice."

"There's something between you and me, Quaid."

"Sweetheart, it's been going on for years. Not always chasing each other, we've sure been aware of each other. You make me happy, Cynthia. I've never felt like I do when I'm with you." He kissed the top of her head. "You can have any guy you want and yet, here I am."

"Oh, yeah, I'm such a catch."

"You are. And I'm crazy about you. And now there's no curse in the way." He tucked his finger under her chin and brought her face up, their eyes meeting. "I want to see you, get to know you, and not just in the Biblical sense."

"Sounds like a plan . . . a good plan."

He kissed her then asked, "So, what's your mother going to say when you tell her you're keeping company with that ruffian, Quaid O'Fallon?"

"Would you like one or two lumps of sugar in your tea, Quaid?"

"I think it will go more like, 'would you like one or two lumps on your head, Quaid.' She is not going to be thrilled."

Cynthia touched his cheek. "That is entirely up to Ida Landon."

When Cynthia came downstairs the next morning, Quaid was gone, but there was a note propped on top of the folded blanket that said he went into Memphis to get the *Annabelle Lee*, that Preston was hanging around this morning till he got back, and she should drop off Lucky later, down at the docks when he got there. She glared at the note. "Bossy man."

"Men always think they know what's best for their woman," Sister Candy said as she strolled into the room in white shorts, black bandana holding back her hair, gold hoop earrings, and a big purse over her shoulder. "Heard what happened to Lucky, the story's everywhere. Is he okay?"

"He broke his arm so he'll be a little sore today and probably sleep in."

"Well that gives us time for a little business." She jiggled her purse. "You've heard of bed in a bag, girl, well this here is protection in a bag. We had ourselves a time in

Rockton picking out . . . protection. Even picked up a few clients in the bargain."

"Clients?"

"Supporters . . . for our little congregation. We are very selective." She put the purse on the game table by the window, opened it and pulled out a big ugly-looking gray gun, two smaller ones, and one derringer-looking thing with a mother-of-pearl handle. Gunmetal gray took on a whole new meaning. Sister Candy laid them out, planted her hands on her hips and grinned. "Here we are. Take your pick. Sister Ginger and I are already armed and dangerous and we got these for you. But you got to keep them locked up tight so Lucky doesn't get at them. I realize he's one of those brainy kids who knows more than I ever will, but he's still a kid and curiosity is their strong suit. Don't need any accidents, just protection."

She nodded back to the table. "I think the smaller one is good. Pick it up."

"Oh, God, I hate these things."

Sister Candy rolled her shoulders. "And how well do you like your sleazeball ex, or those slimebuckets who broke your baby's arm?"

Cynthia picked up the derringer. "I can keep this in my pants pockets."

"Better wear loose, or that Quaid O'Fallon guy will go ballistic if he thinks you're packing heat. He's one of those protective types who thinks women belong in the kitchen or in bed. Not bad places to be, mind you. But we got other uses."

She picked up another gun. "This here's a 9mm something-or-other. Beretta maybe. I knew a guy named Beretta. Had a set of ba . . . Bibles he was really proud of. Yessiree . . . they were some Bibles." She handed the gun to Cynthia. "Should fit in that little black bag you carry."

Cynthia held it. "A splash of mauve would do wonders for these things."

"It has what they call a boot grip, good for traction, and I got to tell you that traction part is really true."

Cynthia held the gun in one hand then the other. "Not too heavy. Won't ruin the lines of my Kate Spade." She sniffed the gun. "It smells funny." She swiped a red smudge and her insides froze. "If this is blood—"

"Pizza. Pepperoni. We were in Leroy's van haggling prices and eating. Damn . . . I mean darn . . . good pizza." She looked at Cynthia's wide eyes. "And . . . and we were saying the rosary. Yep, doing that too. We tend to take our mission work right to the streets . . . save the sinners. Amen." She made a quick sign of the cross.

"The derringer and 9mm something it is. How much do I owe you?"

"On the house. Little gift from me and Ginger." Candy pulled two boxes of bullets from her purse. "These are called rounds . . . guess because they're round. Not very imaginative. Go out in a field, someplace far away, and shoot the hell out of a can or something. Remember those 9mm bullets go real far, so you don't want to be shooting some poor cow in the ass."

"Right, no cows in the ass."

"Good morning, darling," came Ida's voice down the stairs. Cynthia's gaze met Candy's and she whispered, "Uh-oh." Candy scooped the guns into her big purse, Cynthia shoved the bullets in one pants pocket and the 9mm thing in the other pocket. The bulges were noticeable. When she got the chance she'd sew up some pants for toting guns.

"What's this?" Ida said as she came into the sitting room and picked up the overlooked derringer. "I used to have one of these." She aimed it across the room and pulled the trigger. A shot rang out and the picture of Stonewall Jackson jumped off the wall, crashing to the floor. Least there was no glass from the last time the man landed on the floor.

"Holy Mother of God," gasped Sister Candy, as Ida blew the smoke from the end of the barrel like they did in old West movies.

Ida smiled and picked up the picture of Stonewall. "Right between the eyes. I still got the touch. Good as ever."

Cynthia shook her head. "Good as ever at what?"

"Sweetheart," Ida said, handing Cynthia the picture then kissing her on the forehead. "A few weeks ago Thelma over at Hastings House blew her grandma's vase to kingdom come. Kept the pieces to remind everyone, mostly Conrad if I remember correctly, just who they were dealing with. A girl's got to take care of herself in this world. We all got another side that comes out when we need it to." She winked and handed the derringer to Cynthia then Ida sashayed her way into the dining room.

Sister Candy stared at Cynthia. "Well I'll be d—"

"Mom," came Lawrence's voice from the hallway. "What was that noise? Sounded like a . . . gun?"

Sister Candy slapped her hand against the hole in the wall as if leaning there to relax, trying to look nonchalant. "How's your arm, Lawrence?"

"Terrific." He tapped on the plaster cast. "This is so neat. I always wanted a broken arm—though technically it's not a break, it's a greenstick fracture. That means one side of the fracture is broken and one side is bent. It's classified as an incomplete break."

Cynthia held up Stonewall, putting her thumb over the circle between his eyes. She faked a grin. "The picture sort of fell off the wall."

Lawrence sniffed the air. "Why are you taking target practice at Stonewall Jackson?" He pointed to the picture. "I can see where you shot him and I can smell gunpowder.

Stonewall was a really good general, mom. Remember to put the gun on safety. I think I need some breakfast." He started for the kitchen.

"Wait," said Sister Candy. "Uh, maybe your mom can take you out for some breakfast, you can show off that cast around town. Bet all the other kids will be green with envy."

Lawrence's eyes grew. "You really think so?"

"You helped save a boat in trouble and even got a glimpse of those desperate characters people are looking for. I'd say that's the stuff boys dream about . . . least at your age. When they get older, well . . ."

Lawrence started for the door. "I'll be out in the car, Mom."

When he left, Sister Candy said, "What Ida said about having another side kind of got me thinking. She's got more gumption than I thought, a bit of a wild side. I've got a plan to help Ida make some cash, she being a southern woman with a sweet little accent and a feisty side. I think she can do a little . . . preaching."

"Ida?" Cynthia said. I don't know about preaching, but she did want to write a book about southern ways."

Sister Candy beamed. "Well there you go. I knew this would work out. Some things are just meant to be."

Chapter 14

With blue skies overhead and the Mississippi calm as a puddle, Quaid cut the engines and guided the *Annabelle Lee* to the O'Fallon dock. He tossed the lines to Hank who tied off the tow, the *Sea Ray* bobbing to starboard. Rory sauntered out of the office, Bonnie on his shoulder. "Mighty sweet cruiser you got there, boy. Newest purchase?"

"Salvage. Seems the guys from last night's events never came back; they abandoned her. I paid the dock fee in Memphis to get her out of hock, then did a quick patch job to get her this far. She needs work, the engine's screwed up from the river water, but nothing we can't handle. We needed a chase boat with muscle, now we got it."

"Well, this one is a humdinger." He slapped Quaid on the back. "Guess I'll know where to find you today, sweating over the engine." He nodded to the gravel road. "And here comes your helper. I think you and Lawrence have a bond."

"That kid's a hell of a lot smarter than I'll ever be."

Rory laughed, "You and everybody else on the planet. But he's still a kid. Hard to remember that when he's talking like some college professor. I better get Sweet Pea some juice, she's getting fussy and none of us want this baby fussy . . . Lord have mercy if that happens. Since you're hanging around here today, I'll mosey on up to Hastings House. See how my repairs are holding together."

Rory said *hey* to Lawrence, then headed back to the office with Hank. Quaid said, "You're sure looking happy for a kid with a bum arm."

Lawrence held it up, grinning. "All the kids signed it. They thought it was neat that I was in the papers." Lawrence stopped, his face suddenly paling. "What's the *Sea Ray* doing here? Are . . . are those guys back?"

"No way, those men have no reason to come after you. But it looks like the boat's ours. Someone who saves a vessel in peril has a preferred maritime lien on that vessel if it goes unclaimed. So far those guys haven't shown up."

"Ours?"

"You helped save her, didn't you? Guess that gives you a right, if you help fix her up."

Lawrence scuffed his shoe against the dock. "Except Mom's sending me away to school."

"You don't want to go?"

"The guys think I'm cool now, and that's good. And I sort of met this girl at the market, Katelyn Moore, when Mom was shopping for vegetables. Mom's making me soup, says it'll make my mending bones stronger." He made a face. "She's a great Mom, but she really sucks at cooking."

Quaid sat on one of the pilings as gulls swooped and dragonflies darted about. "Girl?"

Lawrence reddened, ear to ear. "She . . . she has a telescope up in her attic and there's an eclipse coming up."

"And she smells good and has pretty silky hair and soft eyes?"

Lawrence's jaw dropped as his eyes nearly popped. "You know her?"

Quaid put his hand on Lawrence's shoulder and bit back a grin. "That's the way all girls are and they turn guys like us to putty."

"Are you putty over Mom?"

Oh, hell! Did Lawrence see him with Cynthia last night? How could he talk his way out of that one? "Why do you ask?"

A sly grin played at Lawrence's mouth. "A question answered with a question. Lawyers do that when they have something to hide."

Having a smart kid around was good and not so good. "I'm not exactly a putty kind of guy but—"

"Mom says you're a hottie. I'm not exactly sure what a hottie is but I don't think it has anything to do with temperature and more to do with men and women and sex. So, does this mean you're going to marry my mom? If you are, that's okay with me, but can you hurry up and do it so you can talk her out of sending me to boarding school?"

"I think I'm being played."

Lawrence grinned. "Maybe a little. And now we own a boat together so I really can't leave here. I'll get a life jacket and we'll start fixing her up. Let's change the name of the boat from *Moneymaker* to *Cynthia*. Maybe that will soften Mom up."

Quaid laughed. "You really think so?"

"No, but it's worth a try." Lawrence climbed onboard the *Sea Ray* but Quaid didn't move for a second, considering what Lawrence said about the marriage thing. Lawrence knew something was going on between Quaid and his mom and that didn't feel right. It didn't feel honorable. Oh, he and Cynthia cared for each other but fooling around with Lawerence so aware just didn't seem like the right thing to do. What kind of message did that send to an impressionable kid? So now what? Give up Cynthia just when things were going good? Dang!

By late afternoon, as he and Lawrence sat under a river maple on the dock drinking RC Cola and eating MoonPies, Quaid made up his mind to take the plunge and make things right . . . least try to. He took another drink of cola and said, "This is what's known as Tennessee cuisine."

"In New York my favorites are cannoli down in Little Italy and the noodle shops in Chinatown."

Quaid reached in his pocket, took out a Swiss army knife and handed it to Lawrence. "Rory gave it to me, used to be his, and his dad gave it to him. I'll teach you how it works when your arm's better. How to keep it oiled and how to use it without losing body parts."

Lawrence looked at him with huge eyes. "It's an heirloom and you're giving it to me?"

"Can't think of a better person. You were one brave kid out there on the water yesterday. But you got to promise me not to mess with it till you can use both hands. Think of it now as a good luck charm."

"Did you have it with you yesterday?"

Quaid grinned and ruffled his hair. "You bet. Made us both lucky."

Preston strolled down the dock, hands stuffed in his khaki shorts, sporting a red and yellow floral shirt today. He stopped and laughed. "Bet you two had to work really hard to get this dirty."

Lawrence beamed. "But we fixed the engine. As soon as we get the hull patched we'll take her for a spin. Want to come with us?"

"You bet. But now it'll have to wait for dinner. Your mom made soup and sent me to get you. I tried to tell her I'd do the cooking but she insisted. Been chopping and simmering all day I think we can feed the whole Landing if we wanted to."

Quaid stopped mid-chew. "Uh-oh, I forgot about the soup."

Lawrence licked his thumb. "I didn't, but this stuff has vegetables beat by a mile." He stood. "I'll wash up in the office to get rid of the evidence."

When he took off, Preston took Lawrence's place. "How is he?"

"Good, but still afraid. Hear anything about our missing presidents?"

"Nothing here or in Memphis. They vanished and with good reason."

"Demar thinks Jett is connected to these guys."

"But how and which one and why?"

"We have a hunch on which one, and you're going to love this."

"Beau Fontaine of the Charleston Fontaines, right?"

"How'd you know? There are strangers all around with the new construction going on."

"The accent comes and goes and he can't cook for beans. What kind of guy wants to open a restaurant and doesn't know how to cook, at least a little? He knows good food well enough but on preparation he's clueless. And since I look eccentric and harmless he can't see beyond that. It never occurred to Mr. Fontaine that I know exactly who he is. Magnum is a great cover." Preston gave a half smile, the look in his eyes more shrewd than Quaid realized before.

Preston took a MoonPie from the box and cracked open the wrapper. "Lawrence is right, these are better than vegetable soup. I'm thinking we should shuttle the boy between us. The bad guys are ruthless. If they're willing to toss a kid overboard and kidnap a baby they're capable of anything, and right now we have no idea where they are."

Lawrence headed off with Preston, and Quaid finished the last of his RC, then went back to work on the engine.

The sinking sun glared through the cockpit door, casting long shadows across the salon and into the engine room, and then suddenly there were no shadows. "You fed my son marshmallow crap and cola for dinner? Men have died for less, O'Fallon."

He wiped his hands on a rag and came out into the living area.

"Well?" she growled.

Well, hell! Shorts, sandals, hair piled on top of her head with strands falling, giving her a sexy look. Fresh as summer lemonade on the front porch. "We named the boat for you, that's got to count for something."

"Like a bribe to keep Lawrence here and not at boarding school? He already tried that and . . . and do you always work without a shirt on?"

"It's hot in here, generator still broken. So, did the bribe work?"

She let out a long breath. "He has friends now, even a girlfriend. Katelyn. Good grief, he's eight. I am not ready for a Katelyn. And did you have to give him a knife?" She set a basket on the counter then faced him and held up her hands in surrender. "I know, I know. This is not the city and boys do boy things here, and he did pinky swear he wouldn't mess with it till you showed him how."

"And I believe him."

Cynthia looked him in the eyes. "And I do too. I had my first sharp scissors for cutting material when I was seven, so I can't complain too much."

He grinned and so did she, as if thankful for this precious time, with no one drowning, no ex's to get rid of, no immediate confrontations. A perfect moment that just sort of happened out of the blue, when the world turned a little slower, felt a bit mellower, a lot happier. There weren't a lot of those moments and Quaid appreciated the ones that came his way. All because of Cynthia Landon.

"But you are still not off the hook, buster. I brought

soup, a huge pot, because there's a ton left over and you get to eat it all since Lawrence is full of junk food and I don't know what to do with it."

"I wanted to introduce him to the good things of Tennessee."

Her blue eyes softened, her lips melted into a sweet smile as she gazed at him. "Well, that happened when he met you."

The world stopped a beat, Quaid was sure of it. "You didn't have to say that."

"And I wouldn't have said it if I didn't truly mean it." She smiled, then turned to the cabinets and tried to open a door. "I take it there are bowls for the soup on this yacht, Lawrence says it has everything, that the *Cynthia* is yare. I think he's been watching old movies again." She pulled again. "What's wrong with this?"

Quaid came up behind her, inhaling her breezy scent, drinking in her sweetness, blown away by what she just said, his heart swelling. He unsnapped the catch and whispered in her ear . . . she had the prettiest ears. "It's too hot for soup."

He kissed her neck, a little moan escaped her lips, and his plans for honor waned.

"And it's getting hotter," she said on a sigh that tore right through him as a gentle rock of the boat tucked her body against his.

"I'm still mad at you over the sugar and the bribe." She turned in his arms and faced him—eyes misty, smile a little devilish. "But I think I'm getting over it." She unsnapped her shorts. "You have great powers of persuasion, especially with your shirt off. And I bet there's something more comfortable around here than a Victorian sofa."

His honor crumbled. Having Cynthia overwhelmed him completely. "We'll have fun finding out. Right now I need a shower." His fingers connected with hers at her waistband and he unzipped the shorts the rest of the way. "Wanna join me? I have to warn you, the head is really small."

She cupped his dick through his jeans, the pressure arousing him all the more. "Guess we're not talking about the same head." She claimed his mouth in a convincing kiss as her fingers worked his belt buckle. He unbuttoned her blouse and inched the two of them back toward the tiny bathroom, leaving her blouse, then her bra in their wake. His jeans slipped over his hips, her shorts dropped and she kicked them aside. A sandal landed on the counter with a soft thud, another one bounced off the table. He discarded his own shoes, not breaking the kiss, then flipped on the water in the tiny stall. "I love us both naked," he said against her lips.

"We have underwear."

"I hate underwear." He peeled down pink panties, taking his time, savoring the view. He removed his briefs. "*Now* I love us both naked."

"I love seeing you aroused."

"You show up and that's what happens every time."

Her fingers closed around him. "To think I'm responsible for this is pretty powerful stuff, Quaid O'Fallon."

"Let's find out just how powerful." He backed her into the confined shower, sliding the door shut behind them, the cool drops a welcome relief from an August inferno coupled with the one they created on their own.

He took the clip from her golden hair as the droplets trickled over her face and off the edge of her chin. "This is very cozy."

His hands slid down her back, his fingers massaging the indent of her spine, and he cupped the smooth twin mounds of her derriere, pulling her into him. Her legs parted as their bodies met, his erection cuddled against her navel. He grabbed a soap-on-a-rope from a little bracket overhead.

"Smells expensive," she said as he lathered, the sensual odor filling the little area as he gently smoothed suds across her shoulders, over her breasts, down her middle. "You're teasing me."

"I'm loving you." His hand slipped to the juncture of her legs.

"Not fair," she said through clenched teeth. "I want the soap."

"But I'm not finished." He hooked it over her head, the rope dropping between her breasts. He took her hands and slid them between their bodies, then to his mouth, kissing one palm then the other, then lifted her hands over her head, holding them both in one of his.

Her eyes rounded in surprise, her cheeks pinked. "Oh this is really not fair."

"I want to look at you uninterrupted, and you keep interrupting." He ran his finger down her middle and she squirmed.

"You think because you're stronger and bigger you can get away with this, turn me on and I don't get to do anything to you?"

He kissed her. "Yep, that's pretty much the plan. And you can't retaliate against a man with a bruised rib. That wouldn't be sporting." He fondled one nipple, making it hard, then the other. "I think you like this."

Her eyes clouded. "Quaid," she whispered. "This is too much."

"But there's more, sweetheart. Lots more. We're just getting started." His fingers slid into the tight curls between her legs. "Do you want me to touch you?"

She whined, "If I ever get out of this I'm going to torture you, tantalize you, messed up ribs or not." She whimpered as he slowly slipped his fingers in, her hips rolling into him, wanting more.

"I love making you feel good." The water slowed, trickled then stopped. "Dang."

Her eyes fluttered. "Wh . . . what happened? Things were just getting good."

"We used all the water in the holding tank. This isn't the Hilton." Reluctantly he let her hands go and slid his fingers out. As she grabbed his shoulders. "You have me so turned on my teeth ache."

He wedged from the shower stall and found big white towels, thick as a rug, in the cabinet under the sink. He handed one to her then reached back for another till something stopped him . . . tightening around his wrist. He yanked.

"What the . . . ?"

In a split second she grabbed his other wrist and secured both behind his back, then turned him around in the little space, backing him into the little sink, grinding her middle against his erection. "Revenge."

"How'd you do that?"

"Soap on a rope, and you're not the only one with clever fingers, Quaid O'Fallon. Seamstresses tie knots all the time." She gave him a siren's smile. "Oh, this is going to be fun."

He struggled. "What if something happens? I need to be able to take care of you."

"Oh for God's sake, I am forty. Lived all these years without you, I can manage another ten minutes." She kissed him, slipping him her tongue. "That's all the time we're going to last here, if that, and quit struggling or you'll hurt yourself more. Just relax."

He pulled for all he was worth, his ribs aching, not caring. When the wet slippery rope gave, he relaxed. He'd let her have her fun and enjoy it too. If he needed to get his hands free, he could. Whether she realized it or not, that's what Cynthia counted on. He took care of her and Lawrence, kept them safe. What else would draw someone like Cynthia Landon to Quaid O'Fallon? He took her trust seriously.

Cynthia studied Quaid just as he'd done her. "You're all wet. I'll have to fix that."

She dried his face, his shoulders then his front, reviving the tight curls of hair across his pecs. His solar plexus flexed as she dried him in long, slow strokes, then she hunkered down.

"Legs . . . I have to dry your . . . legs." She licked his penis and he sucked in a quick breath. "That is not my leg."

"It needed attention. It looked lonely." She dried one leg then angled for the other. "Next time we do this it's in a big huge bathroom with air conditioning and—" She cracked her head on the sink.

"Ouch."

"Dammit, are you okay?"

"Yes, but I need consolation." And she took his erection into her mouth.

"Cynthia!" he hissed her name and every inch of him stiffened. She licked him, making him harder still, then she took all his length again, faster, holding him tighter between her lips, loving the sensation of pleasing him.

"I never did this kind of thing with Aaron." She looked up at him and winked. "You're my first. I think I like it, least with you I do."

"That's it."

He shrugged out of the rope, brought her up slowly but emphatically till they were face to face. She huffed, "You . . . cheater."

"You vixen."

"You could get out of that rope all along."

"You can harangue later." He ushered her into the salon and grabbed his jeans.

She grabbed him. "You are so not leaving me like this, Quaid O'Fallon. You play with me, tease me, get me hotter than the hinges of hell and—"

He held up a condom. "I'd grin but I don't have enough skin left. And I'd throw you over my shoulder but my ribs aren't up to it."

He stole a kiss, then tore for the bed in the next compartment, dragging them both onto the soft mattress, him on top.

She took the condom from his hand. "Up, up."

"Babe, if I was any more up this thing would be a lethal weapon."

"Up as in away from me a little bit so I can get the blasted condom on."

He sat back and she rolled on the latex, her fingers shaking, his breathing erratic, her insides screaming for him to be there.

"You are one luscious woman." His eyes smoldered.

"Words later, action now." She held out her arms to him and he just sat there. "Quaid?"

"I'm coming."

"Good God, not yet!"

He rolled his eyes. "I meant I wanted to look at you and then I was—"

She grabbed his forearms. "I don't care what you meant. Now, dammit, now." She froze. "Can you do this with bruised ribs?"

"Honey, when it comes to making love with you, I could do it in a full body cast." His mouth devoured hers as he slid into her in one long hard thrust, her legs widening, widening again to take in all of him. She gripped his shoulders, her hips lifting from the bed to meet him. He roared deep in his throat, the intense sound of male pleasure filling her head, her heart. Knowing that she satisfied him to that extent pushed her over the edge as he ground out her name in climax.

Her limbs quivered and there wasn't enough oxygen in the little cabin, the heat oppressive. She felt dizzy, nearly faint. His magnificent body gleamed in the sunlight with a fine sheen of male sweat.

"Holy shit, girl," he panted against her neck, adding a kiss. He didn't move, letting the moment between them linger so they could commit it to memory. Slowly he pulled himself from her, breaking the connection, making her feel alone again. She hated it, and being alone had never bothered her before. He flopped back on the mattress, the gentle swells of the boat soothing, hypnotic.

"I think we just christened your boat."

"This has a bottle of champagne beat all to heck." He discarded the condom. Chuckling, he rolled to his side facing her, their bodies close. "Do you have any idea how much I like you?" He tweaked the tip of her nose.

"I'm glad you're here and part of my life, I really am." She grinned. "You do know that an older woman landing a younger man is quite an accomplishment."

"I'm landed?"

She crawled on top of him on all fours, her knees at his hips, her hands at his shoulders. She peered down at him. "You're on the hook or maybe I'm the one there, wiggling around trying to figure out what to do."

"I love it when you wiggle."

"Then we'll just wait and see what happens next."

Chapter 15

Demar flipped a slab of spareribs, the meat sizzled on the hot grill, getting ready for the dinner crowd. He slathered sauce across the chicken and turned the sausages, the incredible aroma wafting into the evening air. He loved cooking, Slim's, the people, Sally. Sally . . . Fear gnawed his insides. How much longer could he hold on to her while playing the Jett game? He hated hurting her, really hated the possibility of losing her altogether, but Jett was a good lead on the case, at least he hoped so after all this.

He turned up the radio, the announcer introducing a new after-midnight program starting tonight, " 'Southern Spice,' putting heat in your relationship to keep it on fire."

He didn't need heat, he and Sally had all they could handle in that department, except Jett wanted her share, too, and was getting more insistent every day. The big question was, how long could he put her off without her getting suspicious and how long would Sally tolerate his less-than-loyal behavior?

He loaded ribs, sausage and chicken into the smoker, then tossed a helping onto a tray for an early dinner order. He took it inside, the night waitress not on duty yet. Keefe and Ryan sat at the bar, no one else in the place, just platters of uneaten food. "Messin' With My Lady" hummed from the jukebox. Demar put down the tray. "What happened? Where'd everyone go?"

"Out," Ryan said. The look in his eyes and Keefe's stopped Demar cold. "We're here to fix something for a friend, and didn't need an audience."

Damn, this was no friendly encounter and had nothing to do with food. He was about to get his clock cleaned, and these two pretty boys might have a polished appearance but their eyes said they were pissed as hell. That translated into taking care of Sally and *really* taking care of him. "Look," he started in a low voice. "I know why you're pissed and—"

"We think it's time you packed up and left town on your own steam," Ryan said.

"Or we can lend some assistance," Keefe added. "It's your call." They stood facing him.

"You haven't talked to Quaid, have you?"

"We don't need Quaid. He's got his hands full at the moment."

Demar backed up, keeping both guys in sight. "There's an explanation."

"Yeah, the harder the dick the softer the brain. You're going to take your cop gal and get the hell off the Landing."

Demar backed his way to the other side of a table. "This is business. Jett's not what she seems, she has connections with someone here and is—"

"You have fifteen minutes to pack up your crap and get out of town."

Keefe and Ryan circled the table and Demar stopped. Best to face a fight head on. "I'm not going anywhere, and you've got this all wrong. I'm here to help—"

Keefe swung and connected with Demar's jaw. Some cushy soap star! Demar replied with a jab to the ribs and suddenly Quaid came between them, pulling them apart. "What the hell are you two doing?"

Keefe rubbed his gut. "This jackass is two-timing Sally with some bimbo from Nashville. We were extending a one-way invite out of town."

"Ah, fuck a duck," Quaid groused at Keefe. "I didn't even know you were in town." He took him in a hug.

"Just got here. Got a play to put on. Thought we'd take care of some trouble then go looking for you."

"Except you're the ones causing trouble, just like old times." Quaid snagged the plate of food from the bar and dropped it onto a table with a hollow thud. "Demar's on our side, I just forgot to tell you."

"You forgot?" Keefe griped.

"Let's eat, I'm starved. Grab the stack of napkins off the counter."

"I'm back one lousy hour and you're already barking orders," Keefe grumbled and went for the napkins.

"Somebody's got to keep you in line since it looks like we're all here on the Landing for good." The three slowly exchanged looks, grins and nods.

"'Bout damn time," Ryan added.

Keefe added, "Especially since I volunteered us to build a new baseball field."

"I knew it." Quaid pulled out a chair, sat and tore off a chunk of rib. "But first off we have to get Dad, Mimi, and Bonnie straightened out and that's where Demar here comes in." He motioned for Demar to take a seat then continued, "He's not messing with Sally, he's playing Jett for information. She used to be his partner back in Nashville and we think she's connected to the guys at River Environs and using the information she can get from him to find Mimi."

Ryan nodded to Demar. "And you're using her to find the bad guys. A game of cat and mouse."

Keefe drummed his fingers. "You're stringing one woman along and trying to hold on to the other at the same time? Hell, man, you should be the one on a soap opera."

Ryan leaned across the table to Quaid. "With all that, it still didn't cross your muddled brain to tell me what the hell was going on?"

Quaid shrugged. "Slipped my mind. Got other stuff to think about."

"Like Cynthia Landon," Demar said, Ryan and Keefe chuckling.

Quaid grabbed a chicken leg. "Any of you got a problem with that?"

"Not me," Demar said, holding up his hands. "I got enough women problems at the moment."

"Hey," Sally said as she and several customers entered the front door. She ignored Demar, making him feel guilty as hell for putting her through this.

She came over to Keefe, and folded her arms. "Denzel Washington is nowhere to be found in this town. We all looked one end to the other and no one's seen that hunk of man around here. The only thing in the town square is the new flagpole on top of the founders' memorial, which is nice but certainly not Denzel Washington. You lied to me, Keefe O'Fallon."

Keefe rolled his shoulders. "Did I say Denzel Washington?" He took a bit of chicken. "I meant Dan . . . Dan Washington. Going to open up a hardware store on the corner. Thought you'd like to meet him since he'll be right across the way."

Sally slapped the back of Keefe's head with the flat of her hand. "That is not funny. You know I like DW. You're back an hour and teasing me already. Next time it's hotdogs for you. You can forget barbecue." Sally strolled off as the returning customers reclaimed their seats and the food they'd left to find the movie star. Quaid chuckled and said in a low voice to Keefe, "You said Denzel Washington was in town and Sally didn't take you out and shoot you dead for sending her on a wild goose chase?"

"A chance we had to take. We needed to talk to Demar alone. Reports of spotting DW in town on his way to New Orleans emptied the place in ten seconds flat."

"So now what?" Ryan asked as he snagged a sausage and turned to Demar. "Do you have anything we can use?"

Demar leaned over the table. Lightnin' Hopkins' "Another Fool In Town" kept the conversation from being overheard. "I talked to a cop friend in Nashville. It seems Jett got a call one day and ten minutes later took personal time and left for here. Obviously this has nothing to do with having the hots for me, but using me. Since cell phones don't work on the Landing, I got the phone records from Hastings House, thinking she'd placed calls from there to her contact, but there was nothing unusual for a B and B— just calls to here, tourist places in Memphis, boat rentals, Ivy Acres and the like, same sort of calls coming in. Thelma says Jett's had no visitors since she got here, but there are people coming and going at Hastings House all the time and Sally saw her meet with someone in the woods but didn't get a good look. Said he sounded like someone from up north."

Ryan took a gulp of beer. "Then we're no closer than before. What do we do?"

Quaid wiped his mouth with a napkin. "Didn't help that I pulled those two assholes off that sinking boat."

Rory said, "You couldn't let them drown."

Quaid gave him a look that suggested he could have done it without a second thought. "They nearly killed Lawrence, stole Bonnie, would kill Mimi in an instant.

They're slime, drowning's too good for them. I'm looking forward to meeting up with them again . . . soon. Very soon."

Demar said, "Quaid and I think her contact is Beau Fontaine, a new southern gent in town who might really be the third president we're looking for. I need to go through Jett's room and see if I can find a connection. Don't want to accuse the wrong guy and let the real contact get away. Tomorrow night I'll tell Jett I want her to meet you guys at your house since you're my new friends. She'll go for it because she's after info on Rory and Bonnie, and this meeting gets her closer. You keep her busy, tell her I had to help Slim, that gives me time. I'll get the key from Thelma." He nodded at Keefe. "You're an actor, you can do this."

Quaid leaned in further and whispered, "Well, we got to try something. How much longer can the plumbing problems at Hastings House continue before Jett catches on? We are hell-and-away out of time."

The next night, Demar watched the lights wink on in Hastings House, the old brick Georgian-style house probably looking the same as it did during the Civil War, except for electricity, heat and running water. Nice additions.

He waited in the bushes, watched Jett leave, then crept around to the back. Opening the door, he slipped inside. Easy conversation drifted from the front room where Thelma entertained her guests with after-dinner coffee and liquors. Demar made for the back stairs. They creaked under his weight, but then the whole house creaked. At a hundred-and-fifty years old the place had the right.

He hurried down the hallway carpeted in orientals, turned the corner to Jett's room, unlocked it, pocketed the key and relocked the door from inside. Sweeping his penlight around he tried to get a feel for where she might keep something important. For sure she had her PDA with her but there had to be something in the room that would help. He checked by the phone, no scribbled phone numbers. He held the penlight in his teeth then riffled through the writing desk. Zip. Cops were good at not carrying identifying information on them. Damn. He went to the closet and dug through pants and jacket pockets and heard a key turning in the door.

Holy crap! Jett? Couldn't three guys keep one woman busy for one stinking half hour? Keefe was not winning any awards for tonight's performance that was for damn sure. Demar slipped into the closet and drew it closed behind him without latching it. A light went on, he could see it under the door and around the edge.

He heard the phone being picked up, then Jett said, "It's me. No, still nothing. Everyone's real closemouthed. I'm meeting Demar at the O'Fallon's tonight, they're good friends. In fact, I was half way there and something occurred to me: Rory O'Fallon does not seem all that upset about Mimi. Either he's not in love with her anymore or he's got her stashed somewhere near here just like you think he does. I'll go through his house if I get a chance. I doubt if she's there, if your bugs haven't picked up anything. Stay where you are, I'll call you later."

The phone clicked into the rest, footsteps, then water running. The bathroom. He had to get out of here. If she went to the closet for a jacket or whatever and found him, it was all over.

Demar inched open the door, crept into the room, reached the main door and stepped into the hall as Sally rounded the corner, his hand on the knob, the door still open, his heart in his throat. Fuck! Fuck! Fuck!

Sally stopped dead, the color draining from her face. "Well, isn't this a nice little coincidence. I wondered if you were here. When you weren't in your apartment or at the bar I figured as much but thought I'd check it out anyway."

"Demar?" Jett said as she came to the open door. "I didn't hear you come in. I thought I locked this door?"

Demar smiled at Jett. "I came to get you. When you didn't make it to the O'Fallons I thought you might be sick. I came here to check on you."

"Well, isn't that the sweetest thing I ever heard," Sally said. "And exactly what were you planning on checking, Demar? Jett being such a frail little waif and all." Anger blazed in her eyes but hurt lingered deeper inside.

Sally came up to him. "I hate your guts, Demar Thacker." She said to Jett, "I hope you two are happy together because you so deserve each other."

This time she sounded more sad than angry, and Demar wished it were the other way around. The last thing on earth he wanted to do was make her sad . . . actually it was the second to the last thing. The very last was to not find Mimi. He couldn't live with that on his conscience.

How would he ever get Sally back? When this was over he had to—somehow. Jett seemed to buy the situation. In fact she seemed to revel in it, and that was the good part. Least there was one, sort of. Sally stomped down the hall and he felt his heart crack. Christ Almighty, did life get more complicated than this?

Jett stood in front of him, her face taking Sally's place—except no one could ever do that. She drew up to him, her chest to his, and purred, "You really came to check on me?" She undid the top button on her blouse. "Well, I think you can check all you want, sugar."

She dragged him inside and closed the door, leaning against it, blocking the way out. She undid the other buttons, her red blouse parting, revealing her lacy bra against lovely brown skin—except it wasn't Sally's lovely brown skin, and that's what mattered most. How the hell was he going to get out of this?

"Let me show you how much I appreciate you coming for me, Demar." Jett licked her lips and swayed her hips as she came toward him.

Oh crap! Oh, crap! "We're supposed to be at the O'Fallons."

"And I want to go, all I need is just ten minutes, baby, to show my appreciation."

"Fire?"

Her eyes widened. "What?"

"Yeah, fire. Don't you smell it? This place is old, it'll go up like a match." He took Jett's arm and ushered her away from the door so he could open it. "Smell." He sniffed. "Yeah, fire." He pointed to the hall. "That way."

"Demar I don't smell—"

"Subtle, very subtle. I'll tell Thelma."

"But—"

"She'll take care of it. Got to protect the house and we sure don't want to be here in a fire. Remember the last time we were together in a fire. We nearly didn't make it out."

She paled. It was totally rotten of him to play on her fears but her little plan was headed for bed, and he wanted no part of bed with Jett.

"I think I smell smoke," Demar said to Thelma as he whisked Jett toward the front door. Thelma's eyes met his and she gave a slight nod and said, "Got a batch of scones a little over done, that must be it."

Demar stopped with Jett in the foyer of the big house. "Well there you go. Not as bad as I thought, but you can never be too careful."

He checked his wrist, which didn't have a watch but he hoped Jett didn't catch it. "We're late for the O'Fallons, yep, really late. They'll be looking for us. Have a nice evening, folks," he said to Thelma's guests and escorted Jett out the front door, closing it soundly behind him.

She pulled up short on the front porch and stared at him. "What the hell was that all about?"

He shrugged. "Burnt scones. Come on, baby, the O'Fallons are waiting for us."

Blind Boy Fuller's "Lost Lover Blues" blared in the background as Sally took the plate Cynthia offered to her. Sally aimed at Demar's smiling picture duct-taped against the back wall of Slim's, did a windup pitch and let go, smashing the china to pieces.

She smiled hugely, cupped her hands together and held them up in triumph to half the female population on the Landing—who had booted the non-female population out an hour ago. They cheered. The women then saluted with shots of bourbon or Kool-Aid or whatever, and gulped them down. Sally said, "I got the big stinking weasel right between the eyes with that plate. I think I need another: I'm getting the hang of this."

Cynthia passed another plate as Sally asked, "You sure you don't mind me smashing your wedding china against Demar's thick head? It's Chantilly, it's really a beau . . . beau . . ." She couldn't get her tongue around the rest of the word so she went with, "nice pattern."

"Every time I look at it I think of Aaron. When I found out the scumbag bankrupted my loft, I smashed our every-day china and downed two bottles of peach schnapps. Better and cheaper than a shrink and since he picked out that china I didn't mind. That's why I suggested this. His mother—who thinks her son is the baby Jesus—picked it out." Cynthia nodded at the photo. "Go for it, you're doing us both a favor."

Sally took a swig of Johnny Walker Red, aimed and let another plate fly across the room. It crashed, a chunk of the picture ripped, and the women cheered again and did another round of shots.

Sally hiccupped and hurled a cup, the fragments blasting into the air.

Sister Ginger said, "You'll find a great guy, Sally, someone who appreciates you. Ida found her Beau and couldn't be happier, though I honestly think Preston is a much better match. He's so in love with her, and Beau . . . well Beau's in love with Beau."

Sally shook her head. "You sure know a lot about men for being a nun."

"Sometimes men come to us for . . . therapy. Our sisterhood is real big on therapy."

Sally said "Well, I'm done with men and this time I really mean it. I'm heading off to Seattle. Got a good job offer with an investment firm that I can't pass up. And I'll be back to visit but I can't stay here." She smashed another plate, feeling sad to the bone.

Thelma said, "You should call into that new radio show down in Memphis, "Southern Spice," ask what to do about Demar. That woman, Tennessee Tess, has great advice."

Sally nodded. "She's all about pleasing your partner in bed and keeping marriage and relationships fun and exciting, and not letting things get stale. I was listening to her last night. Never knew there was such a thing as Bare-ass Bingo and I lived in New York for years."

Jennifer Webster said, "She does Bedroom Blog every day. Scorched my monitor, burned up right there on my desk, had to get a new one."

Her cousin, Betty Ann, added, "And she has that sex position of the week web page. Tried it with my Harry. I think I'm pregnant."

Effie said, "Good grief. Thought I left all this stuff behind in California. What happened to living in the Bible Belt?"

Sister Candy laughed. "'Southern Spice' deals with what's below the belt, girl."

Sally tossed another plate. "Wonder if she has any suggestions on what to do with a big bastard who's cheating on you?"

Sister Ginger got the phone from behind the bar. "Let's find out."

It was a little past midnight as Demar headed to the O'Fallons' dock after dropping Jett at Hastings House. Quaid, Ryan, and Keefe sat on pilings, Rory with Bonnie in his arms sat on a log washed up from a flood, the chunk of wood that now served as a bench.

They all nodded and Keefe said, "That was damn quick. I'm surprised Jett didn't insist you come up to her room for . . . whatever. So, why'd you have Thelma call us and say to meet you down here?"

"It's safe to talk here." He nodded at Rory. "Your house really is bugged."

"I knew it," Rory hissed. "Christ in a sidecar, a man can't even have the privacy of his own house."

Demar stuffed his hands in his pockets. "The reason I know is that when I was going through Jett's room she came back early. I hid in the closet and overheard a phone conversation. She mentioned your house being bugged and told the person on the other end she was going to the O'Fallon house and she'd look around for something that might lead them to Mimi. So, I gave her something. I left a note by your phone that said, *Hastings dry dock, Thursday,* 7. I put 'M' under it."

Keefe said, "She asked me where the bathroom was when she was here."

Ryan grinned. "Well damn. Think whoever she's working with will go to the dry dock looking for Mimi?"

"Sounds too obvious," Quaid said. "She'll never buy it, might even tip her off that we're on to her. She is a cop after all."

"I agree." Demar nodded. "Except it's the best I could come up with on the fly and Jett doesn't know we're on to her so she's not suspecting anything. Inviting her here was a good idea. We lured her exactly where she wanted to go, to your house. There's no reason for her to think we're laying a trap for her, more like we're dumb hicks."

Bonnie fussed and Rory stood and paced with her. "So now what? We wait at the dry dock and see who shows up?"

Demar said, "I made it seven, left out the A.M. or P.M., so we'll have to keep watch both times. I figured that was before and after the dry dock crew's working day, so it should be easier to spot someone snooping around. We'll have to tell Conrad we're using his place."

Ryan gathered Bonnie from Rory and took his turn at pacing as Demar added, "There's an apartment at the dry dock, right over the office and it's suitable for a meeting or maybe hiding out, so it fits the note that Mimi could be there. Conrad stayed there for a few weeks before Thelma made him come back to Hastings House and warm her bed. Can't believe they've been married three weeks now. Took them a while to get together but once they did they didn't waste much time."

Rory said, "When this is all over we'll throw them one wing-ding of a party. Right now we've got to finish up things here. We'll wait till Jett's contact shows his ugly mug and we have one of the bad guys for sure. We keep tabs on him and he'll lead us to the other two."

"What is Jett's connection?" Ryan asked. "I don't get that part."

Demar said, "I don't either. Why would she risk everything to get involved in this?"

Keefe said, "Take a look at her clothes, her makeup, her hair; that is one high-maintenance woman. A cop's salary can't touch it."

Demar added, "We'll find out soon." He nodded up the road. "What's going on at Slim's? I heard a lot of hooting and hollering on the way down here."

"That's where the women are and why they aren't down here with us. Sally's throwing dishes." Keefe took his turn with Bonnie. "At your picture. I believe the woman's a little pissed. She told Cynthia what happened at Hastings House, who told Thelma, who called here, and Effie and Callie took off to lend moral support. Every female within a five-mile radius is there. They all think you're dog dirt, by the way. What the hell did you do to cause a dish-throwing party?"

Demar moaned, and he wasn't a moaning kind of guy unless in the sack with Sally with a hell of a lot to moan about. "I was sneaking out of Jett's room and Sally showed up, my hand still on the door. She suspected I was with Jett since I wasn't in my apartment or at the bar."

Laughing, Quaid took Bonnie. "Oh man, you are so totally screwed. It's going to be great to see you two get back together."

Demar grumbled, "I'm glad to supply you with evening entertainment."

Rory put his hand on Demar's shoulder. "When this is over we'll get you squared with Sally. The sheriff here is useless as tits on a bull. The town's growing and you are the man for the job, we all know that. Don't you worry about Sally. There'll be some groveling involved and jewelry . . . always jewelry, but we'll make it work."

Rory glanced at his sons. "Can't have you be the only one not married after all this."

Ryan and Keefe grinned then stopped and looked wide-eyed at Quaid. Ryan said. "You're marrying Cynthia Landon? Holy shit, when did that happen?"

Quaid opened his mouth but nothing came out. Demar chuckled because it felt a hell of a lot better than contemplating his mess with Sally. "Well, I'll be damned."

Quaid shook his head. "Wait a minute, I didn't say I was marrying Cynthia."

Rory reclaimed Bonnie. "You are so in love with that woman. You forget to eat half the time, forgot to tell your brothers you and Demar were on the same side, and you walk around with that glazed look in your eyes like you don't know if you're coming or going. Either you're in love or you got a serious case of gas."

Rory started up the road toward his house. "Let's call it a night, I'm bushed. Quaid can take the first watch at the dry dock tomorrow. I'm betting the farm all this marriage talk has killed any chance of him sleeping tonight."

Chapter 16

Chapter 16

Quaid sat on the front porch of the O'Fallon house, rocking, worrying, sweating his ass off and it had nothing to do with a hot August night on the Mississippi. What the hell was he going to do about Cynthia? Could he really ask her to marry him? He couldn't believe he was considering such a thing. They'd been back on the Landing a whopping two weeks. Her divorce was barely final. For a man who'd never contemplated marriage for more than thirty seconds this was a little sudden.

Rory came outside in the old ratty robe that Thelma had been trying to throw away for the last twenty years. His gray hair stood out in all directions and his eyes were still the kindest Quaid had ever seen.

Rory plopped into the wicker rocker with a soft grunt. "Going to sit out here all night, worry yourself into a lather, or you going to ask her to be your wife?"

"But—"

"Here's the way I see it, boy. You don't have much of a choice. There's a smart kid involved who doesn't miss a trick. You are going to have to either fish or cut bait with his mama. Not right to do otherwise."

Quaid raked back his hair in total frustration. "I should

just break it off with her. I can still see Lawrence once in a while and—"

"The real trouble is, you don't think you're good enough for Cynthia Landon." He tossed a paper into Quaid's lap. "Maybe this will help give you a boost of confidence."

"I can handle things, Dad, you have enough on your plate right now without worrying over me."

"Hell, boy, you can handle anything, but a nudge up the ladder once in a while doesn't hurt any of us. That's what family's for."

Quaid unfolded the official looking blue-backed paper. He held it up to catch the light from the old porch lamp that had been on since the first night he got here, lighting the way then just as it was now. Quaid read, sat up straighter and shook his head. "You can't just give me O'Fallon Transport."

"That there paper doesn't say boo about giving, it's business. I'm selling it to you, some paid out each year from the profits. And before you go rambling on like some fishwife, hear me out. Ryan, Keefe and I talked this over. They don't want to run the business. Ryan and Effie are setting up their architecture firm here and a branch in Memphis. Keefe is teaching theater at the high school, doing summer productions on the showboat, and there's talk of him picking up some summer stock gigs in Memphis. Callie's already doing research on her book."

Rory put his hand on Quaid's shoulder. Quaid remembered the first time Rory O'Fallon had done that, twenty-years-and-two-months ago, and had said, *Boy, you're coming home with me.*

"We want you to have the business, keep it in the family. I don't want the headaches anymore, I've got me a baby and wife to tend to. I'll help with the office, your brothers will run barges from time to time, but the operation is all yours. You got the feel for it, Quaid, the knack. You got river running in your veins just like I do. You're my son."

Quaid couldn't talk, a lump the size of Tennessee lodged in his chest. "I . . ."

Rory's hand gripped a little tighter. "You just go into Memphis tomorrow and pick that gal of yours out a pretty little ring and make her and her son and yourself real happy. Hellfire, you all deserve it."

Rory pushed himself from the chair and ambled his way back inside, the only real home Quaid had ever known. He leaned back and stared into the darkness, the sounds of the night and the Mississippi drifting his way. He had no idea what lucky star he'd been born under to wind up in this very spot, but he was damn thankful . . . real damn thankful.

He drifted off, till the first rays of sun zapped him in the eyes. He gazed across the dewy grass, through the trees to the river . . . always the river. And now he was part of it. He folded the deed neatly, slid it into his back pocket and made for Hastings dry dock, slipping in through the small stretch of woods that separated Conrad's place from the O'Fallons' dock. A little shiver crept up his spine . . . make that *his* dock.

Crouching behind a mulberry tree, he ate a few berries, mulberries being his favorite. He had a good view of the parking lot in front of the dry dock office and boats bobbing in the river: some pleasure craft like his *Sea Ray* waiting for repairs today, and one big tow. A cabin cruiser hung in midair, suspended from a lift, another rested in a cradle. A big tow occupied a dry dock waiting for the welders. Conrad's business was good. The man was working like a maniac to make it that way.

Quaid suddenly spotted Beau Fontaine. He kept to the

trees on the other side of the parking lot and peeked into the windows of the weathered frame building. The brass top of Beau's cane caught the early morning sunlight.

Quaid inched forward into the clearing then walked toward Beau. "Looking for something?"

Beau spun around. "Why . . . why Quaid." He forced a smile. Quaid knew one when he saw it. "You sure as heck know how to scare the bejeebers out of a man," his southern drawl more southern than ever.

"Conrad doesn't come here till nine. You looking for something . . . like Mimi?"

Beau's eyes rounded. "That missing woman? My, my why would I ever do a thing like that?" He shook his head slowly as if considering the question, then stroked his chin, covered in a neatly-trimmed graying beard. "But now that you mention it, that does make a lot of sense. You see, the reason I came down here is that I was out for my morning constitutional as I always do and I spotted someone sneaking around. I followed him down this way because he seemed secretive. I must have lost him or he saw me and just took off." Beau held up his cane. "I don't move as fast as I used to."

"Did you get a look at who the guy was?"

"I do believe it was Preston. Couldn't imagine what he was doing here. He's kind of a strange duck. He puts on this Magnum front and acts kind of eccentric and I personally don't think he's that way at all. He's kind of sneaky. I've heard him on the phone talking about your family and Mimi. Now I know he's working for you and all, but maybe he's not, if you get my drift. I'd keep my eye on him if I were you. He's not what he seems." Beau tapped his cane to the ground. "I best be getting back to Ivy Acres. Ida's getting real good at making coffee."

Beau sauntered back up the gravel road, using his cane

more than when he came down. Maybe he was just tired or maybe he wasn't what he seemed. Or, maybe he was right about Preston not being what *he* seemed.

A retired schoolteacher could always use cash, and the three executives hunting for Mimi had lots of it to keep them out of the slammer.

What was true, what was crap?—that was the question.

Cynthia propped open the door to Slim's, letting in the early morning breeze and letting out the smell of beer and barbecue. Both were fine but needed refreshing from time to time. A low moan came from the bar. Sally warbled, "Ice, I need ice, my kingdom for an ice cube."

Cynthia found a baggie behind the bar, dumped in ice cubes and put it on Sally's head. That she was still in the same horizontal position, face-up on the bar where Cynthia had left her the night before, helped keep the baggie in place.

"I think I'm dying."

"You sort of smell that way but mostly it's wishful thinking. You should have let me get you upstairs last night. There's a pitcher of stuff here marked *the hair of the dog that bit you—love, Dad*. Says to chug it and you'll feel better."

"Remember those guns the nuns fetched from Rockton . . . get me one."

Cynthia parked on a stool. "For you or to use on Demar?"

"I'm deciding. You know what I'm also deciding is we need a party around here. Conrad and Thelma eloped three weeks ago and we've all been so caught up in the Mimi situation that we didn't celebrate. We need to celebrate and it would get my mind off you-know-who."

"Girl." Cynthia gazed down at Sally as she stared up at the ceiling, bloodshot eyes, baggie on her head, face the color of the wicked witch. "You are so not in a condition to celebrate anything. You celebrated enough last night to last all this year and next."

"That was a wake, now I need a party." She cut her eyes to Cynthia. "Come on, help me out here. Make a sign and put it on the door. Seven o'clock tonight. We'll get Preston to cook." She burped. "I'm leaving anything f-o-o-d to you. This is not my day for that. Heck of a way to curb an appetite. Wonder if Fat Fighters knows about this?" She again cut her eyes to Cynthia. "You can't refuse a dying girl's wish."

"Besides," came Effie's voice from the doorway as she and Callie walked in. "You never know, it just might turn into an engagement party."

Cynthia smiled. "You two want to celebrate your engagements? Now it really is getting to be a party."

The two sat at the bar beside Sally, exchanged looks then Callie said to Cynthia, "Not ours, yours. We didn't know if we should tell you but Quaid's freaking out. He backed over Keefe's SUV on his way into Memphis this morning to get the ring."

"R . . . Ring?"

"He fed Max tofu and Ryan dog food for breakfast. And . . . he wore a plaid shirt and khakis into town."

Cynthia felt the blood drain from her face. "Plaid? Khakis? Quaid? Ohmygod."

Effie gritted her teeth. "Scary stuff. But if you're going to turn him down you'll have to be . . . gentle. I think he's on the edge. Not that we want to know your answer, that's your business not ours."

Sally slowly righted herself, keeping the bag plastered to her head. "Like heck, of course we want to know. What kind of women would we be if we didn't want to know stuff like that? This is the Landing, everybody knows everything." Three pairs of eyes focused on her. "It's the truth and you all know it." She pointed to Cynthia. "Well, give. What's it going to be?"

"We've been together two weeks, and a lot of that was not all that together so much as running into each other."

Sally huffed, "Oh for heaven's sake. You probably had a proper engagement to that Aaron guy, and bridal showers at Tavern on the Green, and the big fluffy wedding and look where that got you, married to an ass. Sometimes you got to just go with it, girl, let things happen."

"And if I'm wrong I'm not just messing up my life, but Lawrence's, and every time I let a guy in my life it goes right to hell in a handbasket. I can't do that again."

Sally sat cross-legged on the bar. "And when your life went to hell who pulled you out this time? I'm willing to bet it was Quaid, that's what he does. Takes care of everyone."

Effie took Cynthia's hand. "But the real question is do you love him?"

"He's . . . young."

Sally grinned. "And the problem is . . . ?"

Cynthia slid from the stool and paced. "I don't know what to do."

Effie ushered Cynthia to the door. "Go home, slip into something pretty and think . . . think real hard. Where are you going to find a man better than Quaid O'Fallon and do you really love him?"

Cynthia suddenly found herself on the other side of the door to Slim's as it closed soundly behind her. Now what was she going to do? This was not how she envisioned her day going at all. What happened to helping Sally feel better, putting the finishing touches on that mother-of-the-bride dress, and maybe doing some target practice, she still hadn't done that. Guns . . . ick. But a necessary ick if butt-brain Aaron ever showed up again.

She got into the Blue Bomb, fired it up, backed into a

tree, nearly ran over Beau Fontaine taking his morning walk, and headed for Ivy Acres. What to do?

And two hours later as she sat on the front steps and Quaid's Jeep rolled into the circle drive in front of her house, she still wasn't sure what to do. Her last marriage was such a huge mistake, what made this any different?

Quaid opened the door and got out and her gaze met his. Her stomach flipped. Stupid question. Quaid made it different. He even wore a stupid plaid shirt for her.

He plopped beside her and said, "You look gorgeous. You always look gorgeous." He stared straight ahead, then ran his hand over his face a few times and pulled at the shirt.

"You look like hell. Are you okay?"

"Terrific." He let out a ragged breath, swallowed, then turned to her. "Look, I don't know how to do this. I don't have a clue. I can grab people off sinking ships, rooftops, out of trees, can fix any motor man's created, hunt, fish, survive in the wilderness for weeks with nothing but a knife but—"

"Yes."

He wasn't breathing.

"Yes, I'll marry you?"

Air escaped his lungs. "Good God, why?"

"Because I love you."

Lawrence bolted from behind what was left of the rhododendron. "Yes!" He jumped up and down in the driveway. "We're getting married!" He threw himself into Quaid's arms. "You're my dad, the one who really counts, like Rory was with you." He faced Cynthia. "We're getting married. Kiss him. Come on, do it. That makes it official. And a ring." He turned to Quaid. "Do you have a ring? You gotta have a ring."

Quaid pulled a black box from his pocket.

"Oh, this is great. Now put it on her finger, you're sup-

posed to get down on one knee and say *My darling woman,
I love you with all my heart, will you marry me?*"

Cynthia massaged her forehead. "Lawrence, what in the
world have you been reading now?"

Quaid shrugged. "Sounds better than anything I've
come up with." He knelt on the step below her. "Cynthia
Landon, would you do me the honor of being my wife?"
And he slid the emerald solitaire on her finger.

Lawrence beamed. "Holy cow, holy cow, we're engaged.
I want to wear a tux to the wedding. Guys look great in a
tux. Like Gatsby. Katelyn will like it. I'll tell Grandma."
He ran into the house, the front door banging shut behind
him.

Cynthia sighed, "I need a rest, I'm hiding his library
card."

Quaid arched his brow. "Grandma? The fly in the ointment?"

"Then it is her ointment, isn't it? Besides she's still asleep,
she was in Memphis till late last night." Cynthia kissed
him, her head swimming, her heart pounding, feeling totally happy. "I love you, Quaid O'Fallon. I didn't realize
how much till right now. I'd be honored and thrilled to be
your wife. Truthfully you are the most wonderful man I've
ever known." She framed his face between her hands and
grinned, feeling nearly euphoric. "Now was that so hard?"

He smiled a really terrific smile that warmed her heart
and sizzled the rest of her. "Yeah, nearly did me in but it
was worth it."

Sister Candy and Sister Ginger came to the door. Sister
Candy said, "Oh my God, he's on his knees. He did it, he
did it, he really did it."

Sister Ginger added, "We've got to call Sally so she can
tell everyone."

The sisters went back inside and Cynthia pulled Quaid
up beside her. She leaned against him, gazing at the ring

sparkling in the sunlight. "It's beautiful. It matches your eyes."

He rubbed his hands together. "I'm glad you like it. I didn't know which one to pick. Diamonds are nice but you're more colorful than that."

"I'm colorful?"

"You're really dazzling," he said in a rush of words. Then he nodded to the hedges where he'd fallen. I'll get gardeners over here this week to spruce up the grounds. The inside of the house needs painting and the floors should be refinished."

"Sounds like you've been giving this a lot of thought."

"And we should get married as quickly as you're comfortable with."

"Don't you want to enjoy the engagement for a while?"

"We get married and then I can move in here and make sure you and Lawrence are safe from Aaron and those guys from the boat. We'll get this house back the way it used to be. I think you'll like that, and Ida too. I'm not wealthy but I have enough money to take care of you and you'll be safe with me, but of course you know that, that's why you're marrying me. I can afford to send Lawrence to that private school if that's what you really want and—"

"Whoa, whoa. Wait a minute." A chill crept up her back. "You don't have to do any of that."

"Of course I do. That's why I'm here."

Reality fought its way through her brain presently drowning in pure bliss. "You think I'm marrying you so you can take care of me, protect me and Lawrence, make things right?"

He shrugged, matter-of-fact. "Sure."

"You don't think I really love you, do you." It was a statement, not a question. She knew him and how he worked . . . he was the protector, the savior, the one who made the world around him perfect. It was like payback for Rory saving him. "Damn you, Quaid O'Fallon."

"I think I liked *the most wonderful man* part better."

She yanked at the ring but it didn't budge, so she stuck her knuckle in her mouth, licked it and pulled off the ring.

He looked bewildered. "What are you doing? Doesn't it fit?"

"It's not the ring that doesn't fit, it's you. You have such a low opinion of me you really think I can't take care of myself, and such a low opinion of yourself that you don't think I can really love you?"

"Cynthia, you're terrific, wonderful, beautiful, incredible. So why in the almighty hell would you want to marry me, not that I'm complaining, I'm just seeing it for what it is."

"I might as well marry a pit bull."

"Well, sort of . . . but I smell better . . . usually."

"Dear God! I truly love you but you refuse to believe me. Well, Mr. O'Fallon, until you can get it through your thick skull that I can take care of me and Lawrence without your wonderful supervision, and that I love you with all my heart and this marriage has nothing to do with being a pit bull, our engagement is over."

"Over? But . . . What more do you want from me? Name it, I'll make it happen."

She smacked her palm against her forehead. "See, this is why I cannot have men in my life. I marry one who takes, takes, takes and never gives anything back and then I almost marry one who gives, gives, gives and won't take anything in return."

"But . . . but I really do love you."

"And I believe it, but I can't marry a man who believes I'm doing him a favor by becoming his wife." She yanked open the door and slammed it behind her.

* * *

"Well, fuck," Quaid muttered. He felt as if he'd been zapped with a bolt of lightning. One minute he was doing damn good, the woman of his dreams had agreed to marry him, making him more happy than he thought possible, and the next minute he was face-down in the dirt, wondering how in the hell he got there.

Lawrence came back onto the porch and handed him a cookie. "Wow, what did you do? Mom is so pissed off. She's slamming doors and grumbling about men and stomping around like a crazy person. Preston's hiding in the pantry. I could hear you arguing all the way in the kitchen."

"I think I just had the shortest engagement in history. I blew it. Forget the tux." Quaid took the ring from his pocket and looked at it, Lawrence peering over his shoulder. "It's really pretty. You tried, you said the right stuff. I don't get what happened."

"I thought I was doing the right thing and then bam!"

"Your brothers have nice girlfriends . . . least Mom says so. Maybe you should talk to them."

Quaid thought of the ribbing he'd take from Rory, Ryan and Keefe for screwing this up. Demar would sympathize, since his love life was in the toilet too. Quaid glanced at the door and Lawrence said, "Don't do it. I wouldn't go in there if I were you."

"Good point."

"Guess you're not calling the boat *Cynthia* after all?"

"More like *I Wore Plaid for This?*" Quaid gave Lawrence a squeeze then kissed his head. "Don't you worry about a thing, sport, I'll fix this somehow."

Quaid dropped the ring back in his pocket, got in the Jeep and headed for the dock. When he pulled into the parking lot, his brothers, Rory and Demar were waiting. Oh boy!

"Well," Rory asked when the Jeep pulled to a stop. "How'd it go?"

"Don't ask," Quaid said, then waited for the ribbing to start . . . but it didn't. "Aren't you going to start with the smart-ass cracks?"

Ryan shook his head. "Are you kidding? Do you know what hell Effie put me through before she agreed to marry me? I moved all the way back to San Diego before we straightened things out."

Keefe rolled his shoulders. "I messed things up so bad with Callie and was in such a state that I handed Bonnie over to kidnappers. Gee that was fun."

Rory rocked Bonnie in his arms. "And my woman's still on the lam, and the only way I can see her is if there's a plumbing problem." He winked at Quaid. "Like I said before, the road to getting the right woman is a damn minefield and things aren't going to be any better for you tonight at the wedding reception at Slim's for Thelma and Conrad."

Demar held up his hands. "Oh, no. Count me out. I'm not going anywhere near Slim's."

Keefe said, "If you don't go you'll look like a coward. Just don't bring Jett, we don't need bloodshed."

Demar leaned against a piling. "I'll take the seven o'clock watch tonight over at the dry dock, then come over just to wish Conrad and Thelma all the best. But I got a feeling that Quaid spotting Beau this morning had something to do with Mimi."

"Or," Quaid offered, "he really was taking that walk like he always does and Preston is the connection along with Jett."

"We need to keep our eye on all of them. Beau and Preston will be at the party so that won't be hard. Jett's another story. I'll try and keep track of her."

Ryan slapped Quaid on the back. "Do us all a favor, big brother, just don't wear that god-awful shirt. Where the hell did you get it anyway?"

Quaid slapped him on the back in return. "Your closet."

*   *   *

Standing on the bar, Cynthia grabbed the roll of white streamer paper from Sally and nailed it to the ceiling of Slim's with enough force to jar dust from the rafters.

"Hey," Sally yelled, holding up her hand, her eyes squinting shut. "You're killing me here, girl. I've got the mother of all headaches." She pointed to the ice bag she'd strapped around her head using one of the sisters' bandanas. "Remember me doing shots, throwing plates, flat on my back on that bar." She nodded to her former resting place. "Think tape, or glue or chewed gum . . . anything but a hammer."

She handed Cynthia the gray roll of duct tape that she'd used last night to fix Demar's picture to the wall. "Double it over and make it sticky on both sides. Nice and quiet like, okay?"

Cynthia let out a deep sign. "I'm not getting over this broken engagement thing too well. I'm in the mood to beat up something . . . or someone."

Sally gave a sideways glance. "What's that mean?"

"I've learned a lot from Quaid."

Sally snickered and Cynthia blushed. "And not just the sexy stuff though the man sure has his share." She tore a chunk of tape with her teeth and stuck a swag of crepe paper to the ceiling. She threw the tape, then the streamer roll to Callie standing on a table. She stuck up another swag, then tossed the paper and tape to Ginger, who threw it to Candy as they festooned the ceiling with dips of crepe paper. Bells, doves and hearts hung here and there, white balloons in the corners.

Callie jumped down from the last table and gazed around. "I like it. A little cheesy—make that a lot cheesy—but it's fun. Conrad and Thelma will be surprised and we all need a break from the craziness going on around here."

Sally slumped into a chair. "Are you kidding, it's flipping terrific. We raided everyone's garden for flowers and begged for white tablecloths and vases. We've mastered the art of instant wedding reception. We should go on *Oprah.*"

Effie said, "Preston's doing lasagna and putting the finishing touches on the cake. He and Lawrence are headed up to Ivy Acres to get a cake plate from Ida. Beau was supposed to drop it off but had to go into Memphis for business."

Callie fluffed a tablecloth over one of the wood tables and Effie set a vase of flowers in the middle, as the door opened and an older man with gray hair, unshaven chin and hollow eyes strolled in as if he owned the place. Cynthia's heart beat faster and her palms started to sweat. Could she really deal with this man? Then she thought of Quaid and how he'd dealt with Aaron. Yeah, she could so do this.

The man grumbled, "I'm looking for Cynthia."

"And you found her," Cynthia said as she forced a grin and walked toward him. She tried to keep the anger from showing in her eyes. "I thought it was time we met."

He gave her a steely look. "I'm here to pick up my money. You said Quaid left money for me."

"I lied. I told you that to get your sorry, lying, arrogant ass here. I figured it would work because I'm willing to bet the bank you've hit Quaid up for money a lot, knowing he's a sucker for family, and unfortunately that includes you."

Sally's eyes covered half her face. "Pete? You're Pete? We haven't seen you on the Landing in twenty years. My, my, you have not aged well. But I guess the real problem is that you've aged." She faced Cynthia. "How'd you know he was hitting Quaid up for money?"

"I married Aaron. I know the type."

"I'm out of here." Pete turned for the door but the sisters blocked his way, and they weren't looking too sisterly.

Sally asked, "How'd you find him?"

"Preston knows more than how to bake a mean lasagna and dress like Magnum," Cynthia said to Pete. "Tell me, did you use the money you got from Quaid over the years to pay gambling debts from betting on the ponies? Poker? Craps? Black jack? Texas Hold'em?"

"So what if I did. What business is it of yours?"

Cynthia felt dizzy. "You said that to the wrong person." She glanced around. "Where's my purse? I need my gun. Men like you make me sick."

Pete's eyes widened. "Gun? Who the hell are you? What do you want with me?"

Sally said, "You can't shoot him, dear, your son will be back, bad example."

Effie added, "And it's messy."

Callie said, "Not if we bury the body first."

Pete went white as the streamers overhead. "What the fuck. This has gone far enough."

Cynthia said, "Here's the problem, Pete. Quaid can stand up to anyone but he can't stand up to you because you're his grandfather. So, I figured we could stand up to you for him. Think of this as comeuppance by proxy. You screwed with Quaid's head and his self-esteem when he was a kid, and it's our turn to make that right. You're going to apologize to Quaid."

Sally said, "I think something public is in order."

Pete hissed, "You can go to hell."

Callie said, "That would be where you're headed and we can arrange it."

Effie added, "I could draw up plans for a gallows, we could hang the son of a bitch."

Sally got Cynthia's purse and retrieved the derringer. "I

say we just shoot his balls off. Bet that could wheedle a great apology."

Pete wobbled and held onto the back of a chair. "Fine, I'll say I'm sorry just to get you bitches off my back."

Cynthia gasped. "Now you made us all mad. Ever see six women mad all at once?"

Sally got her baseball bat and paced. "*I'm sorry* is what you say to your woman when you can't get your dicky up for her. We need something more, something like *Hi, my name is Pete and I'm a rat's ass* so everyone knows you treated Quaid bad, didn't feed him, made him steal to survive, break into places to sleep for the night. Made him into a hellion."

Cynthia growled, "Because of you Quaid doesn't think he's good enough for me. You nearly ruined his life and now you're ruining mine."

Effie said, "I could design a pillory."

Sally grinned, the ice pack sliding to the left side. "That will work."

Cynthia said to Pete, "You're going to make things right with Quaid and undo the damage you caused."

"Then all will be well," Sally added. "Except for Demar, he's still a pig." She turned to Effie. "On second thought, draw up plans for that gallows. Just in case we need it."

Cynthia took the derringer from Sally and slid it into her pocket. "I'll be standing in front of you with my little pea shooter. One little mess up and I'm taking Sally's sage advice and you can bend over and kiss your balls good-bye."

Chapter 17

The air filled with the scent of diesel fuel as Quaid watched *River Boy* pull from the dock and churn her way toward Vicksburg to pick up a payload. He helped Hank roll a cable onto the *Annabelle Lee,* then fueled her up for a run tomorrow. Taking a break, he checked the repairs to the *Sea Ray* that Conrad had finished up earlier. What a honey of a boat with 320 hp, a terrific cabin and some pretty terrific memories.

He did a mental sigh. What the hell was he going to do to get Cynthia back? He loved her, but that wasn't the problem. As much as he tried to convince himself, he still didn't really believe she loved him. He knew in his heart—even if she didn't realize it—that she wanted him because he could protect her and Lawrence. And that was okay with him. Why couldn't it be okay with her?

He gave Hank instructions for the night and told him he'd be at Slim's for the party if Hank needed anything. Quaid walked up the road to home, the evening sun at his back, Max trotting along at his side just as he'd been there for Rory every evening. They turned for the big frame house, till Quaid heard a commotion in the town.

Now what? He didn't care; he was too tired and frustrated to care. He took two steps toward the house then knew he couldn't just walk away. He'd always care about the Landing. Crossing the road he made his way past Slim's. Something at the new flagpole held everyone's attention. Maybe they got one of those flags that had flown over the White House and everyone was there to celebrate and . . . "Holy cow!"

Quaid froze. "Pete, why are you tied to the flagpole? What are you doing here?"

"Get me out of this," Pete sniveled. "And I'm not tied, it's duct tape. That fiancée of yours taped me here. She's a damn lunatic."

Cynthia sat on a chair in front of him. "Ah, ah, ah," she said, wagging her finger at him. "You really don't want to say things like that, Pete."

"Now tell Quaid why you're here," Sally coaxed. "You don't want to make Cynthia . . . upset."

"No, not that!" Pete crossed his legs as if trying to protect his dick. What was that all about? Effie, Callie and the two nuns—who never looked less nun-like than now—stood next to Cynthia.

"We're all waiting," Cynthia encouraged, nodding at the growing crowd.

"All right, all right. My name is Pete and I'm a rat's ass."

"And," he continued, "I am sorry I was a piss-poor grandfather to Quaid and treated him like crap and drank and beat up on him and said really shitty things to him."

"And," Cynthia growled, looking more pissed by the minute.

"I'm sorry. What more can I say." He eyed Cynthia then Quaid. "All right, all right, I can say more. I'll never bother you again I swear it, especially if you got anything to do with this Looney Tunes woman in front of me. How the hell did you wind up with this wacko? You're a smart guy, made something of yourself. You can do better than this nut case, Quaid. Run, get the hell away from her."

Everyone laughed, some slapping Quaid on the back. Then he laughed, and it felt as if it came from the depth of his soul, as if something snapped into place that he never thought would. Seeing Pete taped to the flagpole and the people in town gathered around, supportive and pulling for him, meant a hell of a lot. He wasn't sure how Cynthia Landon had pulled this off but she did it for him—all for him.

Quaid took the new knife he'd bought to replace the one he'd given to Lawrence, and cut Pete free. "Go home," he said to him in a quiet voice. "And don't come back."

Pete didn't even look at him but ran toward an old Chevy at the curb. He drove off, the door on the driver's side still hanging open. The crowd began to drift off to get ready for the party, no doubt, but he snagged Cynthia's hand and drew her close. "What was all this about?"

She smiled up at him, looking totally pleased with herself. "You took care of Aaron for me, I took care of Pete for you."

"Another one of those things that make us even?"

"More like I wanted you to know just how much I really love you, and that I can take care of things right nicely when I have to. In fact, I'm getting better at it all the time."

"I love you, too. God, I love you and you obviously love me. So marry me."

"You need time to realize you are a fine man. That you are respected and looked up to." Cynthia slid from his grip and strutted her very lovely stuff toward Slim's, knowing he was watching and teasing the hell out of him. He loved seeing her all sexy and flirty and what the hell did she mean that he needed time. How much time?

"Quit drooling," Rory said as he came up beside Quaid, Bonnie in the stroller. "You got yourself a real catch there, boy. Now you got to figure out how to keep her."

Bonnie started to fuss. Quaid quickly unbuckled her and scooped her into his arms. "Are you taking Bonnie to the party tonight?"

"Dropping her at Hastings House. The racket at Slim's would be too upsetting."

Bonnie scrunched up her face and Quaid said, "Uh-oh. Got a bottle? Tell me you got a bottle."

"Didn't think I'd be out so long. Then I caught the Pete show and I couldn't miss that."

"Except now she's hungry and we're all going to pay."

Bonnie looked at Quaid then Rory, took a deep breath, and yowled. Three people ran across the street to get away from the racket. Max crouched and put his paws over his ears. Rory yelled over the noise, "You carry Sweet Pea, and it's a good thing she likes you or she'll yell louder than ever, I'll push the stroller. Head for home and get a move on. If we don't get her quiet quick people will think it's one of those tornado warnings."

And three hours later, as Quaid shoved open the door to Slim's, he felt as if he'd been caught in a tornado. One look at Cynthia dressed in yellow silk that clung to her lovely curves, gold earrings, hair in some fancy do, made him feel as if he'd been dropped right on his head. She handed out beers and laughed and swayed one way then the other to "Howlin' For My Baby." He stared, not able to take his eyes from her. He'd been doing that a lot lately.

"See something you like?" Keefe said as he placed a beer in Quaid's hand.

"Yeah, and how the hell do I get her?" He watched Conrad and Thelma dance together and then dance with others. Ryan got his sax from his case and broke out with "Cross Road Blues" and Sally joined him, belting out the tune like no one else could. Callie snagged Keefe for a dance and Demar came up, looking like death warmed over, as Sally finished the song and disappeared back into the crowd.

Demar said, "You know that job offer Sally got from Seattle? She's taking it. She's already packed, luggage in the car. Slim's ready to beat me to a pulp, not that I blame him. She's leaving tonight after the party. Did you know Cynthia and Lawrence are going with her, keeping her company on the drive out? Something about giving you time. What the hell do you need time for?"

Quaid felt his head swim. "I don't, and how in the hell am I going to convince Cynthia of that? Have you seen Jett?"

"Guess who showed up at the dry dock at seven tonight? First Beau, then Jett." He gave Quaid a knowing look. "They are our connection."

"No wonder Beau tried to finger Preston. I'm betting Beau's the missing accountant. If we keep our eye on him and Jett they'll lead us to the two guys who got away."

"Since they found nothing at the dry dock and you showed up there, Beau and Jett might put two and two together and realize we're on to them. They're going to be scrambling to find Mimi any way they can."

Lawrence came up, big smile, hair combed. "This is a great party. I don't like the mushy doves and hearts stuff but the music's good and we're cooking really great food. I'm helping Preston in the kitchen. He taught me how to make lasagna." Lawrence said to Demar, "Your girlfriend's a good cook, and she loves Bonnie. Wanted to hold her, but I told her she was at Hastings House. She went to visit. I better get back to help Preston set out the food."

"See," Demar said. "Sally's even good in the kitchen. I didn't know she could cook. I can't lose her. I don't know what I'm going to do but I can't."

Clyde Miller sat at the old upright and he and Ryan

started in on "Wild Thing." The place erupted, everyone laughing and singing, Sally dancing and swaying, making her way over to Demar. Quaid backed up, giving Sally room, and bumped into Cynthia. The two women danced around the men, reminding them what they so didn't have . . . *them*!

The music got louder, Cynthia rubbed her front to his back, making every muscle in his body beg to have her. Sally ran her hands through Demar's hair and kissed the back of his neck, the crowd cheering. The music ended, everyone clapping and laughing.

Quaid snagged Cynthia around the waist. "What do you think you're doing?"

Sally laughed. "Practicing a little "Southern Spice." Showing what you two are pining for."

Demar's eyes devoured her. "All this and you can cook too, damn. I didn't know that."

"Only if a microwave's involved, baby. I can't boil an egg."

Demar's eyes cleared and his gaze fused with Quaid's. "Sally was singing, she couldn't have been in the kitchen with Lawrence."

"Oh shit, *that* girlfriend," Quaid said, running behind Demar toward the back.

"What do you mean, that girlfriend?" Sally yelled, trailing behind with Cynthia. Quaid stopped in the middle of the little kitchen. "The food's here, but where're Preston and Lawrence?"

Moaning came from the storage closet and Quaid opened it to Preston struggling to sit up.

Ryan, Keefe and Rory came in as Quaid helped Preston to a sitting position. "What happened?"

Preston rubbed the back of his head. "Someone hit me from behind. I'm getting real tired of getting whacked on the head. But I got a look at the guy's shoes—saddle shoes."

Quaid and Demar exchanged confirming looks as Preston continued, "They said something about PayDay's ready. That's a candy bar. What's a candy bar got to do with knocking me out?"

Quaid said, "It's a boat like *Moneymaker*. Where's Lawrence?"

Preston looked worse. "Isn't he with you?"

Quaid glanced at Cynthia, her face suddenly gray. "They took my son? Why?"

Demar said, "He must know something important."

Preston said, "I went to my car to get a platter. Lawrence must have overheard something then he came back in here. Guess they thought he was with me and didn't realize he was in the kitchen."

"Stop!" Cynthia held up her hands. "What the heck's going on? Where is Lawrence and who took him?"

Quaid said, "Lawrence told Jett that Bonnie is at Hastings House. All you have to do is look around and you can see that everyone from there is here at the party, which means . . ."

Demar finished, "Which means Bonnie is with her mother. Everyone knows Rory wouldn't trust his baby with a stranger. Jett is in cahoots with the missing bank presidents, and Beau Fontaine is one of them."

"My Beau," Ida said from the doorway, Sally, Effie and Callie standing beside her.

Demar said, "Now those two have Mimi and Bonnie and Lawrence."

Quaid took Cynthia's hand. "We know they're on a boat and we'll get them. The *Sea Ray*'s ready and we'll have tows on the river watch for *Pay Day*." He kissed her. "Stay here. Sit tight. It's going to be okay, I swear it will."

Rory started for the back door. "Quit your dang jabbering, time's a wastin'."

* * *

Cynthia felt all the blood in her body turn to ice as she stood there in the little kitchen. "They have Lawrence, my baby?" She swallowed. "Hang tight? If that isn't a perfectly male thing to say."

"Beau Fontaine took my grandson," Ida said, her eyes narrowed. "That no-good son of a bitch used me, and I'm going to get even if it's the last thing I do. I have my gun, two actually; let's go find him."

Cynthia blinked. "T . . . two?"

"Did I hear gun?" said Sister Candy, Sister Ginger beside her.

Sally pulled herself up tall. "We'll get a boat down at the dry dock. Conrad has a bunch." She faced the sisters. "We have bad guys to chase."

Effie said, "Except those boats have holes in them, that's why they're in dry dock."

Callie nodded. "Then we get a boat without a hole. There's got to be something."

They all stampeded out the back door and got to the parking lot cluttered with cars from the party. Gridlock comes to O'Fallon's Landing. They headed for the docks, till Cynthia saw Max jumping and barking at a car that was trying to wiggle between other parked cars to get out. The white Lexus convertible on the other side finally made it free then took off down the road, Max galloping full tilt behind it.

"Holy shit!" Cynthia gasped. "Lawrence is in the trunk of that car. That's why Max is going nuts. He never chases cars."

Sally added, "That's Jett's car." She pointed. "Follow that dog."

Cynthia jumped into the Blue Bomb, then Sally. Effie, Callie and Preston got into the second seat, and the sisters climbed in and helped Ida into the third seat, facing backwards. Cynthia smacked the dash three times and the engine caught. "Good car." She floored the accelerator, sideswiping two cars and a truck, and aimed the Bomb for the two-lane.

Max was losing ground but not giving up. Lightning zigzagged through the sky, rain dotted the windshield. Sister Candy said, "We're losing them, step on it."

Cynthia grinned. "Oh we won't lose them, it's raining and we have a car full of Southerners."

Sister Ginger yelled, "You're slowing down a lot. What are you doing!"

"My son's in that car, I don't want him hurt. I'm keeping my distance. Just wait, it'll be okay."

"Sweet Jesus, we don't have time to wait."

They took one curve then the next, coming up on Hastings House to the left. A white streak tore across the road in front of the Lexus.

"What was that?" Preston yelped as the convertible swerved, skidded then slid off into the ditch. Cynthia slammed on the brakes. "That was Grant. God Bless that Yankee!"

Everyone poured out of the Buick. Jett scrambled from her car and started to run, and Sally tackled her in a full body slam that threw them hard against the pavement with a solid thump. Cynthia popped the trunk and Lawrence scrambled out into Ida's arms. Relief washed over Cynthia as Ida kissed her grandson, tears on her face. She held him tight as Max caught up, licking Lawrence's face. Ida sniffed. "Thank God. Now where's that no good Beau Fontaine? I'm going to blow him from here to kingdom come."

"Amen," the sisters said and crossed themselves.

Sally sat on Jett's back as Preston said to her, "Where are Mimi and Bonnie?"

"I'm not telling you anything," she spluttered from the ground. "Now get this pig off me."

Sally said, "You have one minute to tell us everything or

we'll drag your sorry ass to that river over there and throw you in."

"Besides," Preston added. "If we don't get the others there's a chance the DA might try and stick you with all that's happened, like kidnapping, extortion, you name it. That puts you in prison for the next twenty years, being someone's bitch. Cooperation is recommended."

"Fuck! I didn't sign up for this."

Sally slapped Jett's head. "No 'F' word around the kid."

"Just getting information, is all I was going to do," Jett huffed. "Uncle Edward . . . Beau . . . has Mimi and Bonnie and his partners are picking them up at some derelict dock down the road. They've been hiding out at this old house. Lawrence overheard me talking on the phone saying Mimi was at Hasings House, I thought he was with Preston. I was going to let him go, I swear."

Cynthia shook her head. "I don't know what dock that is. Docks aren't my thing." Everyone nodded their heads in agreement.

Lawrence said, "That's Captain Valentine's dock by Stevie's Ridge, where Quaid took me to look at the meteor shower. The dock's overgrown but it's there."

Cynthia patted Lawerence's head and said to Preston, "You're still groggy. Stay with Jett. Get up to Hastings House and have someone patch you through on the VHF to Quaid, and tell him what's going on. Lawrence stays with you."

"But Mom!"

Preston protested, "What are you going to do?"

Cynthia gave him a half grin. "I don't know, we'll make it up when we get there, but if Quaid doesn't get to the dock in time we're Bonnie and Mimi's only hope. Once they get on the river and duck back in some tributary we'll never find them."

Ida handed Preston her gun, which looked like a small

cannon. "I'm sorry I chose Beau over you. It's the Landon curse, you know. We never seem to get it right." She smiled at Cynthia. "Till lately."

Everyone piled back into the Bomb, Cynthia smacked the dash and they tore up the road. "This is a mighty fine riding car," Sister Ginger said. "I so appreciate a nice ride, don't you Sister Candy?"

"There's Valentine's house," Ida said, pointing to the left. "And there's the overgrown dock across the road."

Cynthia made a sharp right, the Buick bottoming out, making her slow down. More rain dotted the windshield and they spotted an SUV. "That's Beau's car," Ida said. "The dirty rotten jackass." The women scrambled from the car and raced toward the dock.

"Hold it right there," came Beau's voice from behind. They stopped dead and faced him, toting a gun, now pointing it at Ida. "Drop your purses. I know you all have enough fire power to arm a small country."

Ida huffed, "If I ever get my hands on you, Beau Fontaine of the Charleston Fontaines, I will stomp you flatter than a bug on a windshield."

He waved his gun toward the dock. "Walk slowly to the end. We have Bonnie so don't try to be cute. You don't want anything to happen to that baby, now do you?"

Quaid had the *Sea Ray* wide open, tearing through the water that looked more gray than blue, reflecting the clouds overhead. Rory said into the mike, "This here is Rory O'Fallon on the—" He glanced at Quaid.

"*Cynthia.*"

Rory grinned and continued, "The *Cynthia*. We're in pursuit of my baby and fiancée who have been kidnapped onboard the cruiser *Pay Day*. Over."

"Rory," came a reply. "This here is *River Rat*. We just passed Valentine's old place. The boat you're looking for is there. Seems to be quite a commotion on the docks. A bunch of women."

The five men exchanged looks as Rory said, "Christ in a sidecar. What the hell's going on?"

Quaid ran his hand over his face. "Just a guess but I'd say the women weren't sitting home and holding tight."

"There," Demar said, pointing to the shore up ahead, Quaid turning the boat in that direction.

Keefe used the binoculars. "I see Sally, Cynthia, Effie, Callie, Ida and those two sisters. Do women ever listen?"

"To each other," Ryan offered as Keefe added, "Mimi's got Bonnie in her arms and they're on the back deck. There are two guys with them and Beau's holding a gun on the girls."

Rory's face tightened and he whispered, "Daddy's coming, Sweet Pea."

A minute later that seemed more like a million, Quaid cut back the engine and the *Cynthia* glided up to the stern of *Pay Day*, the boat dipping and rolling in the mounting waves. Rory said, "We can't risk gunplay with Little Bit there." He climbed onto the bow followed by Ryan and Keefe, all surefooted from a lifetime on the water. Looking a little green, Demar said to Quaid, "I'll take the wheel, you go on deck. I'm not the river man, I'm the barbecue man."

Quaid grinned and slapped Demar on the back, then joined his brothers and his dad. Rory yelled over the building storm and rumble of the engines, "You can't kill everyone. It's over."

Beau yelled back from the dock, "All we need are those disks. We'll keep the baby till we get them." He nodded to Mimi on the boat, struggling to keep her balance as were the two men, the boat pitching one way then the other. "Hand the kid over to my partner."

Mimi's auburn hair tangled in the breeze, her face white as the foam on the water. She clutched Bonnie closer.

Rory's jaw tightened, his hands fisted at his sides. Then suddenly he relaxed, a slight sly smile on his lips. What the hell?

He said, "If that's the way you want this to go down, fine by me." Mimi's gaze fused with Rory's across the distance. He peered hard at Mimi. "Give him Bonnie."

Her eyes bulged, her expression suggesting Rory was out of his freaking mind. She held Bonnie tighter still.

Rory continued, "We've been through so much together, Mimi. Please trust me one more time. We need to end this. I bet Bonnie's real hungry."

Mimi swallowed then her eyes suddenly cleared and she gave a barely discernable nod. She faced the man beside her and he pocketed the weapon, now leaving two guns. Mimi handed the baby to him. Even from where Quaid stood, he could see Bonnie scrunch up her face, turn red, stiffen every little muscle of her body let out with the most god-awful scream Quaid had ever heard.

Startled, Beau and his buddies stared at Bonnie, giving Rory, Keefe, Ryan and Quaid the split second they needed to jump to the *Pay Day*. Mimi snatched Bonnie, Rory grabbed the gun, Keefe tackled one guy to the deck, Quaid and Ryan body-slammed the other.

Quaid saw Beau grab Cynthia and aim his gun toward her and his heart stopped, till Ida whacked Beau over the head with a chunk of driftwood, crumpling him to the ground in a groaning heap. She peered down at him. "No one messes with southern women and their families, Beau Fontaine. No one. If you were really from Charleston you'd know that."

Chapter 18

Demar got out of his car, the town just starting to come awake, the sky blue, the morning air fresh. He stared at Slim's. He'd been with the Memphis police all night giving statements and getting the guys from River Environs squared away. And of course there was Jett to deal with. She'd been a good cop till her uncle convinced her to make some money the easy way. Five to seven in a Tennessee lockup was not the easy way especially for an ex-cop.

Sally's car was parked in front, trunk open, boxes inside. Damn. He ran his hand over his jaw. How could he make this right? How could he convince her he really did love her?

Well, he better damn-well think of something. He stepped onto the porch and zeroed in on Sally inside, boxes piled to her eyes. "Well, as I live and breathe if it isn't—"

"I'm sorry." He held out his hands to stop her so he could get this all out. "I'm sorry I lied to you, that I led you on, that I hurt you in any way—and I did, in so many ways. I know right now it looks like I love my job more than you and that's not true. I was afraid if we didn't crack this case soon, Bonnie, Mimi and Rory could wind up dead. I couldn't put our happiness above that. I couldn't live with myself if I did, and truth be told, you'd hate my guts if I made that decision and let anything happen to the people you love. Sally, I want to be one of those people you love."

"Well—"

"I know this is the second time I deceived you and that sucks. But the good times, when I told you I loved you, I swear I meant every word. I'm staying on the Landing, running for sheriff. I think folks trust me to do a good job and keep them safe. I want to date you, court you, treat you like a queen, but if you go I won't get a chance to do that. Stay. Give me one more chance. I'll make it right."

She put the boxes on the bar and smoothed back the hair that had fallen across her lovely face. "Are you finished?"

"Yes."

"I was going to say—before I was so rudely interrupted—if it isn't Demar Thacker, the man I'm going to marry." She nodded at the boxes. "I'm bringing them back inside."

She smiled at him and he sat on a stool before he collapsed on the floor. "Well dang, girl."

"That's all I get? Well dang?" She sashayed over to him and wrapped her arms around his neck. "Rory stopped over here earlier to make sure I understood what you were up to with Jett and that without you he wouldn't have his family back with him now." She brushed her lips across Demar's, and he was sure he'd never experienced a more wonderful sensation.

Her lips smiled against his. "I love you. I want to be your wife. I want to have my own investment firm here in town and with the new construction and houses going up I'll have clients. And, I want to work here on the weekends and sing the blues with Ryan, and have you in the audience so I can sing to you."

"A dance pole?"

"No dance pole."

"Think Ryan would design us a house here in town? Your office on the first floor, an apartment for us on the second?"

"And what if *us* becomes more than two?"

"Kids?" A bubble of sheer happiness slid up his throat. "We'll make it a really big apartment. You can be close to your work and your family. I want you to be happy, Sally. Whatever you want is fine with me."

"You know what I want right now? Breakfast. I am starved."

"Eggs? Bacon? Cornbread? A real Tennessee breakfast."

She patted her hip. "Fat Fighters would not approve."

He scooped her into his arms. "I love you just the way you are, every delicious inch of you. We can think healthy tomorrow, today we splurge." He kissed her, feeling better then he'd felt in a really long time.

She tossed her hair and gave him a wicked wink. "You know, I think we need something in that storage room for our breakfast. Wanna come take a look with me?" She held him a little tighter. "You are my hero, Demar. You are the best."

"The best *what* is the question," Quaid said as he came inside.

Demar laughed deep in his throat. "Guess that's between us."

Quaid said to Sally, "I came to welcome you home . . . again. And from the look on your faces I'm thinking there's going to be another wedding. Congratulations?"

Sally snuggled into Demar's arms. "I think that's a safe bet. But the real reason you're on my doorstep this morning, Quaid O'Fallon, is to make sure I'm staying, and that means so is Cynthia." She shooed him away like a bug.

"Go find your lady and Demar and I will meet up with you later."

Demar carried Sally off toward the kitchen and Quaid poured coffee into a Styrofoam cup, then headed for the dock. He was settling into a pattern, one that he loved, but without Cynthia in his life he felt empty inside.

Hank gave him a little salute as he untied the mooring lines for *River Runner*. Her engines engaged and she headed upriver to Rockton to pick up a string of barges. Hank whistled as he swept the dock and Rory drew up beside Quaid, their eyes following the tow.

"Good worker you got there," Rory said.

"Another kid without a home finds one." Quaid watched as Hank hauled a coil of new line onto the *Annabelle Lee*. "He's staying in a backroom in the office. He needs better, a room of his own—and he's not the only one."

Rory's brow rose. "Sounds like you're going somewhere with that."

"How's Mimi?"

Rory laughed, a full rich sound without a hint of worry for a change. "Clucking around the kitchen fixing Bonnie breakfast, deciding if she wants to paint the kitchen something called mauve rose or touch-me-not lilac. Said she thought about redecorating the place all those months she was hiding out. Planning for the future kept her going and not lose hope."

He patted Quaid on the back. "I think your room's slated for buttercup yellow, if it's okay with you of course."

"Ryan and Effie are building a house in town, Keefe and Callie have plans for a house on the next bluff. I saw the blueprints. I think you're going to be a granddaddy real soon. And I'm going to buy Valentine's old place."

"It's a derelict, boy. You'll have your work cut out for you." He laughed. "But Captain Valentine sure threw some hellacious parties there in his time." He looked to Hank.

"It's got a few outbuildings, if I remember right. Nice place for someone needing a place to stay." He looked Quaid dead in the eyes. "How does Cynthia fit into all this?"

"Wish the hell I knew." Quaid stuck his hands in his pockets. "That woman is a complete mystery. She loves me, I love her, Lawrence is terrific, blah, blah, blah. And then nothing. All I know is when Beau put that gun to her, I nearly had a heart attack. I want to marry her but she says I have to love myself. What am I supposed to do, buy myself a fancy car? Dress in expensive clothes? Hell, I already did plaid, what more does the woman want? I don't get it."

"I'm looking at touch-me-not lilac and something yellow, and have no idea what's wrong with the paint already on the walls. But all I can tell you is that having the woman you love beside you is worth walking through the fires of hell. Tomorrow we're going to Nashville and turn over the disks, then all we'll have to worry about is each other, Bonnie and paint chips."

"There is a string of barges needing pickup down at Greenville. Think I'll take the run and bring Hank along. Maybe some river time will clear my head. When are you and Mimi tying the knot?"

"Next week. We've wasted enough time. Cynthia's making Mimi's dress." He put his hand on Quaid's shoulder. "You have a good trip now, you hear. Nothing like the river to set things right."

Cynthia sat at the kitchen table stirring peppermint tea, staring off into nothingness, listening to the afternoon drone of insects outside the window. Ida sat down beside her and let out a deep sigh. "Now aren't we a pretty picture, you mooning over Quaid, me in a tizzy over how to get Preston back."

Cynthia cut her eyes to Ida and grinned, and she hadn't

felt like doing that all day. "Well bless my stars, my mama's in love."

Ida chuckled. "And to add to it, I get sass from my daughter. Truth is, I've been pining for that man for a bit now, even with Beau around. Just didn't know how to set things right, and I still don't." She picked up a sheet of paper in front of Cynthia. "What in the world is *raison d'être?*"

"Fall out from sending Lawrence to French lessons. It's fifteen reasons why I shouldn't send him to boarding school. Found it tacked to my door when I woke up this morning. It's not that I want to send him away, but he's really smart. I can't just ignore that."

"No more than you can ignore he's a little boy and likes being with you here on the Landing."

"Then I propose a compromise," came Lawrence's voice as he walked into the room, hair ruffled and sun-streaked, his cheeks rosy. "I got some ideas. I'll do summer camps for eggheads. That's what Katelyn's parents do. The high school teachers tutor her outside of class and there are enrichment classes at the colleges in Memphis. The choir director gives Katelyn piano lessons, the teller at the bank teaches her accounting, Sally's teaching her economics. I thought Ryan O'Fallon could teach me how to play the sax. He sure can make that baby wail."

"Wail?" Cynthia swallowed a moan. "I'm being outmaneuvered by an eight-year-old."

"Who has thought this out very well," Ida added, with a wink at Lawrence.

"Katelyn and I instant messaged till midnight to get this together," Lawrence said with a sheepish twinkle in his eyes.

"Well," Cynthia sighed. "I suppose we can try and see how it works out. I'd hate sending you away, I'd miss you and—"

"Yes!" Lawrence yelped. "I'm going to tell Quaid before he heads out to pick up a payload and then I'm going to stop over at Katelyn's."

"Math problems?"

"She's teaching me how to fish." Lawrence shot out the front door as Sister Candy and Sister Ginger came down the stairs, suitcases in hand. Ida stood. "Oh, my goodness. You're leaving us?"

Sister Ginger gave her a hug. "The house is painted, your lovely bed and breakfast has guests, you have a job that's doing well, and the other sisters want us home."

"So many needs to tend to," Cynthia offered, then hugged Sister Candy. "You've been a wonderful help with everything. I don't know what we would have done without you."

Sister Ginger said, "That's the way he would have wanted it. You know where to find us if you need us." Sister Candy winked at Ida. "And Sister Ginger and I have been discussing your getting Preston back. Perhaps a love letter read on the radio, a little something theatrical since we're dealing with Magnum. Always good to give a man what he wants."

The door closed behind them and Cynthia said to Ida, "I hate to see them go. But I don't get the letter on the radio"

"I hate to see them go, too. They're wonderful girls. Perhaps you should have some more tea, dear." Ida led her back to the dining room table then pulled a flask from behind a pot of white gardenias sitting on the windowsill. She poured the contents into Cynthia's tea. "Take a drink, a big drink."

Cynthia pinched the bridge of her nose and closed her eyes. "Now what? I think that's getting to be my mantra."

"Well, dear, you see, Sister Candy and Sister Ginger aren't really nuns, they're like sisters of the night. They were the other women in your father's life and felt bad that he left us in dire straits, so they came here to help out. They're—"

"Call girls."

"The sister act was a cover. The *he* they kept referring to is your dad. He treated the girls nice, and truth be told he did the same to me. He simply didn't get the *forsaking all others* part of the wedding vows. I didn't know who Candy and Ginger were either, till they came up with the radio idea."

Ida took Cynthia's hand. "'Southern Spice' is *my* radio show. I'm Tennessee Tess. Candy and Ginger thought about doing it themselves but simply don't have the time. One of their clients is a producer of a radio station in Memphis and—Well, you get the picture."

"Everyone listens to 'Southern Spice,' Mother. Everyone."

Ida blushed. "Including Preston. Isn't it great, and that no one knows who I am makes this oh so much fun! I wear hats with a veil at the studio, adds to the mystique. I'll have to come clean with Preston, of course, especially if I do an apology to him on the air. I believe he'll get it even if I don't use his name; he is a private investigator after all. I do believe we've finally broken the Landon curse. I've found Preston and you have Quaid. He's a fine man; I regret that I misjudged him. I heard about Pete and the flagpole. You must love Quaid very much to have done that and I'm sure he loves you too."

"He thinks I love him because he can take care of me."

Ida chuckled. "Oh my goodness, he is one of those macho types, isn't he? Then it's up to you to convince him otherwise. And if you truly love him you'll make it happen."

She kissed Cynthia on the cheek and nodded at the untouched tea. "I hope he doesn't stay pigheaded too long, dear, for everyone's sake." She stood. "And now I have a letter to compose."

Cynthia felt her stomach roll. What was she going to do? She didn't want Quaid to marry her because he was the great protector . . . sounded like a stupid campaign slogan. And she didn't want him to think she was doing him some sort of favor by marrying him. Both reasons for marriage were completely unacceptable.

She took the tea to the sink and dumped it down the drain. What happened to simple love without so much baggage? It didn't exist. Then again maybe it did, and she was the one complicating the hell out of everything.

Quaid stood in the pilothouse gazing at the charts and not really seeing the information there at all. If he didn't start concentrating he'd run aground in no time, not too swift for the guy who ran the company. He looked to port. The lines were free and he heard Hank's footsteps on the metal stairs leading to the pilothouse. Giving the engines more power, he headed for the channel and the deep water, till Cynthia opened the door and stepped inside.

"Okay, why do you want to marry me? I want to know right now. It's important."

He stared at her, not because he didn't know the answer to her question but because she took his breath away, just like she always did. Suddenly there was a scraping sliding sound and the *Annabelle* ground to a halt.

"Oh, crap."

"That's it!" She threw her hands in the air. "You don't have an answer except 'Oh, crap'? You can't even come up with one thing?"

"I just ran the tow aground at my own dock." He looked to port and saw Hank, laughing his ass off. "Why isn't Hank here and what are you doing here?"

"Getting answers, at least trying to. So . . . answer me." She paced the little room. "I'm older and I'm not wealthy and I have a lunatic for an ex and my mother is "Southern

Spice" on the radio—do you believe that? But you can't tell anyone, and I don't even have a job, though I'm thinking about opening a shop in Memphis to sell—"

"I thought this was my question?"

She stopped pacing. "Well you didn't do too great with your original answer."

"Okay here we go, one more time . . . though I don't exactly mind repeating it. I love you because you're honest and brave and trustworthy and you're a good mom and—"

"No, no, no." She held up her hands as if warding off an attack. "Good mom is not the reason to get married."

"Honest, brave and trustworthy were in there, too."

"Sounds like a Saint Bernard."

He put his hands on her shoulders. "Here it is. I love you, and I think you feel the same about me, and you being a good mother to Lawrence is important. It tells what kind of person you are, which is a damn fine one. Why are you making this so difficult?"

She bit her bottom lip and he wanted to take her in his arms and hold her except . . . "I need to know, Cynthia. You're making us both nuts."

"I'm afraid. There, now you know. Terrified. Petrified clear through."

"Of me?"

She punched his arm. "Of course not you. I'm afraid of making another bad decision. I think that's been the trouble all along. I don't trust myself. I don't want to louse it up. I married the wrong guy, bought the wrong car from the wrong guy, had the wrong guy for my lawyer, and I don't want you to be the wrong guy. I love you too much for that. I got over the others but I know me, and I couldn't get over marrying you and then losing you. I have to get it right this time, Quaid. I got to quit lousing it up."

"You really think you'll lose me?"

"You got to admit, I've got a sucky track record going here."

He sat her in the captain's chair where she'd sat the night of the storm. A tow out in the channel churned on by, sending rollers their way, rocking the boat, making her look apprehensive. He held her for reassurance. "I love you and I love myself. I'm not sure what that means but I'm working on it."

She didn't look so good; guess he needed to convince her more. "I just bought myself a big old house I always wanted and I hope it will make you happy too. Got a hell of a third floor for a sewing loft." She looked worse, a little green—actually a lot green. He wasn't doing well at all. "I'm not going anywhere, Cynthia."

"Oh, dear. But I sure am. Oh, God." She pushed him aside and ran for the door, yanked it open and tossed her cookies.

He came up behind her, holding her. "Babe, you really don't like boats, do you? Ginger tea is supposed to help, or those patches. You poor thing."

She turned around and pounded his chest. "I am not a poor thing, I'm pregnant."

"What? H . . . how?"

She gave him an evil look and he rephrased, "I mean we used protection. Not that I'm not happy about you having our baby . . . actually I'm sort of ecstatic. He grinned. "Make that real ecstatic. But this is a little unexpected."

"Well, the best I can figure is it happened in the bushes when you were climbing the trellis and nearly killed yourself. In my sexual exuberance to jump your bones I tore open the little blue foil pack with my teeth. I don't think that was one of my better ideas. They should add a warning, do not tear with teeth."

He leaned back against the door to the pilothouse, the

sun warming his skin, Cynthia's news warming his heart and his soul. "Are you okay with this?"

Her lips relaxed, the first thing relaxed about her since she got in the pilothouse. "Yes, as a matter of fact I am. I always wanted another child. Aaron didn't want the first, so two were out of the question. But a baby is not the reason to marry, Quaid."

He nodded. "But it is a reason to be damn happy." He draped his arm around her and drew her close. "And you've made me the happiest man on earth, Cynthia Landon. I love you, want to spend the rest of my life with you and our kids. Will you please marry me?"

"Yes! I think I should do that."

"What do you think Lawrence will say?"

She laughed against his chest. "Oh, Quaid, he'll probably want to deliver the baby. Do you think we're up for all this?"

He framed her beautiful face in his hands. "As long as we're together we can handle anything."

Epilogue

Rory stood in the doorway of Ryan's room, watching his three sons get ready for his wedding. For a second his heart beat a little harder, squeezed a little tighter, and he saw them as three little boys playing together, having fun, the loves of his life. He was one lucky man to have kids like his sons and Bonnie.

Quaid said to Keefe, "That's not the way you do a bow tie. You have worse fashion sense than Old Miss Buzzy."

Keefe laughed. "Who the hell's that?"

"Someone who doesn't massacre bow ties." Quaid took the tie and knotted it neatly around Keefe's collar. "There—at least you won't be a total embarrassment."

Ryan said, "How'd a badass like you know how to do a bow tie?"

"I'm engaged to a woman who designs wedding apparel. It's in the air."

Rory came into the room and gazed at his sons. "Got to admit you all clean up pretty well. Your mama would be proud. I know I am. This is my wedding day, next month you three get hitched in a triple wedding."

Ryan, Keefe and Quaid chuckled and Ryan said, "It was either that or flip coins to see who got married first."

Rory laughed too. "Well, it's going to be some blowout. Don't think the Landing will ever be the same."

And deep inside he realized that after these weddings nothing would be the same. "For a lot of years now it's been the four of us, the four O'Fallons."

"And it's always going to be the four of us," Keefe said. "We're just getting bigger."

"And better," Quaid added.

Rory nodded, complete happiness welling up inside him. "There is nothing, absolutely nothing, better than family."

Take a look at Kathy Love's
I ONLY HAVE FANGS FOR YOU.
Coming next month from Brava!

"Why are you so scared of me?" Sebastian asked softly.

She shifted away as if she planned to move down a step and then bolt. He couldn't let that happen, not before he understood what had brought on this outburst.

"Wilhelmina, talk to me." He placed a hand on the wall, blocking her escape down the stairs.

She glared at him with more anger and more of that uncomfortable fear.

"You can bully your mortal conquests," she said, her voice low. "But you can't bully me."

Sebastian sighed. "My earlier behavior to the contrary, I don't want to bully you. Or anyone."

'You can't seduce me, either," she informed him.

"I don't . . ." Seduce her? Was that what all this was about?

"Do you want me to seduce you?" he asked with a curious smile. Maybe that was the cause for her crazy outburst. She *was* jealous.

She laughed, the sound abrupt and harsh. "Hardly. I just told you that I *didn't* want you to seduce me."

"No," he said slowly. "You told me *I can't*. That sounds like a challenge."

Irritation flared from her, blotting out some of the fear. "Believe me, I'm *so* not interested."

He raised an eyebrow at her disdain. "Then why do you care about me being with that blonde?"

"That blonde?" she said. "Is hair color the way you identify all your women? It's got to be a confusing system, as so many of them have the same names."

He studied her for a minute, noting that just a faint flush colored her very pale cheeks

"Are you sure you don't want me to seduce you?" he asked again, because as far as he could tell, there was no other reason for her to care about the identification system for his women.

She growled in irritation, the sound raspy and appealing in a way it shouldn't have been.

Sebastian blinked. He needed to stay focused. This woman thought he was a jerk, that shouldn't be a draw for him.

"Why did you say those things?" he asked. "What have I done to make you think I'm so terrible?"

Her jaw set again, and her midnight eyes locked with his. "Are you going to deny that you're narcissistic?"

He frowned. "Yes. I'm confident maybe, but no, I'm not a narcissist."

She lifted a disbelieving eyebrow at that. "And you are going to deny egocentric, too?"

"Well, since egocentric is pretty much the same as narcissistic, then yes, I'm going to deny it."

Her jaw set even more, and he suspected she was gritting her teeth, which for some reason made him want to smile. He really was driving her nuts. He liked that.

He was hurt that she had such a low opinion of him,

but he did like the fact that he seemed to have gotten under her skin.

"I think we can also rule out vain, too," he said, "because again that's pretty darn similar to narcissistic and egocentric." He smiled slightly.

Her eyes narrowed, and she still kept her lips pressed firmly together—their pretty bow shape compressed into a nearly straight line.

"So you see," he continued, "I think this whole awful opinion that you have formulated about me might just be a mixup. What you thought was conceit, which is also another word for narcissism," he couldn't help adding, "was just self-confidence."

His smile broadened, and Wilhelmina fought the urge to scream. He was mocking her. Still the egotistical scoundrel. Even now, after she'd told him exactly what she thought of him. He was worse than what she'd called him. He was . . . unbelievable.

"What about depraved?" she asked. Surely that insult had made him realize what she thought.

"What about it?" he asked, raising an eyebrow, looking every inch the haughty, depraved vampire she'd labeled him.

"Are you going to deny that one, too?" she demanded.

He pretended to consider, then shook his head. "No, I won't deny that one. Although I'd consider myself more debauched than depraved. In a very nice way, however."

He grinned again, that sinfully sexy twist of his lips, and her gaze dropped to his lips. Full, pouting lips that most women would kill for. But on him, they didn't look the slightest bit feminine.

What was she thinking? Her eyes snapped back to his, but the smug light in his golden eyes stated that he'd already noticed where she'd been staring.

She gritted her teeth and focused on a point over his shoulder, trying not to notice how broad those shoulders were. Or how his closeness made her skin warm.

He shifted so he was even closer, his chest nearly brushing hers, his large body nearly surrounding her in the small stairwell. His closeness, the confines of his large body around hers, should have scared her, but she only felt . . . tingly.

"So, now that we've sorted that out," he said softly. "Why don't we go back to my other question?"

She swallowed, trying to ignore the way his voice felt like a velvety caress on her skin. She didn't allow herself to look at him, scared to see those eyes like perfect topazes.

"Why are you frightened of me, Mina?"

Because she was too weak, she realized. Because, despite what she knew about him, despite the fact that she knew he was dangerous, she liked his smile, his lips, those golden eyes. Because she liked it when he called her Mina.

Because she couldn't forget the feeling of his fingers on her skin.

She started as his fingers brushed against her jaw, nudging her chin toward him, so her eyes met his. Golden topazes that glittered as if there was fire locked in their depths.

Once again she was reminded of the ill-fated moth drawn to an enticing flame. She swallowed, but she couldn't break their gaze.

"You don't have to be afraid of me," he assured her quietly.

Yes, she did. God, she did.

Here's an advance peek at Nancy Warren's
"Nights Round Arthur's Table" in
BRITISH BAD BOYS
Available now from Brava!

The night was quiet and still. She liked the dark, though she was intensely aware of the man beside her. Once she stumbled over a rock she hadn't seen and he grabbed her hand to steady her.

He didn't let go. She could have pulled away, but she liked the feel of him, the sturdy, capable hand, the warmth of his skin.

"I bought one of your books today, when I was in town."

"You did? I thought Max was going to lend you one."

"I decided I'd like to have my own."

"Well, thank you. Which book did you choose?"

"*Tying Up Loose Ends*, I think it's called."

The book that first put her on the *Times* list, but she didn't tell him that. "Well, let me know what you think of it."

"I will."

After that, they didn't talk much.

When they reached her cottage, he still didn't talk, merely turned her to him and took her mouth.

Okay, so she'd guessed it was coming, had spent most of the short walk wondering how she felt about it and whether she'd stop him if he tried to kiss her. Now she knew that he wouldn't give her time to stop him and how she felt about it was indescribable. It was even better this time. He was so warm, so strong, his mouth both taking and giving.

Drug-like pleasure began to overtake her senses. It had been so long since she'd felt like this. Excited at the possibilities of a man, wanting, with quiet desperation, to be with him. Held by him, taken by him. She began to shiver and he moved closer, so her back was against the stone wall and his warm body pressed against her.

Her hands were in his hair, wonderful, thick, luxurious hair. Her mouth open on his, wanting, giving, taking. She felt him hard against her belly and experienced a purring sense of her own power. And also a stabbing sense of regret.

She couldn't do this, she reminded herself. Her book. Her book was her priority. If and when she finished the novel, then she could think about indulging herself like this. Not until then.

So she tipped her head back out of kissing range and looked up into that dark, intent face. "What was that about?" She'd meant to sound sophisticated and slightly amused. A woman who got hit on all the time on every continent. Instead she sounded husky and, even to her own ears, like a total goner.

"I'm interested. I'm letting you know."

"Telling me with words would be too mundane?"

"Words are your world. I'm more a man of action." Oh, man of action. Oh, aphrodisiac to her senses. She'd always gone for the cerebral types, but there was something about a man who tackled the world in a physical way that appealed to her on the most basic level. His words from dinner came back to her. He'd kill to protect those he loved. Every other man she'd been with had been of the pen is mightier than the sword persuasion, mostly, she suspected, because their swordplay was so minimal.

Arthur was a man who would make her feel safe. When she crawled into bed, terrified of the fruits of her own imagination, she could see herself burrowing against his warm skin, his arms coming round her in comfort.

Then she gave herself a mental slap. What was she doing? Always imagining things. Arthur ran a pub. Was obviously single and probably took a fancy to every unattached woman who rented the cottage. How convenient.

She shook her head, with mingled irritation and regret. "I'm here to work. I really don't have time for . . . anything personal."

"That's a shame." He ran his warm, leathery palm down the side of her neck so she wanted to press against it. Rub at him like a kitten.

"I have to finish this book. I can't afford any distractions."

"I'm glad I distract you," he said, a thread of amusement running through his voice.

"You are?"

"I wouldn't want to think I was the only one feeling . . . distracted."

And now a look at Jamie Denton's
THE MATCHMAKER.
Available now from Brava . . .

Ash brought his hand to her cheek, unashamed that his fingers trembled as he drew them lightly over her satiny-soft skin. "God, I've missed you," he whispered.

Greer looked up at him, her eyes filled with a longing to equal his own. That was all the invitation he needed.

He dipped his head, his mouth brushing across hers in a light, feathery kiss. He expected a protest, but instead her lips were soft, welcoming. Pressing his advantage, he deepened the kiss before she thought to change her mind.

Her hands landed on his chest and he half-expected her to push him away. Instead, she curled her fingers into his shirt and hauled him close. He didn't hesitate to pull her into his arms and hold on tight when she slid off the stool, wreathed her arms around his neck and pressed her too-thin body against him.

Emotion flooded him. He'd spent too many long nights thinking about her, dreaming about her, cursing her for leaving him. To finally have her in his arms, tasting her, was nothing short of heaven.

She dug her hands into his hair and swept her tongue across his. Blood pounded hotly through his veins, threatening to burn through the thin threads of his restraint. She was in no physical condition to make love but, God help him, that's exactly what he wanted from her. He wanted her hot and naked, wanted her legs wrapped tightly around his waist, welcoming him inside her slick, wet sheath. He wanted to hear his name on her lips as she came, needed to feel her body clench around his, milking him until he had nothing left to give her. He wanted her raw and wild, begging him for more until neither one of them had the strength to do more than breathe.

He slid his hands to her bottom and lifted her. She moaned in his mouth, the sound as sweet and intoxicating as the feel of her denim-covered legs wrapping around his waist. Shoving the barstool aside with his foot, he set her on the countertop and nudged her bottom forward. His dick throbbed painfully within the confines of his trousers and he nearly came out of his skin when she rocked her hips, rubbing herself against his erection.

Smoothing his hands from her bottom, he slid them over the deep indentation of her waist. She was too thin, he thought again, sweeping his hands upward along her rib cage. Dangerously thin.

Although it nearly killed him, he ended the kiss and pulled her arms from around his neck. He took a step backward, hoping the distance would cool his blazing libido.

Greer stared at him in confusion. Her passion-glazed eyes nearly had him ignoring his good intentions. He dragged his hand through his hair. "When was the last time you ate a decent meal?"

Her honey-blonde eyebrows slanted downward. "What?"

He took a good long look at her. Her collarbone appeared more prominent, so did her cheekbones, for that matter, creating a deep hollow in her cheeks. "How much weight have you lost, Greer?"

With a trembling hand, she reached up and twisted the

length of her hair into a loose knot. "Don't worry about it. I can take care of myself."

"Bullshit. If that were the case, then you wouldn't feel like nothing more than skin and bones. Christ, Greer, you're so thin you could put an anorexic to shame. What gives?"

She narrowed those gorgeous blue eyes. "None of your goddamn business." She slid off the counter and bent to pick up the stool he'd knocked over.

"You look like you haven't slept in a month," he said, taking the stool from her and sliding it back to the island.

"I'm fine."

Yeah, then why the hell wouldn't she look at him when she said it? Because she'd never been able to lie to him, and that apparently hadn't changed.

He snagged her wrist and pulled her to him. "The hell you are."

"Leave it alone. Leave *me* alone."

He ignored the warning in her voice. "What are you doing to yourself?"

She tugged her wrist free of his hold. "Surviving," she fired at him vehemently. "No thanks to you." Regret instantly filled her expression. "Ash. I'm sorry. I didn't mean—"

He scrubbed his hand down his face. "Yes, you did," he told her. Whatever hope he'd been harboring about convincing Greer to come back to him evaporated in that instant. And it was high time he pulled his head out of his ass and accepted the fact that his wife would never be able to forget that he'd been the one to put her in the hands of a monster.